WASTE

WASTE

Andrew F. Sullivan

5220 Dexter Ann Arbor Rd.
Ann Arbor, MI 48103
www.dzancbooks.org

First US edition: March 2016
ISBN: 9781938103407
Book design by Michelle Dotter

Library of Congress Cataloging-in-Publication Data

Names: Sullivan, Andrew F., 1987- author.
Title: Waste : a novel / Andrew F. Sullivan.
Description: First Edition. | Ann Arbor, MI : Dzanc Books, 2016.
Identifiers: LCCN 2015033328 | ISBN 9781938103407 (paperback)
Subjects: LCSH: Murder--Fiction. | BISAC: FICTION / Literary. | FICTION /
Crime. | GSAFD: Mystery fiction.
Classification: LCC PR9199.4.S846 W38 2016 | DDC 813/.6--dc23
LC record available at http://lccn.loc.gov/2015033328

Printed in the United States of America

10 9 8 7 6 5 4 3 2 1

To Ed and Shelley Sullivan,

This has nothing to do with you.

You ain't never been no virgin kid;
you were fucked from the start.

Patrick Stickles, "A Pot in Which to Piss"

Larkhill, Ontario

1989

1

The drill whirred twice before the battery died.

"Useless. Mastercraft ain't worth shit. Gimme DeWalt any day."

The two figures loomed over the body in the middle of the woods. Their shadows hid amongst the trees. Their beards were full of sweat and old smoke. One leaned down and slapped the body across the face.

"Connor, you dumb shit, open your eyes. Connor!"

Connor Condon always hated his name. He hated the concussive force of those two C's crashing out of his mother's mouth every time she was pissed, back when they'd lived in his grandmother's apartment. The sound chased him from room to room, rattling the dusty shelves and weaving its way through porcelain bears to find him hiding under the pullout couch he shared with his mother.

"We need you to wake up, and don't you dare puke again."

It wasn't until sixth grade that Connor's name truly became a curse in the outside world. The new bus driver, Marlene, believed she had to take attendance. Her tongue seemed far too big for her mouth when she drawled out his name through pierced lips.

"Tommy, just slap his face to wake him up. One good slap."

All Connor heard were titters of laughter from the backseats. The bus driver's massive tongue had mangled his name somehow. Kids stopped sitting beside him. Connor Condom. The name followed him for years, hunted him down hallways and trapped him in bathroom stalls, kids breathing down his neck, asking if his father was a Durex or a Trojan.

"Probably would have been easier if he was wearing clothes."

A Thursday. It was a Thursday in tenth grade when they pulled the plastic bag over his head on the bus. The driver was too busy navigating a left-hand turn to see Connor's face slowly turning purple as the bag pulled tighter and tighter. Connor remembered now that there was a green Chevy stalled in the turning lane. Before he passed out and smashed his face against the window, he noticed there was a receipt for Kmart in the bottom of the bag.

"Did you bring extra batteries, Al?"

For the next week, they had Connor in the hospital, measuring his breathing and brain activity every hour. They drained fluid from his brain on the second night. Connor did not remember that week. Two weeks later, he emerged with a new learning disability, a severe lack of hand-eye coordination, and a constant migraine. He walked home from the hospital.

"This happened before, remember? They're on my belt, if you'd take three seconds to look somewhere other than your own dick. Slap the kid again."

Astor Crane never called him Condom. He didn't offer him lube at the bus stop or ask him why all his relatives eventually ended up in the sewer. What he did offer was a smoke on the roof one night after he found Connor pitching pigeon nests at the super's car five floors down. Hours later, in Crane's apartment, Connor sat and watched Eddie Murphy on bootleg VHS, unable to stop talking about pigeons. Crane just nodded along as he chopped plants on the coffee table, asking questions and laughing in the appropriate places. Astor asked if he wanted a job.

That was five years and endless baggies ago.

And now Connor was here, somewhere in the woods with major head trauma and three broken ribs. They'd busted through the front door while he was in the bath, soaking his feet and playing the drum on his beer belly. Connor didn't see any faces, only thick gray hair and long beards like ZZ Top. He'd puked on the way down the stairs, chunks of it sticking to his chest hair. A purple horseshoe from the Lucky Charms he'd had for dinner lodged inside his belly button, half digested. One of the men was carrying a drill. Connor could feel the hundreds of pine needles collected in his leg hair. Tiny cuts from the rocks and roots he'd been dragged across as they pulled him deeper into the trees.

Astor wasn't here to help him now.

"Connor, we aren't supposed to kill you outright—you know that, don't you, you little hairy gash? Stay still, now."

The two stood over Connor. Snow began to fall. One of the grey beards leaned down, his vest covered in dandruff and snow. Connor reached out to grab his hand.

"Tommy, you got the goddamn drill or what?"

Snowflakes fell into Connor's eyes, but he'd lost the ability to blink. He felt them melt one by one down his face as the drill buzzed and buzzed, ploughing through the patella and deep into the meat behind his kneecaps. Little eruptions of purple and yellow spurted from his flesh. The sensation did not touch his brain like pain, just in scents that no longer made sense. The beards smelled like burnt meat, his own blood like apricots.

"We haven't killed you, have we? That's not allowed. Only our second non-screamer. That's impressive, but don't start thinking there is a light at the end of this bleak-ass tunnel."

Connor could no longer see. Too much snow built up over his eyes.

"Here it is. You crawl out of here alive, consider all your debts repaid, all your capital returned to you, and all our apologies intact, signed, sealed, delivered. The man on high says you are in the clear. If you don't...well, you take that up with whoever you want. I gotta piss."

Connor heard them stumble off. He tried to close his eyes, but the muscles did not respond.

There was no moon. Connor lay there in the dirt and the pine needles, trying to connect each thought to the next. His jaw clicked as he tried to speak. Snow gathered in his hair and in his wounds, turning the flakes pink. Each breath was animated by the cold. Connor did not try to crawl. The holes in his knees filled with melting snow. The vomit on his chest was frozen tight against his skin. Somewhere in his brain, dead cats and grandmothers and rainbows collided. He lay dreaming with his eyes open, his mother pouring red wine into giant vats of diet cola, broken girls in veils dancing in circles around his body in the snow, the black night a backdrop for hallucinations that crackled like busted televisions.

He would be buried in snow. He would drown slowly as flakes melted on his lips, trickled down his stubborn tongue, and filled his lungs with fluid. Connor did not worry about these things. Sliding in and out of consciousness, he prayed the newspaper would not print his full name for the world to see. Nameless, faceless, half eaten by dogs, suffocated in a plastic bag until every brain cell began to fail, Connor Condon would take all these things, as long as no one misspelled his name in the obituaries, as long as his gravestone remained untouched, history slowly fading on locker doors, birth certificate eaten by mice, every trace of him erased.

2

"So they find this kid, right? What's left, 'cause it's probably been months. He's frozen solid."

Jamie Garrison was barely listening, but the little skinhead just kept talking. Moses Moon's head was covered in angry ingrown hairs fighting to push through the skin. Two hours listening to the kid shoot bullshit while they hosed down the prep room and rolled the waste bins full of fat and trim outside. Donnie would be opening the butcher shop in the morning. He would find a mistake no matter what they did, and Jamie would blame Moses.

"Nothing tried to eat him?"

One of the streetlights in the parking lot was busted. Moses stood shivering in the cold, his toque barely covering his head, ears bright red. Frost beaded on his pants. Jamie tossed his keys from hand to hand, watching his breath rise up to the flickering light.

"Maybe a bear, I don't know, all right? Can we just get in the fucking car, J?"

Moses hopped from foot to foot. His jacket was made for spring and it was December.

The car smelled like frozen sanitizer and pork shavings. It was an old Cutlass that Donnie had sold Jamie the summer before. Moses went straight for the radio, listening to nothing, just twisting the dials. They sat in the spinning noise while Jamie waited for the car to heat up. Static and random notes bleated from the speakers.

Jamie put the car in drive. He always made sure to find a pull-through whenever he parked. The reverse gear had crapped out on him in the spring. There were two hernias, one accident, and a lot of pushing since then, but Jamie swore he was getting the hang of it.

Jamie made his way across Larkhill, swerving around potholes and the occasional drunk. Moses lived down by the highway, in one of the old motels strung up like discount Christmas lights along either side of the six lanes. The kind of place where the bloodstains were bleached out of the carpet by Czech cleaning ladies and the bathrooms had condom catchers built into the toilets. Jamie had almost moved down there before Scott offered his basement as a temporary fix.

The car made its way down Hepburn Street, past strip malls studded with porno stores and discount tax offices, avoiding old shortcuts through apartment complexes now patched up with plywood windows. Larkhill's downtown stretched and bloated through the core of the city, dotted with grocery stores and half-empty townhouses with bed sheets for curtains.

"So what's the story with this dumb fuck in the woods?" Jamie asked. Stopped at a light, he watched the old ladies shuffling in and out of the downtown bingo hall, its storefront windows illuminating row after row of blue hair and gnarled fists wrapped around dabbers and hearing aids. A few men sat amongst them, along with the younger welfare set, babies in their laps. Jamie's mother was probably in there right now, keeping an eye on Mrs. Kasper, who'd won the last three nights straight. No one was that good at bingo.

"He was fucking old, man. Crypt keeper. Like your age."

Out on the street, faded HELP WANTED signs dotted some of the windows, but there were no store hours posted. Sharkey's Pawn Palace was about the only place open on the block, a sad little window filled with stiff iron bars and snapping teeth painted onto the glass.

"Remember who's driving you home, if you can, Mosey. Might be important in the future."

"Oh, I'm aware as hell. I can always just bum a ride next time. Got the good old thumb."

"Last time you did that, you got your ass kicked, if my ancient brain recalls correctly."

"I got jumped. Wasn't even in the car yet. They just swarmed me down by the park at Vista and Lawrence." Moses sighed. "It wasn't even that dark out."

"Just be glad you still have all your teeth, man."

They were getting closer to the highway now, apartment buildings and row houses giving way to warehouses and old industrial lots. Larkhill used to have twelve different manufacturing plants and three different head offices for minor corporations. The fields told a different story now. Gray lots covered in concrete and the last bits of loosestrife fighting off the cold. A few were fenced off with barbed wire strung through thick chain link. Dead grass and rotten foundations guarded by rusted forklifts. The ground here was filled with sulfur and asbestos and who knew what else, all of it bubbling under the crabgrass.

"Your teeth. I told you about Brock, right?" Jamie said. "Bottle of Ice hits him right in the mouth, and he's always got that jaw of his sagging open, like everything's a joke."

"He got beaned in the mouth?"

"In the fucking mouth. A forty of Max Ice right in the teeth. They call him Jack-O now. Looks like Halloween every time he cracks his mouth open."

"He's just gon' leave it like that?"

The streetlights toward the highway flickered on and off at intervals. No residents around to complain. Scattered boxes from dumped loads and old overstock stood in frozen piles by the doors to docking bays, each coated in faded spray paint. The letters were too long and jagged, the faces uneven, the smiles bent at odd angles.

"Says it's too expensive. You should see his mouth though," Jamie said.

"Can he still eat, and like drink and all that?"

"Yeah."

"At least he doesn't have to eat from a tube or something like I saw this girl on TV once. She was from Albania?" Moses said. "Or one of those places we should just bomb into glass. Someone we shoulda wiped out years ago. Someone no one cares about except the tabloids."

It was dark on the roads. The streetlights were gone. Only staggered telephone poles stood with loose nooses of wire dangling up and down the street. The ditches were full of leaky plastic bags that old ladies got their nephews to dump when they didn't want to pay the city to haul them away. Paint cans and adult diapers seeped down into the water table. Up ahead gleamed the long strip of motels, buzzing and flicking their signs to draw everyone out of their holes.

"So she is totally messed up and in this home for girls that can't talk good."

"So like deaf girls and…"

"No, not deaf. I'm talking like impediments. And so there was a fire there, and the fire alarm was not connected. Mounted on the wall, but fuck, nobody decided to plug it into anything."

Jamie squeezed the steering wheel tighter.

"You're kidding."

"This is true! It was on the TV, like, a few nights ago, I swear. The fire alarm isn't connected because these are backwoods people who shouldn't even exist, and guess what? No batteries in the smoke alarms. Turns out the dude running the place was like a total cheapskate—how much you wanna bet a Jew? Do they even have Jews there?"

"Moses, what I tell you about the Jew shit?"

The car still smelled like watered down blood, runoff from the cutting boards that dripped onto their clothes. Jamie flipped on the high beams as they approached the motels. Moses and his mom had a room at the Dynasty, the biggest one on the strip. Five stories of pigeon shit and oversized bay windows decorated in thin lines of purple neon, the letters lit up in bright orange like a landing strip. It was right next door to the Stow-and-Go storage yard.

"Most of the kids end up dying due to like the smoke," Moses continued. "They're asleep. They don't even know what's happening."

"What kind of school is this?"

"I think it was just like a home or something," Moses said. "But there is still this one girl and her dirty little gypsy ass. She can get herself a glass of water even if she can't ask for it. But all the staff there just run straight out when the fire starts. I'm talking nurses, doctors, the guy who changes the piss pans, all of them. They all just book it and totally forget the kids."

Jamie stared straight ahead at the road. He tried looking in the mirrors. Buzzing AM voices underscored Moses's high-pitched rant.

"Yeah, okay, Mosey. I get it, all right?"

"And so this girl tries to get out on her own. And she falls in the fire—this is what they said on the show. Her whole face goes up like kindling. Melts like butter. Melts her whole mouth shut for some reason. The way her skin burns it all drips down like candle wax. She's still got her nose and her slanty-ass eyes, but her mouth just doesn't exist. Isn't there anymore. Just gone."

Jamie did not look at Moses. He stared at the speedometer's sickly green light, watched the arrow flicker toward eighty kilometers.

"Moses, why? Why is this something you would tell me?" Jamie said.

"All I'm saying is Brock fucking Jack-O-Lantern Cutcherson should be happy he only lost a few teeth, because this girl has to have tubes hooked up to—"

There was a blur in front of the headlights and Jamie jammed the brake. Moses slammed against the glove box, popping it off the hinges. His face left a greasy imprint on the windshield. The car bucked and thumped into a shape on the road. Jamie's eyes caught a blur of hair before he cracked his head against the driver-side window and then off the cold steering wheel. The car had no airbags. Moses was bleeding from one ear.

"Jamie, what the fuck did you hit? Is that a kid?"

Jamie remembered stories his grandfather told him about moose up north, how the impact usually only broke their spindly legs, sending their massive frames head first through the windshield. By the time the police arrived, usually only the moose lived, its massive head mounted between the front seats wearing a wreath of cracked glass. Sometimes the kids in the backseat were still screaming when the cops pulled them out.

"No, not a fucking kid. Too big to be a kid. My neck, goddamn."

Jamie pulled himself up in the seat. One of his headlights was busted. The other clicked on and off as he tried to put the car in park. Moses opened the car door.

"What are you doin'?" Jamie asked.

"I gotta see who we hit."

"We didn't hit anyone. A car doesn't stop when it hits somebody," Jamie said.

"Well what is it, then?"

The crash rearranged every bone in Jamie's back. His shins burned and buckled as he kicked the door open and his vision blurred once his feet hit the ground. He sat with his head between his knees, fighting the urge to puke up the meatball sub he'd swallowed in three bites for dinner.

"Going to yak?"

"Fuck off, Moses."

"Hey, I'm not the one who fucked up your ride. My neck is pretty messed up, though."

Jamie stood up and stretched his arms over the roof. He laid his face on the cold metal. "That's why you're supposed to wear a seatbelt."

Moses walked toward the front of the car. "Don't freak out, all right, it's just a—oh, goddamn!"

Jamie moved to the front of the car. Each time the busted headlight flashed, Jamie spotted the blond fur and massive paws crushed beneath his front wheels. The grille was imprinted deep into the rib cage. A long tail with a brush at the end of it poked between Jamie's boots.

"You see its teeth, man? Imagine if we hadn't killed it," Moses said.

Jamie never went to the zoo as a child. He only knew about zebras and giraffes from TV.

"You killed a fucking lion, J."

The head was massive, the snout dwarfing even Moses's large, lopsided egg. The gums were black and pink, still coated in a thick layer of saliva. The mane was long and tangled, but the lion looked well fed. No mange or patches of discoloured fur. Each paw could have suffocated Jamie in his sleep. The two men stood over the body, their shadows flicking across the two-lane road.

"Is it dead? I think it has to be dead. It's dead, right, J?"

Jamie could tell by the eyes. Massive yellow and black eyes, the lids frozen open, but snuffed out. No flicker. The pupils no longer reacted to the changing light. A tire had crunched through the top of the beast's rib cage, splintering the bone and popping organs until all their juices ran together. Steam rose from the congealing puddles.

"A fucking lion, J. Shit, wait until I tell—"

"You aren't telling anyone shit, Moses."

"Do you think we can fit it in the trunk? I know this guy from down the hall, he has a brother out on Keewatin. The guy does taxidermy."

"We aren't going to fit this in the trunk," Jamie said.

"The lion? No, he's too big. So we come back with a truck. You think your brother will come by? Maybe do it for free? I only got like twenty-eight bucks on me right now, and I need some of that for tomorrow. How much you think taxidermy costs?" Moses asked.

"We aren't telling anyone about this. We aren't moving shit. We are dragging this fucker into the ditch before my back collapses in on itself and I end up paralyzed for life."

The car lurched as Jamie lay back on the hood.

"Man, this is money though. This is a lion. You could just even sell the head or something," Moses said. "Make cash. Pure cash."

"And how do you think it got here? Fucking flew over the Atlantic to land in the outskirts of Larkhill? This is someone's pet, Moses."

"Or from a zoo."

"Exactly. Or a zoo. Someone with money, someone who can afford a fucking lion."

A small pool was beginning to form under its head.

"So?"

"So you don't think they'll come looking for this…this thing?" Jamie said.

"If we get it out of here soon, we can like—well, do something."

"And don't you think it'll be all over the papers? Escaped lion in town? And I very much doubt there is going to be a fucking reward for killing it with a Cutlass. What there might be is a trial or a lawsuit, or even just a revoked license and then guess who walks home from work all by himself from now on, getting his skinny, skinhead ass jumped like it's his day job?"

"I get it, I get it. And you think we should just leave it?" Moses said.

"I think Mr. Taxidermy-Up-On-Keewatin might watch the news and might look at your pimply ass and the state of my car and put two and two together with a phone call to the cops."

"Shit. So what do we do?"

They dragged the massive corpse across half a lane before giving up. The back legs and tail still lay on the shoulder. Jamie's back finally collapsed, and Moses's arms wobbled with the effort. The single headlight flicked on and off through their progress. The lion's rib cage had cracked again when they'd pulled it free from the car. Its lungs and heart remained exposed to the cold night air. With no reverse, the car had to stay in place as they yanked the corpse out from under the wheels. Jamie checked the body for any imprint of his license plate. A faded nine was pressed deep into the animal's flank.

The night got colder. No cars passed as they shoved the furry mound a few inches at time. People rarely took the service road down to the motels. It was easier to get there on the highway.

Moses's windbreaker crackled against the cold air. His pants were still wet from the hose. He could feel the frost in his knuckles every time he yanked the lion another inch. After forty-five minutes of pushing and pulling, the two sat on the hood of the car. Their lungs ached from the cold air. Jamie slapped the hood and the headlight quit flickering. Their shadows urged them to head down the road. A long trail of blood stretched across one lane, ending in a furry pile.

"Someone is going to find him. We still have a lion on the side of the road. This is no big secret if you can still see him," Moses said.

"Looks like a slug, bleeding out its ass like that."

Jamie could feel his bones grinding against each other when he stood up.

"Let's go. We ain't going to move it any further talking about it."

Moses no longer felt like talking. Every time he opened his mouth, the cold clenched his teeth. He climbed into the passenger side and listened to the car hiccup as Jamie turned the key again and again. The pile at the side of the road did not move. The one headlight only illuminated a small patch of darkness up ahead.

After the fifth try, the car finally kicked to life. The grunt of the engine allowed Jamie to relax for a brief second before he looked out the window at the body. Moses was right.

No one was going to just drive past a fucking lion.

3

Elvira Moon loved bowling. For four straight years, her team, the Blooming Broads, dominated the women's league, decimating all opponents until Big Tina quit to start her own team, the South Side Splitters, with that bitch Claudia from Couscous or whatever country she'd arrived from in a banana crate. Moses was still in elementary school when this division occurred.

The Splitters snatched the title two years straight before Elvira could steal it back. Big Tina quit bowling after that year due to a ruptured lower colon, leaving Elvira to dominate once again with her devastating accuracy and a bowling ball she'd named the Judge. Instead, Elvira disbanded the team. Her greatest rival, who'd worn men's shoes without apology and never forgot to send her a Christmas card since they'd met at a Tupperware party in '78, was gone. After the surgery, Big Tina moved in with Claudia and quit competitive bowling for good. No true competition remained. In Elvira's mind, the Blooming Broads had won enough free games, chicken wing platters, bowling alley T-shirts, promotional balls, and buy-one-get-one-free pizza coupons to last a lifetime.

With no team to hold her back, Elvira made the rounds every week from Saturday Rock'n'Bowl at Paulie's Pins to Yuri's in-house tournaments held every other Wednesday. Her bowling ball collection took over the china cabinet. All her boyfriends had the requisite alley gut Elvira so admired. It was the same gut her husband Ted Moon had before he quit bowling and moved down to Arizona. In the dark of night, Elvira rested her head on that anonymous island of flesh under the sheets. She dreamed of that big trophy they handed out to every player who bowled a perfect game. It was after his perfect game that Ted had quit. Quit his job, his marriage, his friends, quit her and Moses, everything. Elvira both dreaded and desired a perfect game of her own, longed to see the score trickle higher and higher until every piece had fallen into place and the confetti rained down from the ceiling.

Maybe then she'd understand why.

Moses Moon was ten years old when his mother's skull collided with a fourteen-pound ball some novice released during his back swing. Skipping up and down behind the lanes to psych herself up for the Co-Ed Co-Mingler Tournament, Elvira had three shots of gin in her system when the left side of her skull exploded. The sound of the ball hitting her head echoed through Bronson Alleys, overpowering the clatter of pins and the rumble of the bowling balls thudding into the automatic delivery system. One of the part-time kids who sprayed shoes for five hours a day told the cops it sounded just like one of those English bell towers ringing out the fucking end of the world. Like a reckoning.

The doctors called it an unfathomable and unfortunate case. Early onset dementia was often considered to be at least partially a genetic disease, potentially hereditary, though from which parent was still highly debated. A few experts also pointed to diet and exercise as potential paths to stave off this cerebral devastation. None had encountered a woman who, at the healthy age of thirty-two, was struck down by a lime-green bowling ball and thrust into a life of rapidly decaying brain activity.

Elvira Moon could still feed herself, go to the bathroom, and even knit Christmas-themed outerwear for her young son, but she no longer had the capacity to work in a regular corporate environment.

Hullen Financial decided to let her go with a generous severance package after she began rerouting her calls to an old abusive uncle in South Florida. Elvira Moon spent the majority of the payment on rehabilitating dogs who'd been run over by cars and had lost their legs in the process. On tax forms, half of her income was reported as a charitable donation to the K-9 Mobilization Front. Government audits were performed with little to no follow-up.

After adopting many of these dogs, which her neighbors collectively called the Cyborgs, Elvira often forgot to feed them. Her bowling balls grew dusty and she no longer remembered Ted, who now sang soprano during the dinner hour at the Sacred Crow's Big House Casino in suburban Scottsdale, Arizona. She'd forgotten the perfect game. Much of the responsibility fell to her son, who constructed ramps around the house out of two-by-fours lifted from neighbors' backyard projects. Young Moses Moon learned to feed the dogs on a regular basis and to chase them around the backyard for exercise instead of taking them out for walks, where people would often stare, take pictures, or call the police about that strange boy walking a horde of wheeled terriers, Cocker Spaniels, and schnauzers down the street.

It was often Mrs. Singh who made these phone calls, disguising her voice as a man's and playing the heavy metal music her son liked so much in the background. She was paranoid about the police recording her voice, scared of anyone in a position of authority coming after her or her family. Her father had died in Pakistan after speaking out against a corrupt zoning commission, mysteriously drowning in his own washtub, and since then any man in a suit caused the fine hairs on the back of her neck to stand on end.

Hiding behind her thick burlap curtains, Mrs. Singh had spotted the young Moses Moon stealing boards from her backyard. She had watched him allow the dogs to drop their feces in her gardens, ruining the tomatoes her husband liked so much. The dogs pissed through the cracks of the fence, causing weeds to sprout up in hard-to-reach places. In this neighborhood, she understood the houses were built very close together. In fact, the walls were shared. You had to learn to deal with your neighbors, and even be civil with people who didn't know your name.

Mrs. Singh appreciated these points of etiquette. And yet, every day Mrs. Singh watched travesties occurring on her property. The boy stood unchallenged. His crippled dog army slowly decreased the value of her property, which her husband could have explained was rented and not actually their problem. Unfortunately, since he figured this would only embarrass her, the issue never came up at dinner over platters of salted tomato.

Once on a winter morning, Mrs. Singh had even gathered the courage to approach the door of the Moons' townhouse. She rang the doorbell and was greeted by a towering woman whose blond hair was piled high up on her head. The woman only dressed in a pink loose-fitting gown and high-heeled shoes. She wore headphones, and her purple lipstick made jagged lines across her mouth. The house smelled like old milk.

"Are you the mail lady?"

Inside, Mrs. Singh heard the growing chorus of crippled dogs. She could hear their wheels bouncing down the stairs toward her as each second passed and the tall woman just stared at her. Outside in the rain, children on second-hand bicycles jeered at one another. There was no one around, no one to help pull the mutant creatures off her if this tower of a woman set them loose. Her husband would not return from his shift at the car seat factory for at least four more hours. By then it would be too late, and all he'd find would be her broken body covered in tiny bite marks and the treads of innumerable wheels that had cracked all her aging bones.

Mrs. Singh ran.

After her fifth call to the police, a patrol car finally came by to check in on the Moon household. All the dogs were inside. Moses kept most of them in the basement. He did his best to keep the smells down by hanging air fresheners from the lamps and lighting fixtures. He usually got them for free from car dealerships down by the highway, where he rode his bike to escape the smell of the house. He had to duck around this evergreen forest dangling in every room.

"We've had a few complaints from some neighbors. If we could just come inside to maybe address a few issues, we'll be out of your way as soon as we can. Is your mother or father home at the moment? It's probably best we take it up with an adult."

Elvira told them all about the time her cousin made her eat a snail they'd found on the roof of their apartment building. It had to be magic, 'cause how else could a snail get on the roof? The officers didn't laugh or humor her. They smelled the rotten food hidden beneath the floating forests Moses Moon had constructed. Their notepads filled quickly.

Moses Moon was upstairs packing during this one-sided conversation. At twelve years old, he knew he would be taken away by Children's Aid the moment these policemen finished talking to his mother. He would no longer be able to smoke cigarettes or watch the blurry adult channels on the television. They'd take his mom to a room somewhere where she would be scared and alone and surrounded by machines. These wouldn't be machines like the dogs. These would be cold and silent, and they would never lick your face when you were sad.

Moses Moon knew this like he knew the *Tyrannosaurus Rex* was most likely a scavenging dinosaur and not a major predator. He knew it like he knew his father would never come back from Arizona. This was an undisputed truth he had learned to recognize. They would never let her out of that room again.

"Ma'am, would it be all right with you if we went down to examine the basement? We just want to make sure we do a thorough examination."

Moses Moon also called a cab company he'd found in the Yellow Pages. He didn't give an address, but an intersection down the street. He had two hundred and thirteen dollars he'd been storing away from birthdays and the random bills his mother left scattered around the crowded townhouse. She was always forgetting things, like to shower or to tie up her shoes. Moses had got very good at teaching her to do these things all over again. Sometimes she even remembered the next day. Eventually, she might remember everything.

He packed a bag for his mother too, full of her underwear and socks. He threw in T-shirts and her makeup box and a few cans of her favorite chicken soup. He zipped the bag up and dragged it with his own down the long hallway littered with dog barf and air fresheners that had fallen from the ceiling. He could hear the two men in the basement and the chorus of dogs rattling the heating ducts.

"Moses, did you meet the men who've come to check on the dogs?"

Moses took care of the dogs, but he rarely ever gave them names. Big Bitch, Little Bitch, Jaws, Wheelie. He saw them snapping and biting one another each morning when he went down into the basement. He cleaned up the puddles of piss and the wet turds they hid in the corners, the ones the smaller dogs didn't eat. Kids at school always asked if he'd shit himself and why his eyes were red. Moses would not miss the dogs.

"We're going for a walk, Mom."

Moses grabbed a chair from the kitchen. He dragged it over to the basement door and slammed it shut, provoking another round of howls. He could hear the men pounding up the basement stairs two at a time. They bellowed through the fat of their jowls, but Moses could not make out the words. He jammed the chair under the iron knob of the door.

"We gotta go, Mom."

"Well, I don't have a bag, you know that, Mosey. I have to have my bag before I go."

Elvira was still wearing her nightgown and the high heels she'd bought with the prize money from her first Bowlarama tournament, the one where she and Ted won the couples category in a six-game sweep over the Johnstones. Ted bowled a turkey. It was glorious.

"I already packed it. You've got everything."

"What about the dogs?" Elvira asked.

"I've got people to pick them up. Kids from school and their parents all want to adopt them. You should hear them."

"Are you sure?"

A body threw itself against the basement door and the chair legs dug into the floorboards.

"Yes, yes, I'm sure, grab your bag, let's go, go, go!" Moses said.

Out the door and down through the overgrown garden. The dogs overpowered any other noise on the street. Moses could see the cab sitting at the corner, the driver picking his nails and checking his teeth in the rearview. Elvira ran behind him toward the cab, hopping over each crack in the sidewalk. Moses feared she'd roll her ankle, and then it would be cops, and badges, and bars, and a little room, so he grabbed her hand and pulled her along beside him.

"Just take us down to the highway," Moses said. "I've got fifty dollars, right? That's enough, enough for you?"

The driver had watched a woman give birth in his car the day before. It still smelled like placenta. He didn't blink.

"Just to the highway?"

"Yeah, yeah, we can walk from there," he said. "Right, Mom?"

"We can walk wherever you want, baby boy. We can walk across oceans."

The driver turned down their street, passing the silent cop car and the small children who raced their bikes up and down on the sidewalk in the rain. The whole street was coated in orange leaves, the wet rain making them cling to everything.

As Moses slid down low in the seat, he saw Mrs. Singh peering out from behind her heavy brown curtains. Her window was covered in sticky leaves. She didn't see him, but she smiled at the police car sitting on the street. Moses watched her close the curtains while Elvira kept talking about her sister and the plums in the schoolyard. The cab turned the corner without using its signal. That was four years ago.

4

After Jamie Garrison dropped him outside the Dynasty, Moses Moon puked behind the fake Christmas trees that management left outside year round. The smell of lion's blood and shit still lingered in his senses. He knew if he'd puked in front of Garrison he would've never lived it down. He'd heard stories about Garrison beating up kids behind the Zellers when he was in high school, the arms broken over the push bars of shopping carts, the boots to formerly beautiful faces, the jagged snap of fingers in docking-bay doors.

Before he drove off, Garrison had warned him not to say anything. "You don't even know what a lion looks like, you understand?"

Everyone called the rambling motel Da Nasty. It leered out over the other smaller buildings on the block, five stories of clapboard and stucco. Moses had moved Elvira from motel to motel over the first few years of their exile, dodging the police and Children's Aid while riding his bicycle to school. Elvira started collecting bowling balls again, taking them into the shower with her. There were always complaints from housekeeping staff and neighbors concerning missing credit cards and stolen purses. Aliases like Allison Cooper, Joanna Page, Paula McCartney, and Gina Simmons littered the guest books of the tired, neon-coated hovels along the wide strip of the utility road.

Moses hated elevators. The spaces were too small, the walls always mirrored. Reflection after reflection of his pimply skull refracted to infinity till each pore glared at him. He always took the stairs up to the second floor and walked along the thick orange carpeting running his hand along the wall, looking for an open door, a wallet sitting on a dresser, a purse left in the bathroom. Occasionally he walked in on couples locked in complex positions he'd only seen in the pay-per-view movies. He would only order those after his mother passed out in the other double bed, moaning about her poor doggies and the betrayal of Big Tina.

"Mom, you around? I didn't end up bringing back any food yet."

The room still smelled liked moth balls and Pepto Bismol. The dark purple carpet was covered in cigarette burns. The blinds to the balcony were closed. Most of the balconies in Da Nasty were locked. There were too many lonely men romancing the concrete five stories down. Pigeons and a lone red-tailed hawk now ruled the balconies, slowly coating the rails in white each summer, only to have it washed away by the rain and snow every winter.

"Hey, Mom, you here?"

"Just in the bathroom, baby boy. Just in the bathroom."

"You got any plans for coming out of there tonight?"

"I got the Judge in here with me, too," Elvira said.

It wasn't the same Judge from the old days. This Judge was found at a Salvation Army near the butcher shop; it was bright teal and cracked between the holes. Elvira didn't mind. Moses had scrawled THE JUDGE on it with a Sharpie before he brought it home.

The television blared with piped-in laughter as Moses lay down in the bed. Bill Cosby tried to speak to him about the meaning of life through a blast of static, but he ignored the voice. He could smell the dusted meat sticking to his arm hair, but there was no way to get into that bathroom now. Elvira had locked the door. He walked down the hall past the sound of bashing headboards to the ice machine and plunged his lion-stained hands deep into the ice catcher under the machine.

"What the fuck are you doing?"

A man towered over the ice machine and looked down at Moses. The man's wide gut was mounted over a stiff belt buckle. A long beard covered the top of his stomach. A sword wrapped in a green snake stretched down the knuckles of his left hand. Moses stood his ground, trapped with his hands wrist deep in the cold ice.

"Washing my hands, Grandpa."

The older man grunted and turned to walk back down the hallway. He dragged a wet garbage bag behind him still covered in snow.

Moses pulled his hands out and followed the man down the hall. The carpet was thick and shaggy. It masked his steps. The door to Room 227 slammed closed behind the man's balding head, and Moses leaned against the yellow wall. He could hear someone praying from somewhere behind the wallpaper, the rise and fall of a Hail Mary repeating as Moses tried to forget every fact he'd learned about lions in his grade-school days. Massive, muscled bodies that could grow up to eight feet in length, heavy spines which lined the male's penis, the power of their kills based on brutal strangulation of their prey.

Everything he ever learned watching television at five in the morning with the sound blaring and cigarettes burning the tips of his fingers. This would be the best way to forget lions and rogue members of ZZ Top dragging garbage bags through his motel, his home. The hallway was quieter than normal, the late-night residents still hitting the bars and each other down in lower Larkhill. Moses kept earplugs in a can under the bed for weekend nights, when all the vacant rooms filled with lot lizards and line workers with new paychecks to burn and burn till there was nothing left but ash. The Hail Marys continued and Moses nodded along until they finally stopped.

Lions. He had to forget lions. He walked down the uneven hallways, barely testing the doors. He didn't expect to find any abandoned wallets tonight. Tonight was supposed to be about forgetting things. Forgetting his mother holed up in the bathroom, forgetting the smell of his pants, his father in Arizona, the essay he was supposed to hand in tomorrow at 10 a.m. for World History. He was already pretty good at forgetting which nation bombed which first, but right now all he had to try and forget was the steaming pile he and Garrison had left on the side of the road for the whole world to find.

From inside his room, Moses heard his Mom cackle and cracked what only the most optimistic man would call a smile.

Jamie Garrison awoke in his brother's unfinished basement and tried to climb out of bed. He'd spent the whole night hosing down the front of his car, chipping off the bits of lion flesh that had frozen to the front bumper. He dropped them down the sewer grate at the base of the driveway, trying to slip them down into the sludge of leaves and dead squirrels that caused the street to flood every spring. Scott almost caught him when he backed out of the driveway at 4 a.m.

Renee had coffee going in the kitchen when he went upstairs. The stench of Scott's sanitation gear was everywhere. Ever since she and Scott got married in the summer, Renee had gone all formal, as if she didn't have a school of mermaids tattooed up her spine.

"You see the paper yet?" Renee said.

Someone had found the lion. Somehow he'd left a glove or piece of the car—there were serial numbers on cars, weren't there? Shit, they put serial numbers on everything now.

"Scottie said you should look at this story they got on like page ten, it's buried in there somewhere. Someone you know."

It wasn't like Scott had circled the article for him. Every time he turned a page, Jamie felt the grind of his bones against one another. His neck strained to stay in place, every muscle tensed and bleating for some relief. Jamie scanned past the used car advertisements and into the police bulletins. Someone had robbed the beer store again.

Someone else had smashed ten windows at the new courthouse they'd built over the old J.P. Chemical land.

"Kansas called for you last night, too, like one in the morning again. Her mom know she's doing that?" Renee said. "Five years old, calling the house? She gonna stay with us again any time soon?"

"Uh, this weekend?"

It was at the bottom of the page. Body found in Athabasca Park identified by police. The body was a few weeks old, according to the article. Jamie remembered the name.

"Kansas still obsessed with dinosaurs? I was thinking we could get a T. Rex pie dish or something, saw it at the Bulk Barn. Or maybe..."

Access to local dental records confirmed the man's identity. A long-time local resident, Connor Justin Condon, now considered a homicide by local officials.

"Sure, yeah. I mean, she hasn't grown out of it yet. Go ahead and get the cake...Renee?"

Renee was slumped down on a chair by the sink, her face buried in her chest, a mermaid peering over the back of her collar. She barely made a noise when she slept.

"You there, Renee?"

Jamie pulled himself up from the table and shoved the page of newsprint into his back pocket. He ran a chapped hand through her faded red hair and turned off the tap she'd left running at the sink. The overhead fan in the kitchen turned slowly, raining dust down on everything in the purple light. Jamie could taste it on his tongue.

5

Brock Cutcherson lived in one of the Polish neighborhoods down by the lake where everybody double parked and stole from their neighbors' tiny herb gardens when they weren't home. He rented a basement apartment from the Karskises and often had to deal with stamping feet when he turned his Iron Maiden records up too loud. But it was fuckin' Maiden, so whatever.

Still, the Karskises often invited him up to dinner with their quiet daughter Karina, who wore the desperately needed braces Brock's rent checks had paid for over the last two and a half years. She worked for Macalister and McGowan, an old downtown law firm based out of a former funeral home. They kept her in the basement sorting old files, where she often composed poems on the back of subpoenas before running them through the shredder, never to be read again. She knew her father would not approve. Sometimes she left Brock notes in the shared laundry room, tucked inside the lint catcher.

"So it's like this, right: 'Mr. Cutcherson, although you have never spoken to me alone before, I want you to know I thank you every day for the money you provide my family.'"

"Kind of formal, isn't it?" Jamie said.

He sat on Brock's bed and tried to avoid knocking over half-full containers of Chinese food and McDonald's Happy Meal toys Brock had lined up on the floor like soldiers.

"Well, basically she's saying, 'Let's knock boots, big man, thanks for un-fucking up my mangled mouth.'"

Jamie checked his watch and rocked back and forth on the bed. The longer he sat still, the more he felt each muscle knotting itself tighter and tighter around his bones. Getting out of the car had taken fifteen minutes and he still couldn't turn his neck all the way to the right. Brock's splayed smile stared back at him. Half his teeth were missing after Monday night's bottle accident.

"Face it, you're going to end up marrying that broad and having three little babies with her and moving in with the family and making the pilgrimage see to the Pope and learning the deep, dark secrets of pierogi magic."

"Shut up, Garrison."

Jamie kicked a foot out and sent a bunch of Fraggle Rock toys flying into a corner stacked with dirty underwear. Brock winced but didn't say anything.

"Why do you collect these little buggers, anyway?" Jamie said.

"Happy Meals are cheap as fuck. For three bucks, I get a whole meal."

"Yeah, but you don't need to—whatever. I brought this over."

Jamie flapped the battered piece of paper in Brock's face.

"You remember him, right? The little wiener from back when we lived on Olive."

"Which guy?"

"The guy with the—you know, 'Don't Be a Loner, Wrap Your Boner'—that guy?"

"The chick with the hot dog and her grandma? That's just a story, you know that, right? If you're thinking of the chick, or maybe it was a dude, who knows, but the one with the broom stick? Now I know for a fact that *that* happened. Girl fell right off the fridge. Impaled."

"No, he's a fucking guy, Brock. Took the bus with us. Little bitch who almost got me booted out of high school, the one with the—"

"Oh, shit, you mean Condom," Brock said.

"Yes, yes, exactly, that's the dude. The dude just disappeared off the planet," Jamie said. "I figured he killed himself or something, like years ago, but apparently he was still kicking around here somewhere. Until this."

"Until what?" Brock asked.

"Just read the fucking article."

Brock spent every night from four until midnight slugging boxes of booze down at the liquor warehouse. The place had always looked like a deserted hangar bay to Jamie, even back when he was working there on the day shift. Brock would drive home at night covered in beer and gin, avoiding major intersections and the highway in case he got pulled over, but he always failed to wash his pants till the weekend. T-shirts covered in abstract splashes of red wine and vermouth sat in piles till Brock could no longer leap over them.

"You ever think of buying hangers?" Jamie said.

"I'm trying to read here, stop screwing with me," Brock said.

Jamie swung his feet back and forth over the islands of Chinese food on the floor. They were about the only bones in his body that did not hurt. He closed his eyes. Alisha was supposed to call him about the kid again tonight. And Scott still wanted him out in a couple weeks, and the meat shop was going to call him in for another shift. Behind all these thoughts lurked the lion with its rib cage split open and its intestines spooling out across the pavement. Its eyes were open.

"It is the Condom. Goddamn," Brock said. "What a knob. You remember when he cried 'cause we told him yogurt was just elephant jizz, and—shit, what did one of the girls say to him?"

"I don't remember, but he was a shit stain. Pissed himself once on the bus, remember?"

"That was probably the one time I felt bad about that dude. We razed his ass more than once. And he was always making shit look so dramatic. I mean he probably brought it on himself anyway. But no one deserves this kind of shit," Brock said.

Brock leaned back in his chair and coughed in his hand.

"I saw you fucked the front of your car up."

"Just a raccoon, sent me spinnin' off the road a little," Jamie said. "Might have knocked a tree or a shrub or something. No big deal."

"A raccoon?"

"Yeah, that's what I'm also here about; I know you got all those meds, for the teeth, right? So I was wondering. I mean, my neck is killing me."

"Sold 'em, boss," Brock said.

"What?"

"I fucking sold 'em for pretty good money."

"Well, shit, you know where I can get any? I need something. I won't be able to go to work otherwise."

"Go see a doctor like I did."

Jamie stood up and kicked a few more Happy Meal toys across the floor.

"I'm the one who took you to the fucking doctor in the first place."

"You wanna know who I took 'em to?"

"Why else do you think I'm here?" Jamie asked.

"All right, okay? Go down Olive until you see a one-way for Monroe, and then just cruise down there until you hit the old strip malls that pretty much just have like nothing going on. You know the ones I'm talking about. Well, one has a porno store, and the other might still have a sub sandwich place, but anyway, it'll be an old hobby shop, with um, a sun roof?"

"A sun roof?"

"Shit, um, that's the best I can describe it," Brock said.

"Skylights?"

"Yeah, whatever. Just knock there, it says like Henry's Holistic Hobbies on the door."

"You can remember that name, but not the word skylight?" Jamie said.

Brock smiled his pumpkin smile and pulled a two-liter bottle of Coke out from under the bed.

"You'll recognize the guy 'cause he has a big-ass moustache. He'll want you to call him Larry or some shit. I was pretty messed up when I went to go sell him the stuff so I don't really remember. It won't be his real name, I can tell you that. But he has some righteous stuff. Woulda put old Condom out of his misery, if he knew what was good for him. Now watch this."

Brock took a swig from the bottle and then fired two parallel streams from between his teeth across the floor. When he smiled, all Jamie could see were the holes.

6

Moses didn't mind working the morning shift. He liked the quiet. He liked the smell of sanitizer in the cutting rooms, the glow of the battered off-white cutting boards propped up against the floor. All the stuff in the back was stainless steel—the tables, the carts, the sinks. Sometimes he wandered into the refrigerator with his bike helmet still on, dodging the massive sides of beef that weighed more than he did. They dangled from the ceiling on long hooks that swayed in the breeze from the cooling fans.

"Abraham's son, my man, you gotta get your shit together. What is with the shaved head?"

Texaco Joe took a pull from a cigarette and pushed his way into the refrigerator. He had a giant purple tuque pulled over his head. His lips were chapped and flaking.

"It keeps me cool."

"It keeps you cool? It's like thirty under out there right now. Under the zero."

Moses began setting up the cutting boards and pulling the knives out of the sink. The blades were still sharp from the night before. Sometimes Moses would test them on his fingernails when he was closing by himself. Shaving off tiny little slices to flush down the drain.

"If it was thirty below, you'd be bitching a whole lot more. It's like minus ten."

"I don't bitch, all right? If it is thirty below where I'm from, everyone is dead anyway."

Texaco Joe never said exactly where he'd come from or where he was born. The odds were sixty to forty on Barbados, according to Jamie. Joe had tried to claim he was from Houston and even wore an Astros cap in the summer, but he had never crossed the border in the five years he'd worked for Don Henley at the shop. He couldn't even name any other Texas cities besides Dallas and San Antonio. However, he did own three pairs of cowboy boots. Purple, green, and tan leather. His wife polished them for church on Sundays.

"You hear what happened to your little white-boy friends last night at the barber's? They always skulkin' round there. Bound to happen finally, little shits."

"At the Triple K? What happened to them?"

"Yes, my friend's place. He finally got rid of the—what are their names?"

"Since when is he your friend? You can't even remember his name," Moses said.

"You see this new cut? He did this."

Joe spun in a circle. His hair was shaved almost to the scalp. Smoke from his cigarette gathered around the dangling lights.

"You aren't supposed to be smoking back here, Joe."

Joe just waved a hand through the yellow cloud.

"No one will know. You might want to call someone. I will cover for you, little buddy. You really need to get those little skulls under control.

"You didn't see the blood outside, eh? Down the street? I thought you rode your bike."

"I keep my head down when I ride."

"The two little skulls got broken noses, I think. I was getting a shave too, you know. Couldn't adjust myself to see exactly what was going on. A lot of whap, whap, whap was all I heard. "

Joe punched at the air. Moses sat down on one of the bone cans.

"You might want to call the one with the tattoo on his head. The one with the big mouth. He looks like he got the worst of it."

Joe strutted by Moses and back into the meat fridge, stubbing his cigarette out in the steel sink. Moses didn't move. He knew hanging out at the Triple K had been a bad idea. Logan and B. Rex went there every day after school. Moses usually had to work.

Klips, Kuts, and Kurls. The oldest barbershop on the south side of Larkhill, nestled in between Gerry's Convenience and the local branch of the National Fears and Phobias Crisis Center. Established in 1923 by Luke Hofstadler and his three sons. The Hofstadlers were one of the few black families to set up shop on that side of town. The place had been burned down a few times in the past, though the first two were due to electrical problems and the third involved a drunken reopening party to celebrate the second restoration.

Logan had brought it up when they were drunk and listening to some strange Hungarian folk music his dad had bought at a garage sale. It was two in the afternoon and they were skipping history with Mr. Wallburton, who smoked little Russian cigarettes in his Pinto at lunch while reading harlequin novels. He tore the covers off to hide the titles.

"It's basically a provocation to everything we stand for, you know. Like, spitting in our faces. Collectively, as like, a collective of whites," Logan said.

"We stand for what exactly?" B. Rex said.

"Break down the name, man. They can dress it up in purple letters all they want, but like, what else does triple K stand for these days? KKK."

Moses was sitting on Logan's bed, staring at the David Bowie posters and the Star Wars figures lined up on the bookshelf, trying to figure out how they all fit into this new philosophy boiling under his skin every time he rode his bike past his old neighborhood. No, not a philosophy, more like a feeling, a vibration that made the hairs on his back stand up—the small thin white hairs Moses feared would never grow any darker.

"But we don't even wear sheets. That shit is all played out."

B. Rex had his skinny little arms crossed against his massive chest and was smiling, his incisors twice as large as his other teeth. Moses always assumed that was where he got the nickname until they all got wasted at Cheryl Oppenheimer's birthday—the one where someone ripped the phone jack out of the wall—and watched B. Rex do his dinosaur imitations. None of the boys had been invited to that party. They just showed up.

"Same sort of philosophy, though. Don't you guys think so?" Logan said.

Moses didn't say anything. Boba Fett was pointing a gun directly at his face.

"We don't need to hide our faces," B. Rex said. "We got more pride than that."

"But don't you guys think this is fucked up?" Logan said. "KKK? It just seems like one major, undeniable fuck-up. That's all. And we shouldn't—I don't know. We should do something. Make a stand."

In the end, the three of them agreed it was indeed one giant, major, undeniable fuck-up. It was their second meeting as a group, or organization or whatever it was. Even now, in the back room of the meat shop, Moses wasn't sure what they were supposed to be. He rubbed his chest and felt the bruise above his ear where he'd whacked his head against the windshield.

They started hanging out in front of Klips, Kuts, and Kurls after school. At first they just stood around in the parking lot. Customers walked by without even blinking at the three bald heads covered in ingrown hairs and razor burn. Three skinny white boys weren't going to stop them from getting their hair cut at the same place they'd got it done since they were five. These were lifelong customers with weekly appointments.

It was Moses's idea to get the tattoos and the cigarettes. His idea to start wearing the leather jackets he found at Salvation Army when he was looking to replace the Judge for his mother. They were green and yellow football jackets from one of the old high schools. William Orson Collegiate. Each jacket said EAGLES across the back over a pair of wings. Logan said black jackets would have been better.

It was Moses's idea to smash old beer bottles in front of the door after old Hofstadler had swept up at the end of the day. His idea to break the front window one night with a piece of paving they found in the parking lot. His idea to piss on the door handles and spray paint a purple triple K onto the glass. B. Rex ended up getting the paint all over his hands, leaving a trail of purple spurts back to his house. The police had no problem finding him. The tattoos were the hardest part, though. They should never have tried to do it all by themselves.

Moses had worked from an old book on sailor and prison tattoos in Logan's basement. He'd found it at the library and snuck it past the front desk under his jacket. That night Moses held a busted blue pen taped to a needle. The hot ink dribbled all over his hand. A lighter lay discarded on the floor between empty bottles.

They had drunk all day from Logan's mom's stash of bourbon, the cheap kind that smelled like a doctor's office. Moses told them it was to dull the pain, hoping they would overlook his trembling hands. Moses had inked himself first. Facing the mirror, he ran the jagged pen across his sternum. He could barely feel the needle, but he could see the drops of blood running down his skinny stomach. It was just three letters they'd decided on after the first bottle of bourbon was empty and Logan had finished throwing up behind the coffee table.

Moses didn't realize until the next morning his own letters were backwards. White Eagle Army. It made even less sense when they all woke up sober and found the red and blue welts carved into their chests. WEA. Another unfortunate acronym.

"Hey, Moses! Little Abraham, you all right?"

Texaco grinned at Moses through the door to the meat cooler.

"Yeah."

"You going to do any work or cry about your friends all day?"

"I'm fine," Moses said.

"They aren't in the hospital or anything like that, little man."

No, because Logan's mom didn't believe in the hospital. Neither did his dad.

"I know that, Tex."

"I can cover for you if you want to go and pat their little heads," Joe said.

There was a reason Logan's mom walked with a limp. His father never let her go to the doctor after she fell off the roof putting up the Christmas lights. Logan said she shouldn't have been up there in the first place, but he and his dad were terrified of heights. It was a genetic thing amongst the Chattertons. His mom didn't argue for a doctor. Logan's father set the leg himself and made a cast out of old bed sheets and papier-mâché.

Both Logan's parents had failed out of medical school together after performing bizarre elective operations on each other in the semi-abandoned maternity ward of the university hospital. It was a janitor who found Mr. Chatterton rearranging the tendons in his soon-to-be-wife's hands and called a code blue for the entire building. They were expelled.

"Take the morning off, all right?" Joe said. "You don't need to be here right now, you were here last night. I don't even think you changed your clothes, man. You stink."

Moses looked down at his chest. There was still a smear of blood on his shirt. It must have soaked through his windbreaker the night before. Joe slammed a side of pork down on the bone saw and pulled a white coat over his skinny shoulders.

"Heavy stuff, your friends. You go. I'll say you called in sick. You look like a dead man anyway."

The sun was beginning to rise. Trees cast off the last of their leaves one by one, brown flakes coating the pavement. Moses pushed his bike down the street. Logan didn't live in any of the old apartment buildings on this block. They towered over the sidewalks, casting the whole strip in shadows that only grew as the morning passed. The balconies were covered in alternating patterns of pink and teal railings.

Moses could see the house at the end of the street and the two rusted cars parked in the driveway. Both of them sat up on concrete blocks Mr. Chatterton had lifted from the construction site near his dentist's office. He might not have believed in doctors or mechanics, but Mr. Chatterton wasn't going to let anyone but a professional touch his teeth.

The front door was bright yellow, repainted every summer by Mr. Chatterton. He'd inherited the house from his father, a man whose color wheel consisted of four distinct shades of brown. Logan's grandpa had been the janitor at the coal plant and then the nuclear plant just an hour outside Larkhill. He had eaten the same ham sandwich from the same lunchbox on the same bench for fifty-five years before his heart finally clogged and abruptly stopped. When the night shift took over, they found him with a mouthful of ham still clenched in his teeth.

Each room in the house was another indictment against this man who Mr. Chatterton believed had stunted his childhood—the bright mauve of the kitchen a slap to the old man's disregard for family photo collages framed in macaroni, the lime-green hallway a rebuke to his decree that real men did not ask for a pet rabbit on their fifth birthday, and the teal tiles around the tub a final dismissal of his claim that bubble baths were only for women, homosexuals, geriatrics, and the schizophrenic community.

The doorbell was broken. Moses walked into the rainbow-walled house, the hasty paint showing brown and gray in the corners, old wallpaper peeping through the primer near the ceiling. The brushwork looked like loose stitches, barely holding wounds together. Each room was brightly painted in the Chatterton home, but every seam was frayed—every corner slowly unraveling.

Moans came from the basement in slow gasps. Moses forced himself down the stairs, blocking out memories of bipedal dogs and overweight policemen. A long work table covered in old medical textbooks, a surgical saw, Tarot cards, phone bills, and the annual horoscope for those born in the Year of the Monkey took up most of the floor.

"Logan, you all right? I heard you got fucked up down at the Triple K."

The door to Logan's room, painted in what his father would call a "spritely magenta," was wide open. Logan was restrained on the bed with old utility belts and a bright yellow extension cord. His father leaned over him, glasses dangling on a chain above his son's face.

The wound in the side of Logan's head was still bleeding, a slow seepage around the homemade bandages. Logan was awake. His chest rose and fell against the wide carpenter's belt attempting to hold him in place. A woozy black swastika poked out from underneath the bandages on his head.

"Um, Mr. Chatterton, I just came by to check on Logan," Moses said.

Mr. Chatterton was humming to himself. He held a scalpel in his hand; the same one he'd used on his wife's leg the winter before. It was an old breadknife he had modified in the garage.

"Moses. Moses Moon. Hold on one second."

"What did you do to Logan?" Moses asked.

"Nothing drastic, yet. Just removed some of the debris the silly nurses at St. Joe's couldn't get out of the wound. You'd be surprised how dirty someone's boot can be. The amount of filth we carry around on our persons is quite astronomical—that is, when you look at it on a molecular level. What you might call the nitty gritty."

"Molecular?"

"Yes, Moses. Logan is going to be fine, but I've spoken to his mother about removing those awful tattoos on his head. Would you like something to drink?"

He smiled and pushed his glasses up.

"We'll have to go upstairs for that. I think all we have is water, and maybe some Kool-Aid. Now, back when this was my father's house, and this was years ago…"

Mr. Chatterton's veined hand propelled Moses up the stairs, farther and farther away from Logan's breath, which rose and fell in gaps before disappearing as the basement door closed behind them. The light in the kitchen was dim. Mr. Chatterton turned on the tap but kept on talking. Moses stared at the hand-drawn diagrams stapled to the mauve wall above the cupboards. A woman's hand. A child's foot. Each piece was detailed with small letters, the lines slightly slanted, the ruler slipping in the artist's trembling, veined hands.

"Yes, my father. His house, you know…and well, he wasn't a very nice man," Mr. Chatterton said. "In fact, he had quite a few problems. And he always brought them home."

Moses tried to drink the water quickly. Mr. Chatterton poured him another glass.

7

Jamie Garrison knew he'd made a mistake when Connor Condon began to thrash around inside the plastic Kmart bag. The kid looked like a fish, his big mouth puffing out and pulling in the plastic, his lips fat and purple. Jamie saw Connor's eyes staring back at him in the window. He could see the boy's skin slowly changing color, the muscles in his neck straining to yank the plastic off his face.

Jamie didn't stop though. He just ground his teeth together and pulled tighter while the ninth-graders near the front took up a chant of *condom, condom, condom, condom*...their voices bounced between the syllables. The bus driver wasn't even looking, her eyes burning into the back of a stalled driver's head, her horn blaring at the green Chevy that refused to move from the turning lane. Brock was in the seat beside Jamie and leading the chant with his hands in the air, his mouth dangling open as it always did, his leather jacket reeking of cat piss. Brock flicked his wrists like a maestro and the chant rose.

Jamie kept his eyes on the scummy window and watched Connor's head slowly nod itself into a blank stare. It was then the fear struck, that this little piece of shit might not wake up, that this little pimply ass in track pants and a Ghostbusters T-shirt might never open his eyes again. Jamie took Connor's head and bashed it hard against the window again and again until the handle on the bag snapped. Brock and a bunch of the other kids laughed and said it sounded hollow, like a fucking coconut, man. The condom chant receded and then died out altogether.

Every few weeks they would grow tired of tormenting Connor, forgo all the condoms filled with condiments and the permanent markers they used to draw on his face. Jamie's favourite was the Fu Manchu they gave him for Thanksgiving. Brock used a brown marker he stole from his remedial art class. But then the kid would have to go and do something stupid, start singing the Cheez Whiz song or bring his GI Joes on the bus like it was show and tell. Without fail, Connor Condom would always find a way to draw a larger target on his back, an ever-expanding circle. The longer the gap between his humiliations, the bigger the target would grow, until every eye in the hall seethed at his presence. Teachers looked the other way or smiled behind their attendance sheets. Bets were made on when exactly he would kill himself.

Melissa Hurley knocked on the tenth-grade heads to test if they sounded as hollow as the Condom kid's did. She laughed and poked at Connor's body and then ran up and down the bus aisle, rapping skulls with her thick costume jewelry. Brock played the bongos on his own head. No one, they agreed, sounded as hollow as that fucking Condom kid. Jamie sat back in the seat and kicked at Connor's back. The boy slumped forward and whacked his head on the seat in front of him. Nobody ever sat beside the Condom kid, even when the bus was crowded.

After the bus got to school, even Jamie and Brock ran when they heard the high-pitched wail of Marlene the bus driver, her tongue piercing somehow enhancing the cry that burst from the yellow tunnel of the bus. She stumbled out carrying the boy's limp form. The Kmart bag was still plastered to Connor's face.

There was no suspension, but only after hours of interrogation in the vice principal's office with the blinds drawn. Mr. Georgopolous, with his hairy arms and shining comb-over, slammed his fists on the desk again and again, a fat finger pricking Jamie in the chest every time he asked a question. What had that kid ever done to him, this Connor Condon? What did he do to deserve this? Who else was involved? Why did no one report this until now? Why, in fact, was it the bus driver who had to find the body almost buried under one of the backseats?

Jamie sat still and closed his eyes against the spittle gathering on his cheeks. Mr. Wilkinson, the actual principal, stood against the door with his hands behind his back. Graves Memorial Collegiate and Vocational did not need another visit from local law enforcement. They agreed this would be handled internally.

The questions continued. Jamie had answers for them all but kept his mouth shut. He knew they had no interest in the way the Condom kid always spread out his homemade lunch across an entire table in the cafeteria; the way he raised his hand, always twisting his palm in the air like he was the Queen in a parade.

They didn't notice the smell of his armpits when he pulled himself up the steps onto the bus, the small black hairs that dotted his nose when you got nice and close to his face before you spat on him. All one hundred and fifty ways that hatred festered through Garrison's thoughts and found its expression through drive-by eggings and violent free-for-alls behind the Zellers on Friday nights. Don't forget the cadence of that kid's voice, as if the vocal cords in his throat couldn't commit to one sound before the other, causing them to trip and fall out of his mouth in a bloody, phlegmy mess. Make that one hundred and fifty-one ways Jamie Garrison had learned to hate the Condom kid.

The blinds stayed closed and eventually Georgopolous left in a flurry of damp paper and dandruff. His mistress was waiting for him down at the Pillaros Hotel. That was the word in the halls. Mr.

Wilkinson took over. He sat across from Jamie in the vice principal's chair and placed his feet on the table. The room was hot and sweaty. Mr. Wilkinson didn't say anything for a long time.

"I know what happened with you."

Jamie didn't look up from the floor.

"Saw it in the paper a couple weeks ago, you know. Very surprising," Mr. Wilkinson said. "Something about a fire, right? That you? Tell me if I am getting close here."

Jamie began to rock back and forth in the chair. He tried to stop himself, but his legs wouldn't listen. This room was too hot. Sweat gathered in the hollow of his throat.

"Now, when we brought up your file, I noticed you lived on—what was it? Olive Avenue, down by a lot of the factory lots, am I right? Not the community housing, but pretty close? Around that neighborhood. Unless you disagree, I'm going to assume we have the facts right."

Jamie nodded but kept his eyes closed. He began to regulate his breathing, pulling air in his nose and pushing it out his mouth. The parking lot outside the window sounded quiet. There weren't any clocks in the room. The low, level tick of Mr. Wilkinson's watch helped keep track of the seconds. It took eighty ticks for Mr. Wilkinson to speak again.

"I'm sorry. I had to arrange my thoughts. Always better to speak when one has something to say, rather than saying...well, you've probably heard that old rotten chestnut before, haven't you, Garrison?" Wilkinson said. "What I wanted to talk to you about was the fire. It was your house, right? I know a number of the townhomes went up together, but the origin apparently was yours, on Thanksgiving, right?"

That was the night when the whole place had gone up while everyone was asleep. Smoke filled the hallway, his mother pushing the boys down the stairs, his brother coughing and crying, the windows bursting from the inside due to the heat. Their father stood outside amongst the dead leaves smoking a cigarette and watching the house burn. The bullet hole in his palm was still wrapped in a bandage from a few months before at the abattoir. He didn't say anything as his wife made the boys stop, drop, and roll on the dead grass. The frost melted underneath their backs, freezing again as they waited for the first ambulance to arrive. A burn bubbled around Jamie's mother's neck, fusing the nightgown to her pale flesh.

"Now I know you've had a rough time lately, and your brother, what's he in now, ninth grade?" Wilkinson said. "I know he hasn't been to school in a couple days, so you obviously have some problems at home. Or wherever you're staying at the moment. And of course, that is your own private business. I don't mean to probe."

Silence for five minutes. No tears. Jamie grunted. Mr. Wilkinson just sat with his feet up on the table and watched. A dull, low moan eventually began to spurt from his chest like a dehumidifier. It didn't sound like him. It didn't sound like anything human.

Eventually, in that hot room, a two-week suspension was handed down from one sweaty palm to another. Nothing proven, nothing gained. Jamie walked home to the rambling motel in the cold and told his mother he stayed late after school for homework—a group project on native rights in the aftermath of World War II. She laughed in his face and asked him to change the dressing on her burn. Big yellow bubbles popped every time pressure was applied.

Jamie didn't say anything to his father, sitting on the balcony of their motel room, smoking and dropping the ashes down onto the patio furniture below. The insurance company was still waiting for the arson judgment. Initial reports suggested an electrical fire. It was too cold for anyone to use the motel pool. The remains of a crow circled its clogged filter, the chlorine slowly dissolving its feathers down to the quick. One of the hotel staff kept trying to fish it out with a pole, cursing at the dead bird in Polish. The motel smelled like cheap champagne and old cigars. They called it the Dynasty. They were only there for two weeks before a city councilor's girlfriend popped the waterbed in the room above theirs with her stiletto and the water shorted out the television.

Jamie spent those two weeks walking around town, carving his initials into fence posts and doorframes. He walked past the pawnshops on the downtown strip lined up like children's blocks. Sharkee's Pawn Palace. Jameson Pawn and Loan. The Loan Arranger. Each one packed with festering potential. Someone who thought they'd get married. Someone who thought they'd play guitar. Each dream propped up in the window. Jamie started spending each morning watching crumpled people trickle into the pawnshops, handing over the old dreams they'd decided to surrender, the ones gathering dust like diplomas dangling from bathroom walls. Sometimes he thought to buy them a cup of coffee, but he had no money—only the change he found in the candy machines at the arenas.

The pawnshops were often empty in the afternoons, the owners watching soap operas or cutting dope in the back rooms with men in leather jackets and ponytails. All of those discounted lives gathering dust until someone else came to pick them up for triple the initial price.

Jamie never bought anything.

Sometimes he spent the afternoons at Melissa Hurley's, until her father walked in on them with Melissa bent over her old Easy-Bake Oven and Jamie pumping away from behind. It didn't help that the oven was plugged in and would not stop dinging throughout the entire shouting match. Her father threw Jamie naked down a flight of stairs and tried to whip him with his belt.

It only took four days back at school for Jamie to fuck up again, a knee to the crotch of Harry Knowles that some kids said popped one of his balls. Melissa Hurley had moved on quickly, a whirling dervish of red hair, pancake makeup, and angry yellow pimples in search of the right boy, any boy. Mr. Hurley's heart attack during a sermon on premarital sex only increased her speed.

Knowles was apparently the newest in a long line of conquests, something that didn't faze Jamie until Knowles told him about Melissa mocking the size of his dick. Tiny, man, like a pinky. Like a pencil. Like one of those pins they put under a microscope to show you how small a cell is in biology class, you know?

No testicle was actually popped in the ensuing melee.

Jamie did not bother showing up for his official expulsion. He did not want to sit while Mr. Georgopolous rained dandruff down on his face. He didn't tell his parents either. He didn't even bother going home that night. Instead he hung out under the eaves of the Coffee Time downtown and watched people in wet trench coats and broken umbrellas hand over pieces of themselves to the bearded men behind greasy bulletproof glass for loose crumpled bills and slivers of change. He wanted to reach out and touch them. Women in torn leggings and jagged leather boots paced through the puddles outside, some ducking into cars that smelled like cheap cigarettes and formaldehyde before they reappeared again like doppelgangers with busted eye sockets and mussed hair. Jamie kept his own eyes on the pawnshop windows, watching them swallowing everything up whole, every little piece they were given. He had nothing to give.

Even now, eight years later, as he pulled into the strip mall parking lot, Jamie Garrison's fists clutched the steering wheel, imagining his fingers tautly bound up in the handles of that plastic Kmart bag, watching that fucking kid's face go pink, then red, then purple, until everything turned white and limp in his hands. This was all his fault, that little fucker. The kid couldn't think right after that—couldn't count, couldn't write his name in a straight line, couldn't even piss in a straight line. As Jamie climbed up out of the car with his knees popping and crackling, he could not shake that feeling. The little sniveling face. The small lung capacity. The penchant for minor but permanent brain damage. It was all that kid's fault.

The wide parking lot was spotted with aging pickup trucks filled with older men who lived with their robes open and their families excommunicated. In the summer months, they lingered after hours at the drive-in theater just outside of Larkhill, where no one ever knocked on your window with a flashlight and a badge. The drive-in had been closed for a few months now, so they roamed from one abandoned strip mall to another, writing phone numbers on bathroom walls and pay phones in perfect, tidy script.

A few leered at Jamie through fogged windows. A lone woman scuttled out from the adult video store, white cardboard covering its plate-glass windows. She climbed into her Riviera and began to unwrap a package in her lap. She could not wait to get home. Jamie Garrison tried not to stare at the need exposed so openly around him, wounds dripping with washer fluid and sad, old want. Even now, he still had nothing to give.

8

"He was always satisfied, my father. Complacent. That's how I would diagnosis him. Made no sense. For God's sake, he was born in the Year of the Rat, not the Rabbit," Mr. Chatterton said. "But not at home. At work they could shit all over him, excuse my language, but at home, nothing was ever right, no one was ever right. Not even the television."

Sometimes Moses Moon would dream his father had never run away to sing Bette Midler classics in the Arizona desert. On some nights, after the dull thwap of leaking water beds had faded into a calming tide, Moses Moon dreamed he had a father who would teach him how to fish; a father who would teach him how to swim the butterfly and check the oil in his first car. In the dreams of Moses Moon, his new father was a lecherous professor, a cocky camp counselor, a crotchety TV executive, and a newly minted Ghostbuster, all wrapped up into one unparalleled human being. In these dreams, his true father was always Bill Murray.

"Yes, Mr. Chatterton."

Logan's father sat across from Moses, polishing his glasses on the long sleeve of his shirt. The kitchen was quiet and clean but covered in old drawings, tracings from medical textbooks labeled with nonexistent bones and new tendon systems that would increase power while reducing maneuverability. Mr. Chatterton called them works in progress.

"Now my father always did have a thing about interrupting your elders, one of the few tenets I still uphold in this house. He never did listen, though—that was the problem," Mr. Chatterton continued. "Didn't listen to my mother or me. No, we always had to listen to him. Always."

Logan was still bleeding in the basement. Moses squirmed in his chair, slowly drinking his glass of water. He didn't want another refill.

"Logan never had to play organized sports. He never had to eat the same goddamn ham sandwich every day either. My wife and I—my former wife and I—we always did our best to let Logan choose his own path. Because rules—do you know how many bowls of cereal my father let me eat?" Mr. Chatterton asked. "Just one. Never mind if I had a long day ahead of me. My welfare, my choices, my personal well-being were all secondary to his choices. His choices—the ones he made for me. You understand?"

"I think I understand," Moses said. The water was warm in his mouth.

"Let's just say my wardrobe was never my own. It was always selected for me. As was the paint on my walls, as were my friends. But what friends, really?"

Mr. Chatterton was crying. His eyes were pink and crusty.

"So I always let my son, my Logan—we named him after the mountain. We climbed it on our honeymoon, which seems to be eons ago," Mr. Chatterton said. "How a woman can say so many things one day and yet the next remove herself from your life—how? And all the work we put into rebuilding her leg and her hand. The hand was almost perfect."

Moses noticed the house was too quiet, the stumping gait of Mrs. Chatterton muted, silenced. She wasn't home today. Mr. Chatterton never would have sent her to a real doctor. She didn't even have her own car. Just like bodies, the machine was another mystery for Mr. Chatterton to turn from the functional to the formidable, as he liked to put it. Each car in the driveway had been there for years, slowly dissolving in the rain.

"But then, you and your friends just had to break the boy..."

Moses didn't want to look at Mr. Chatterton's face. It was cracked in too many places.

"My friends..." Moses began.

"Yes, your friends, the ones you brought to Logan, got him mixed up in all these things. I would not let my son grow up like I did," Mr. Chatterton said. "I mean, can you imagine eating only brown, grey, and white for eighteen years—to never know what a red piece of meat looks like, to only find its flavor on your tongue in a darkened restaurant on a date with your future wife from the prairies, the fucking prairies. A woman who had never been to a real restaurant with napkins that weren't made of paper. A woman who will then leave you after your son becomes a violent little shaved monster. Too many experiments. Too many failures, Moses."

Moses took another sip of his water. The kitchen door was locked; Moses could see the key dangling from the knob. The hallway back to the front door was too short, its garish lipstick red illuminating a path to another locked exit. And Logan was still in the basement.

"My mistake was thinking that with no real controls, my son might make the right choices, that he might experience the joys I was denied. My wish was that he wouldn't feel the same dreadful spike of joy when I heard that bastard was finally dead, chewing on the same sandwich he'd been eating since 1965, chewing on the same bullshit he'd always fed my mother and I until she ended up like a catatonic—like the unchanging face of a goddamn fucking mountain. A face that never changes. You ever see someone like that?

"And instead, I have a son like this. All hate and bile. I had a wife, too, but that's gone. She left. She blames me. Me, me, me! Yes, me,

Moses." Mr. Chatterton spat onto the floor. "Back to Saskatoon, of all fucking places for a woman to go—because she doesn't recognize her son. She's part native and so is he, and when he found that out—"

"I don't really know what you want me to say."

Mr. Chatterton settled his glasses back onto his face before stabbing the scalpel deep into the table between them. Moses stood up from the table, considering which drawer held the knives. In another's kitchen, Moses realized, you were always at their mercy.

"My wife can no longer look her only son in the face. She can't look at me. I am the one who made her this way, just like my father made me into what I am now. He never changed, Moses. He stayed static," Mr. Chatterton said. "The same clothing for forty years. The same job, the same meals. He never could abide what happened on this street. Never could sell the land as those cheap little fire hazards sprang up to kill all the trees on the street with their shadows...such long shadows, don't you think, Moses?"

Moses tried to pretend he was talking to Bill Murray, tried to replace the sneer on Mr. Chatterton's face with a smirk and a wink. This was all just a big joke. A scene that had gone off the rails a little. It happens on the set after a long day. That was all it was. Maybe they'd use the footage for a trailer or during the closing credits. It was a blooper reel.

"Yes, Mr. Chatterton. I think maybe I'll go check on Logan. He didn't seem exactly—"

"Exactly what? Exactly perfect? No. And that's what his mother wanted him to be. That's what we were striving to make here. Not perfect, maybe, but pure. And then you and your hate and your bile and all your—why?" Mr. Chatterton asked. "Why did you have to pick him? And she—she was my best chance at reversing years of research! Control over our own destiny! And now it's all fucked up by your little dirty hands. Look at yourself, you little cunt!"

Moses was flying now, his feet gliding down the stairs, his hands tearing belts from Logan's trembling, sweaty body, the overwhelming green of the bedroom bursting cells apart in Moses's pupils.

The basement door popped open behind him. Mr. Chatterton was still muttering aloud about his father—that bastard, that bastard—because he could never say the man's real name anymore, not after nights of holding that rabbit antenna until his shoulders collapsed under the strain, not after all the mornings where oatmeal was crammed down his gullet, not after years of living under the torture of that deadening sameness, an unending loop of the mundane that had caused his mother's mind to rot. After all that, there was no name—there was only that bastard, that fucking bastard and his goddamn ham sandwiches.

Mr. Chatterton drew closer, his teeth shining and freshly cleaned by the dentist. He'd come home from an appointment to find a note about the hatred living in his basement and the wife who could no longer sustain herself as the focal point of his countless little cuts. His son had reacted so violently to revelations of his heritage that he'd split his skull against the bathroom mirror. The note was written in her gorgeous looping hand, but there was no love signed to the bottom. Only her maiden name without a forwarding address.

"You had to make him into one of you," Mr. Chatterton said. "And you know, we really thought it was a phase. We thought he might have just been confused, you know? But it wasn't. No, it wasn't a phase. And she tried to teach him, but he wouldn't listen. What did you think you were teaching him, Moses?"

"Nothin'," Moses said. "I wasn't even there. I told them it was stupid."

The gag sprang out of Logan's mouth and he was sliding out of the bed. He couldn't stop coughing. Mr. Chatterton stood in the doorway, his skinny shoulders casting the room in jagged shadows. The light bounced off his oily scalp. He held the homemade scalpel in his hand, and he drew a line down the side of his arm with it. His hand didn't waver as it moved.

"I tried to raise him in a way that my father would have disapproved, but he has the same hate, just now directed outward instead of…instead of in," Mr. Chatterton said. "It can only push out for so long. For so long that hate can only push out until it reaches the edges of the universe, and it has no other place to go. Expanding till the center can't hold together."

Mr. Chatterton drew the blade down his other arm. Down and not across. No, he drew it down, straight down and deep inside his arm, flicking the blade out once he reached the base of his palm. Mr. Chatterton never did things in small strokes. The paint in each room was always a performance.

"It's like a star, boys. That's how it works. It pushes and pushes those on the outside, swallowing them whole into its burning, burning—but it can't hold all of it for long, and just like a star, eventually it implodes. Collapses in on itself. Have you ever seen that?"

Mr. Chatterton dropped his homemade scalpel to the floor and it scurried under the bed.

"It falls inward, and all that spite, that fucking bile, it gets redrawn, redirected—some would say misdirected—but that is where the hate was meant to go in the first place."

The blood was no longer seeping slowly from Mr. Chatterton. There was nothing slow about it. He staggered against the wall as the two teenage boys climbed up on the bed, scrambling to back away from his collapsing body. His hands were trembling, the knuckles growing pale like his face. He was no longer smiling, but his eyes were still pink, still raw.

"It all turns inward."

Moses Moon knew this would never have happened with Bill Murray.

"It turns…"

It was Logan who climbed off of the bed and kicked his father's head. Mr. Chatterton just shuddered once. There was no hollow noise, only a wet thunk like someone collapsing on a water bed. Neither of the boys ran for the phone. They crouched over the body and Moses tried to close Mr. Chatterton's eyelids with his fingers. Logan slapped his shaking hand away.

"Don't touch that bastard. Don't even touch that fucking bastard."

9

Henry's Holistic Hobbies. Brock had got one thing right. The windows were frosted with yellow dust. AM stations burped up old Buddy Holly songs from the idle trucks in the parking lot. Jamie knocked hard on the glass. Nothing. He slammed a flat palm onto the glass again. The door opened and a rush of hot, mildewed air swept out into the parking lot. A small man stood there with a sheet of baseball cards in his hands.

"You looking to buy or sell? I know the Pirates aren't exactly stellar this season, but I've got the whole team for sale. Topps, of course. The good ones. You want to take a look at 'em?"

"No, I don't really, um, do the card thing," Jamie said.

"Well, come on in anyway. I'm sure we got something you're looking for. Sort of in a transitional phase right now," the little man said.

Jamie shut the door behind him and staggered around piles of model planes and collectible Star Wars figures still wrapped in plastic. There were no shelves left in the store, just busted glass display cases and tiny slivers glinting from the corners where they'd been swept.

"You musta pissed someone off," Jamie said.

The short man smiled, showing a set of dentures under his thick moustache. He couldn't have been more than twenty-five.

"I'm always pissing someone off. Part of my charm, you know?"

"When did this happen? Who did this shit?" Jamie asked.

"Oh, you always know who. That's the point. They want to strike some fear in your heart. If I didn't know who...well, there really wouldn't be much of a point, now would there?"

It looked like a sledgehammer had smashed through one of the walls.

"They do that too?"

"No, that was all me. I'm expanding the store. Can't deal with such a cluttered space. I'm not Henry, by the way, and I don't really know what half this shit is besides the baseball cards," the man said. "I'm pretty sure that's why he left the whole place to me."

"Henry?" Jamie asked.

"My uncle. Crazy motherfucker—just a nut for all things teenage boys love. And I'm not saying he was into them. Not saying that. Just had a Peter Pan complex—never grew old."

Jamie ducked his head under the pipes and followed the little man through a hole smashed into the abandoned unit next door. The place looked like an old dentist's office. A forgotten Nintendo system lay buried under dust and flakes of plaster. There were files on the floor, old X-rays and yellowed receipts for forgotten procedures.

"You can't just tear a place like this apart, can you?"

"When the landlord died two years ago and the family is still locked in some bitter feud over who gets his property rights, one that'll probably go on for another fifteen years and inspire a whole new season of *Dallas*?" the little man said. "Well, then I can do whatever I want. And I don't even know why you're here. You know, if you hadn't said anything, you might have got to see some of the really good stuff in here."

"You never asked me why," Jamie said.

"Well, first of all," the little man said. "I'm the Lorax."

"Like the kids' book?"

"Sure. Let's say that."

Most of the windows were covered with plywood that had begun to rot from the rain and snow. Moisture dripping in from busted skylights had turned part of the ceiling a bluish green.

"Now who sent you to me? I should give him a bonus for the referral."

"I don't think he's really a repeat customer," Jamie said. "It was, uh, this guy, Brock."

"His face all fucked up like a pumpkin?" the Lorax asked.

"Yeah. Hit with a bottle from a car couple nights ago."

"I just lost mine last year," the Lorax said, and clacked his dentures together. He did not elaborate. A draft swept through the busted skylight in the ceiling, rattling the leaves of wallpaper that had come loose from the walls.

"He told me you sold him or no, sorry, he bought—"

"No, he sold to me," the Lorax said. He pushed through tarps and broken two-by-fours that separated the busted offices into smaller compartments. Heavy bright lamps sat unplugged in each section, rows and rows of lamps taken from retirement homes and garage sales. Ugly brass beasts mounted with dogs and dragons and the occasional swan. A faint odor of manure pushed its way into Jamie's nose. He recognized the smell somewhere in the back of his brain.

"You shit in here, too?" Jamie asked.

The Lorax laughed. "No, man, that's not my shit. Best fertilizer known to man. Pig shit. I need it to keep this whole show running here. You get used to it, believe me. Start to pick out the nuance. Like wine or something. But enough of that, you're here now. You can't sleep?"

Someone honked their horn in the parking lot out front.

"Accident the other day," Jamie said. "Fucked up my neck. Don't wanna deal with a doc."

"How bad was it? Inquiring minds and all."

"I hit a buck. Yeah. A buck. Messed the grille up. Gave me and a buddy a mean case of whiplash," Jamie said. "It'll be a bitch to fix if I can't get the cash."

"Remember when I said the dude that owned the place died?" the Lorax said. "Now, he had some money. He wouldn't have let this place fall like it has."

Jamie sighed and tried not to breathe in the pig shit. Cables dangled from the ceiling tiles.

"Impatient, aren't you? Friend with the fucked-up teeth stayed here all afternoon. We even had a little smoke, but whatever. Different strokes, right? I sit in this place all day. Least you can do is let my ass talk before you rip me off and step outside into fresh air."

"I'm not exactly dressed for this shit is all. Shoulda worn my boots."

The stink of pig shit grew heavier as he talked. The walls were damp to the touch.

"I'm a bit of a farmer," the Lorax said. "I always got my boots on."

Jamie noticed the small grey bulbs pushing through the manure under the tarps and the weak daylight punched through the ceiling in scattered patches.

"The holes work better in the summer months, when I grow bud. I just did my first harvest in here. The electrical bills are crazy, but I'm not paying them. That whole family just has a lawyer footing the bill for this place every month while they tear each other to shreds. Really nasty stuff. I think it might have been in the paper once." The Lorax laughed. "If they ever bothered to come down here and check out some of the old man's properties, they'd realize they were just fighting over who got a larger slice of the cow pie."

"And then you'd be up shit creek."

"I'm very familiar with that creek. That mess you saw inside?" the Lorax said. "Vicious mothers makin' sure I stay far up that creek. You ever want to eat any of these?"

The pale blue walls of the operating chamber glowed around the two of them. A painting of a fox and her pups stood against the wall in the corner. Someone had smashed its glass case and drawn a top hat on the fox. The Lorax pushed a bundle of mushrooms into Jamie's face.

"Eat that shit? All I want is some Vicodin, Percocet or something. Maybe some of the reds."

The Lorax laughed and clacked his dentures in his mouth. He turned and climbed back through the gaping hole into the hobby shop. Jamie followed. One hundred special-edition Darth Vader models with hologram cards attached stared back at them from the pockmarked floor. All fake duplicates shipped directly from Mumbai. All gleaming black.

The smell of the pigs still clung to Jamie's nose. "So, you've got it or not?"

"Straight from Quebec. That's the best place to go get it," the Lorax said. "A place where all they eat is gravy and each other. You know some of the early settlers were cannibals in New France? It's true. They like to cut it out of the textbooks. Last time I made some joke about their priests and spent half my time talking myself out of a hole in the ground."

"A hole?"

Jamie was barely listening now. His leg was starting to spasm with memories of the impact.

"An actual hole. They dug it and everything," the Lorax said. "I've been partially fossilized. How many people can say that?"

The Lorax pulled a plastic grocery bag filled with prescription bottles and loose pills out from underneath a counter covered in stickers, shards of glass, and chewed gum.

"We'll go with twenty for now. On the house for a first-time customer."

Jamie watched the little stubby fingers counting out his pills one by one, pushing them into an old prescription bottle assigned to a Mrs. Wanda Chubbs of Burlington, Ontario.

"I don't know if I can just take this shit off you—like, gratis, you know?"

"It's not a debt—it's an investment." The Lorax clacked his dentures again into a smile that only filled the right side of his mouth. Jamie looked around at the shattered display cases. There was a busted fan dangling from the ceiling and the cash register was cracked open on the floor.

"I'll take it. Was it like this when Brock came here? The mess?"

"You ever listen to ZZ Top?" the Lorax asked. "ZZ Top. Music?"

"They're all right, I guess," Jamie said.

The Lorax pushed a children's loot bag across to Jamie. It had a smiley clown face on the front. The smile was offset from the rest of its features, dripping off the face and into the white background. Jamie didn't want to put it in his car.

"Well these guys looked like two rogue agents of the mighty left hand of ZZ Top," the Lorax said. "Tore the whole place apart, looking for who knows what. Took half my harvest when they left. A lot of rage in those two. And the bickering, man. All they did was talk shit, all day. I shoulda seen them coming."

"They were here all day?" Jamie asked.

"Maybe like two hours, but never shut up once."

It had started to snow outside. Jamie could barely see the outline of his car through the dusty window. He pulled out his keys and grabbed the loot bag.

"Hey, hey, hey, you didn't even stick around for my story, man. My story," the Lorax whined. "About the old dude? Remember?"

"Your uncle? The pervert who dressed up like Peter Pan?"

"Damn, you're twisting my words. No, the guy who ran this place. I guess he got all mad and tried stuffing a big bag of something into the dumpster, kind of a big fuck you to the guy who was supposed to pick it up later that day. Sets off a nest of yellow jackets. Whole swarm of them came out of there. Of course, dude is allergic.

"He's lying there and the place is covered with yellow jackets. My uncle says he just watched through the delivery door. A couple of guys down the lot were unloading a truck and they just sat there too. Watched this guy shaking under a cloud. He said it was like the dude was having a seizure. All 'cause he couldn't be bothered to pay for real garbage pick-up."

"So they watched?" Jamie said.

"What were they supposed to do? Go get stung? Come on. Owner starts foaming at the mouth, his face gets all swollen, and they can't do nothing. Took ten minutes for him to die. Ten whole minutes and fucker was so fat they could barely fit him in the ambulance."

Jamie just shook his head and started for the door. His sinuses were filled with pigs and wasps climbing over each other to block out the image of the lion with its backside split open across the pavement. Snow was probably covering it now too.

"Before you go, buddy, anyone you know needs something, you tell them come to me, all right? I can always use more referrals," the Lorax said. "Business is really just networking."

"And what am I supposed to say? Look for the little fuck in the baseball jersey?"

The little man laughed and popped his dentures out of his mouth. It only made his moustache look bigger—a caterpillar threatening to swallow his face whole.

"Just tell them to ask for the Lorax."

Jamie slammed the door on Henry's Holistic Hobbies. His stride betrayed a slight limp to the left, his face set against the pain shooting up his ankle and exploding behind his right eye. The lion was not forgiving. Snow melted on impact with the grass. A Ford in the corner of the parking lot honked in his direction. Jamie gave it the finger and began brushing the flakes off of his windshield. The clown face on his loot bag watched him while he worked.

10

Logan was mad at first.

He kicked the body and strangled its skinny hairless throat. He smashed its skull against his bed post, stabbed its back again and again with the butter knife until the handle broke off against his father's hip bone. The patch of skin on Logan's head, where half an uneven swastika remained, flapped around while he tried to yank the knife back out. Moses just sat on the corner of the bed wondering when Logan's mother was going to come home. She had to come home.

Mr. Chatterton's blood was sticky by the time Logan stopped crying. For a while he lay on top of the body. The lime-green walls were spattered with red spots that slowly turned brown like decaying Christmas decorations.

"We should call the cops, right?" Logan said.

"We call the police, and they see what you did, and they will say, what, suicide? No way."

Logan had a record with the school board. Mainly for petty vandalism of the bathrooms and school parking lot. The boys had set off fireworks and spray-painted cars with Skrewdriver lyrics that summer. They only had the one cassette and they played it till the tape wore through to the other side. "White Rider," the one with Donaldson shrieking about freedom with his teeth pressed against the mic. Most of the graffiti was too messy to read except for the word "Jew" sprayed onto Mr. Goldberg's car and along the auto shop windows. The police were never called.

Logan and B. Rex had egged Goldberg's house the next night, beside the Bargain Bin and the methadone clinic. Moses had spent that night talking his mother off the balcony instead of pitching eggs with his friends. Elvira Moon had threatened to toss the Judge over the edge of the balcony if he didn't begin to give her straight answers about where her husband had disappeared to that morning. She was still looking for Ted Moon.

Logan and Moses spent the entire day staring at the telephone, peeking out from behind the blinds, waiting for someone to expose them. They tried calling B. Rex, who had a car from his grandfather, the same grandfather who took him hunting and taught him how to shoot, how to break an animal down into portable, edible parts. B. Rex would know what to do. He was the one who was supposed to know things. The one whose parents had set up a college fund and even made him lunch for school. No one was home.

Neither of them felt like eating, not after checking on the body in the basement to make sure it wasn't going to get up again. The day moved slowly, the sun charting its progress with their shadows till finally, after a marathon run of *Golden Girls* and uneaten Froot Loops, the streetlights outside began to flicker on one by one.

B. Rex still wasn't answering his phone.

It took an hour to get the body out of the basement. Mr. Chatteron's body seemed to expand with every minute that passed. Logan kept sobbing and then slapping the body across the face, throwing curses down the stairs at Moses. Each tugging motion left another snail stain behind them. The lion stalked Moses up the basement stairs while he tried not to puke. Mr. Chatterton still had his guts intact. Mr. Chatterton didn't belong to anybody anymore.

"We can't leave him in the house. It'll start to smell."

After traveling six blocks with Mr. Chatterton's skinny body folded up like a lawn chair in the back of Logan's old red wagon, Moses realized it was a bad plan. Two sixteen-year-olds dragging a red wagon behind a bicycle like a tiny caravan. The body was barely hidden under a faded quilt covered with loons and maple leaves. Logan's parents had bought it on their first anniversary, when Logan was conceived in a Comfort Inn suite in northern Alberta.

Headlights flashed past the boys in the snow, each car too busy to notice their oozing cargo. Moses had wrapped the body in Glad ClingWrap before setting off. It took three whole rolls and made all of Mr. Chatterton's features look smushed, like a Picasso painting. Moses didn't want to leave another trail behind.

The store was closed when they arrived at Henley's Meats. Texaco had shut off all the lights. Only the hum of the coolers remained. Moses unlocked the back door and pushed Logan inside. The cutting room was cold and clean. Moses flipped on the lights. Logan lay on the floor, pressing his wounded head against the cool tiles. He had been crying on and off throughout the day. He still would not reveal what he'd said to Mrs. Chatterton, only repeating she was going, going, fucking gone, all right, Moses?

Moses didn't argue. He unloaded the body alone. His bones ached from the car accident the day before and there was still lion blood smeared across his shirt. He was tired and his spine tilted to one side when he tried to stand up straight. There were back massagers for rent back at the motel, but Moses didn't like the smell of them—somewhere between female sweat and old feta cheese.

"Should we take his shoes off?" Logan asked.

"Maybe his clothes too," Moses said.

"What're we going to do with them? Burn 'em? Toss 'em in the trash?"

"We can't use the garbage here. I don't want to get in any shit," Moses said.

Logan rolled his eyes and pulled himself up off the tiles, patches of old blood stuck to his shirt. Light bounced off all the steel fixtures and the freshly washed floor. Logan began pulling his father's running shoes off, one by one. All the unwanted pieces. The hardest part was the T-shirt. It took both of them to pull it over Mr. Chatterton's bulbous head. They left his underwear alone. Moses used the detergent, the rinse, and the sanitizer on the body while Logan tied all the clothes up inside the honeymoon quilt and put it back in the wagon. The humid air filled their lungs and left no room for conversation.

"Should we…um…"

Logan eyed the long, curved butcher knives soaking in the sink. The bone saw lurked in the corner, dismantled and glistening, a passive threat until the morning totes arrived full of pork back ribs. They were on sale at half price for the next two weeks.

"No, no, I think he'll fit. He's not very big. You're bigger than he is, height-wise," Moses said. "And he's—well, he's not fat."

"Just around the middle a little bit."

Moses popped one of the lids. Fat, bone, gristle. Chunks of decaying meat, dark steaks and old chickens. Pints of blood dumped off the cutting boards. Pork fat, beef gristle, rotting turkey gullets. All the unwanted parts. The can was full. Too full. The next container mainly held beef trimmings and broken pig bones bleeding yellow. The blood around the sides of the bone can was green like algae. They could bury him under that blood.

Moses tucked his hands under Mr. Chatterton's hairy armpits. He nodded at Logan to grab the feet. Moses would make it fit.

"They just take him away with the rest of this stuff?" Logan said.

"I don't know."

"And then what will they do?" Logan asked. "What do they do with this shit?"

"I don't know."

The body slid into the green muck, bits of bone and fat bubbling around the surface. Moses was used to the smell. The surface congealed around the body like Jell-O as they pushed it farther down. They had to jam the feet under the lid, the long toenails rasping at the plastic. Logan sat on the floor and closed his eyes. Moses pushed and pulled the bone can outside into the snow. Too cold for crows. The moon made everything look clean. No lion waited outside.

"I can't go back there," Logan said. "She isn't coming back, she's never coming back, Moses. I know that, and he knew it too."

Moses put an arm around his friend and sat on the tiled floor. Cold beads of sweat trickled down through the mangled swastika on Logan's head. That tattoo was Moses's fault too. The red wagon sat in the corner, loaded with its bundle of evidence. They'd have to burn it.

"She's never coming back, Mosey. And now, well, fuck. Fuck. What about all the blood?"

Moses got up and began to turn off the lights. He sprayed the floor down with the hose again as Logan sat in the corner, the lemon backsplash mixing with the tears on his face. Logan could not go back to that house, a house covered in clown paint and filled with all those drawings of his mother's hand, a science experiment left half-finished. The sound of the hose finally cut out.

"You'll have to come stay with me."

11

"New developments in the unsettling Athabasca case from earlier this month. Police spokesperson Cheryl Landry reports that the body has now been identified as Connor James Condon, long-time resident of Larkhill, Ontario. Police are asking anyone with any information to come forward at this time. They are also reaching out to family..."

Jamie spun the dial on the radio. His hands were still shaking a bit. He'd swallowed two of the pills before hopping on the road, waiting for an elephant to emerge from the darkness and crack his transmission in two. He should have gone to work, back to the grinders and the saws and the mess. Instead he'd sat in his car all day, playing with the radio, listening to Connor's weeping mother crying on the front steps of the police station with a microphone plunged down her throat as one of the reporters probed her for fifteen minutes. Jamie had parked behind the Pillar, an old hotel that swayed over Larkhill; it's all-day breakfast buffet shone through the foggy windows. Unlike the motels that ran up and down the highway like neon skid marks, the Pillar was an institution, its massive brick walls witness to far more tragedy than any new age wailing wall or truck-stop parking lot. The inside was filled with decaying cornices, glass chandeliers, and women whose boots rode up over their knees. No one ever questioned the large rusted Cadillacs and old limousines that circled the place on

Saturday night, the remnants of something greater now floating around a clogged drain.

Jamie coughed and hacked as he steered his way through the snow. The wipers' rise and fall soothed his mind, which bounced from the wolves tearing Connor apart to the burst lion hopefully now buried under the snow. No one had found the body yet, or no one had cared to call it in. Maybe someone had taken it up to that guy's place on Keewatin like Mosey said.

Maybe someone had set it on fire.

Jamie was already late to pick up Kansas, already late for the dinner Alisha might have planned—another olive branch he'd snap off at its barely healed juncture. More like a twig by this point, with those tiny spring buds gasping for air. To get there, he was driving past the old warehouse that dangled below town like a hangar bay out by the water, its massive gates never closing, the three shifts rotating in and out like rusted parts in need of oil. Old foreign clunkers and massive new Dodge trucks the repo man would be collecting from gravel driveways within a year slowly pushed their way out onto the old baseline road.

Jamie didn't look at the liquor warehouse, its shoddy brown siding torn in places by heavy winds off the lake, its ruptured foundation leaking precious heat in the winter months. He didn't even glance at its truck yard filled with security cameras no one had ever bothered to plug in. He knew there was nothing in there for him, despite Brock's insistence they'd take him back if he agreed to do another interview with Collins. Both Brock and Jamie had been hired on the summer after Jamie was expelled and his family had moved into a new unit down in the community housing, between an abandoned grow op and the local cat lady, who let her pets run wild through the whole neighborhood and piss on everything.

"Every man has got to have a bonsai tree, man. It is the only way you will survive here."

Donnie Henley's parents had never even heard of the Eagles when they gave birth to their first son. The band did not even exist at the time. Don spent the first twenty years of his life blissfully unaffected by his namesake. That was, until "Hotel California" became the anthem at his college. Called to countless keggers, where he proudly chugged along as the more famous Henley warned him he would never leave, Don dropped out after failing three chemistry midterms in a row. His failure also might have been connected to the bong his girlfriend bought him for their three-week anniversary. The girlfriend who would later become his wife and personal trainer. On his weekends off, Don Henley liked to bare-knuckle box in his backyard.

With TACO BELL tattooed across his knuckles and a freshly broken nose, Henley trained Brock and Jamie in the bowels of the warehouse. He showed them how to empty trucks at the slowest pace acceptable by union standards, and how to build a bed of Heineken cases to rest on if they were hung over. The trick was to pad the top row with bags of sawdust and cover it in a tarp. He showed them how to tie the knots that kept five thousand dollars worth of Johnnie Walker Blue Label from crashing to the floor, and he always knew which table to sit at in the dingy cafeteria. Mostly, Don Henley just showed them how to pass the time.

"Now, I know I love my wife—I've known that ever since she bought me a box of ice cream sandwiches after I had my wisdom teeth out," Donnie said one day. "A girl who knows exactly what you desire, in the exact moment of desire, the exact millisecond, that is a girl you want to stay with for life."

Brock and Jamie rolled their eyes. They were still covered in Beefeater gin from when Sweet Pete Colleti had dumped a skid of it across the loading dock. Took three hours to clean up.

"Hey, I don't expect you to up and propose to whatever girl you've got lined up for the night, all right? I'm trying to tell you something important, though. This place is going to drive you crazy if you don't find a way to cope with it. You'll end up driving a forklift right off the dock.

"What you need to survive here is a bonsai tree. My brother has one in his office in Toronto, one of those nice big office towers on Bay. He says they all have them in the office. That's what they use to relax."

"They have trees in their offices?" Brock asked.

"Little Japanese trees, dwarf things. Only grow so big over the course of their lifetime. Sort of look like full-grown trees, only miniature."

Brock said, "Sounds like your brother is a fag, Donnie."

"You only wish, Cutcherson. Got your mouth open all the time looks like you're just waiting for a dick to fill it," Donnie said. "Unfortunately, he's married."

"All right," Jamie said. "So what's your point?"

"Always with the point here, eh, Garrison? You guys are just lucky the whole system shut down, otherwise we'd be unloading Peanut Noir all night," Donnie said. "Point I'm trying to get to is that if you work here long enough, you will go certifiably insane. Maybe it's the fumes from the booze, or the dust, or the fucking monotony, but you will go crazy without a doubt. Whether it's smashing a window or someone's face or jumping off the top row back in storage. And guess who will have to clean that up?"

"You?"

"Yes, me. I will somehow be bestowed with that great honor."

The warehouse was loud that night, but the three still sat in the shipping container talking in harsh whispers. Harry "Colon" Collins would be on their asses to dust or sweep if he found them hiding out in a trailer while the receiving system rebooted the rolling lines.

"So you need a bonsai tree. You need something to distract you, to keep your mind off the fact that you're stuck in this place for the foreseeable future with a lack of females and a whole lot of ugly motherfuckers who you can barely interact with in a civ manner."

The boys said nothing.

"And although I do have a wife, I also have a fucking bonsai tree. And you can always have both, that's the beauty of it."

"Don, this is just fucking confusin'."

"Everything is confusing for you, Garrison. What I'm saying is pretty simple. With these trees, they always just do a little maintenance, a little interaction with nature every day, a little preservation of something that isn't like a millionaire's stocks or his wife's assets in the divorce over his mistress, secretary, whatever. These guys in the big towers, they get to interact with something real. Real natural.

"Now, back at my place, my wife has a nice little herb garden and that's how she does it. But here, we can't really grow shit, can we? Not even like dill. That shit will grow anywhere if you let it. No, we are kinda stuck. Closest thing we got in here is women."

"Like ten of them? All in the offices, all typing away or running from here to there with their files and shit," Jamie said.

"But that's the point, Garrison. It doesn't need to be all the time. These dudes downtown aren't pruning and raking their little trees all day, but they are checking in on them from time to time. That's how you fucking survive here."

"Most of the girls in here got boyfriends already, or are way old. Like older than you, and you're...shit, you been around since what? Civil War?" Jamie said.

"I'm thirty, I'm not the walking dead, all right? But I get you. You don't need to want to date them. You just need to establish a rapport."

"A what?" Brock said.

"Okay, I don't know—a relationship."

"You said we aren't trying to bang these broads, so what are you even talking about, man?"

"I'm talking about decent human interaction here, boys. To connect you with a world that you otherwise would not be able to handle," Donnie said.

"So what do we do then, huh?"

"Just find one of the girls here, like in the parking lot, or whatever, the caf. Start up a little conversation. Hmm, look. All right, you know Candice?"

"Girl who checks the hours, does all that stuff? She's kinda got a—"

"She's got a weird nose, I know, but she's real nice. I check in to pick up my paystub, or see her in the parking lot. Maybe I chat a little here and there, and it's nice," Donnie said. "I got something to look forward to, a relationship to maintain, and that's it. Something at work that doesn't have shit to do with work keeps me from getting all crazy."

"So, you don't wanna ever do anything with Candice? I mean, besides the nose thing, she is pretty fit," Jamie said. "And she's got that tattoo…"

"No, Garrison, I don't. I really don't. Thing is, I do love my wife, truly, deeply, from the fucking root of my cock all the way to my heart and back, but the other thing is, when I'm here, a little female interaction is what keeps me sane," Donnie said. "It's why I don't think they should ever be segregating boys from girls in schools, and why I think so many of the numb nuts working here end up either crazy or bitter as shit about women."

"And what are we supposed to do with this information?"

"Find yourself a bonsai tree, man. Something to maintain. Cutcherson, man, you want to try that girl who processes all the receiving paperwork. She smiles at you, doesn't she?"

"Have you seen her teeth, man? They don't know up from down. They go fucking sideways. The boys call her the Sidewinder," Brock said.

"You aren't trying to knock her up. I go home to my wife and I don't even dream about that girl. It's just about having someone to talk to or notice you who doesn't have a dick."

"Well, like what if she starts thinking it means something?"

"She won't. She's got guys talking to her all the time. She's got guys on the phone, guys on her walk home, guys in her apartment building," Donnie said. "You ever see the shit they deal with? You'll just be another face. And best thing about the bonsai tree is you don't need to worry."

"Why?"

The machines began to groan to life around them, the massive rollers churning the rubber belts into motion again. Don Henley stood up and rubbed his nose.

"Bonsai trees don't bear any fruit. Whole thing is sterilized."

It took Jamie a while to find his bonsai tree. He spent time hanging out in the parking lot, smoking cheap Indian cigarettes and listening to Springsteen, even though Springsteen was a fag too. Sometimes he'd be there until two before calling it a night. The grind wore you out; it got dust deep into your lungs, the booze sneaking into your chest so that every time you sneezed, all you could smell was gin. Emerging in the darkness every night to drive home on roads covered in everyone else's road kill, all the girls you might meet either at work or in classes while you slept the day away. Brock to this day still kept in touch with Jean, the old lady who ran the receiving desk. She said if he ever got married she would just cry.

Jamie met his bonsai tree in the front office when he changed addresses. Payroll needed to know exactly where to send his new statements and find him during an emergency. Jamie had moved out of his parents' place, out of the old living room where his father sat fingering the hole in his hand. His mother talked about nothing but the bingo scores and that time she and Rhonda bought up all the menthols at the hall.

His was a small place near the warehouse, a flimsy wooden box stranded between giant, faceless buildings built from concrete and iron. It came with five appliances and was fully furnished. An old Ukrainian couple rented it to Jamie, the woman doing all the talking, the mole on her chin distracting Jamie the whole time. It bobbed along with her lips, accentuating every syllable. The old man sat by the window in their retirement community, singing folk songs under his breath and swearing quietly at Jamie.

The girl had not even looked at him that first day. She took the form and went back to typing on her typewriter, her thin hands flying over the keys. The false ceiling hung low over Jamie's massive slouching shoulders as he made his way out, back into the stench of stale red wine and rotten beer embedded in the concrete floor.

Jamie didn't need to look at the warehouse to know what was in there. He drove past rows of old buildings, massive tombs to industries that had abandoned town as each decade passed. His wrists felt looser now, his tongue had stopped pushing at each rogue tooth inside his mouth. The radio was a quiet burble in his ear. Only the broken grille of his car and the one headlight probing the darkness ahead reminded Jamie of the night before. The little house filled with paintings of Russian skylines and old teak furniture was only a few minutes away.

Jamie had done what Don Henley told him. He found a way to survive the monotony of the warehouse, the smells of the cafeteria, the constant throb in his ears from the rollers. He dropped comments to this girl with black hair and too much eye makeup as they waited in line for free pizza every third Thursday. Sometimes she would laugh and tell him her name again like it was the first time. Alisha Wugg. He didn't make fun of her name, but his tongue bled against that patient refusal. It bled every time he tried to speak to her. He would stand there with rust growing on his tongue, wondering what her feet looked like naked. And he didn't even like feet—they were the ugliest part of the human body.

Jamie brought a thick black marker to cover up the graffiti about her in the bathroom. He keyed the cars of men who commented on her ass. He never followed her home. He never left notes inside her locker. He didn't ask her if she dyed her hair or why she drew so much black around her eyes. He didn't ask for her number, and he didn't end up drawing pictures of her until he fell asleep on the couch while the television played *Brady Bunch* reruns with the wrong audio track all night. Jamie wanted to do all those things, but he was too tired.

Bonsai trees do not grow for long, but they do require constant maintenance. Don Henley always tried to make this clear. It was his wife he went home to every night. She was the one who fed him ice cream sandwiches and Greek yogurt when his jaw was broken in another unlicensed brawl in someone's barn. Not growth, but maintenance. Pruning, trimming, maintaining a relationship with a little "r" to make the days pass quicker.

Jamie tried to remember that when he found himself waking up in the middle of the night with dreams of her crying about discrepancies in the payroll. The old Ukrainians' house filled with pizza boxes and old underwear. He made lists to begin cleaning, but lost them in the mess. Laundry gathered everywhere, and Jamie's smell began to penetrate the walls. Brock said it looked like home, but back then Brock was always drunk and still living with his mom, so any place with a spark of life in it seemed like home to him. Life for Brock was fluid and messy and filled with those little bugs that weren't quite mosquitoes but weren't gnats either.

So Jamie Garrison trimmed and manicured his bonsai tree, assuring himself it would never blossom. He continued to draw thick black lines over the graffiti in the bathroom about the Wuggly Dog. Each stroke of marker reminded him she wore too much makeup. Jamie's hands grew callused and yellow, ridges of hard flesh gathering in the crevices of his palm where the synthetic rope burned cells like kindling every time he tied a knot. Alisha nodded at him in line for cabbage rolls and he made small remarks about the weather, her dress, the smell of cabbage. Anything.

Sometimes Alisha Wugg laughed, but usually she just raised her eyebrows.

The little house sat alone down by the water. There was a tricycle in the driveway, abandoned in the snow. The Ukrainian couple had transferred the lease after Jamie got married. After giving up the house and their old teak furniture, it only took the couple two months to die. Jamie's car bumped up into the driveway, swerving around the tricycle. Don Henley had always told them the bonsai tree was a safe bet; just another way to pass the time. After all, a bonsai tree was never going to bear fruit. Just something to look forward to in between safety meetings, training new temps, pulling long slivers of glass from your palm with the emergency safety kit tweezers.

"Did you run over my bike?"

She was only five years old and claimed she was too old for a trike.

"Kansas, you know that's a tricycle, don't you?"

Kansas Garrison stood there with her orange snowsuit half zipped up and one mitten on her little hand. The wind tossed her hair across her face. Her bottom teeth made her mouth look smaller than it was, crowded and uncomfortable.

"I know what a trike is. Did you run over my bike?"

Handle bars poked out from under Jamie's front tire.

"Oh."

Don Henley was wrong about those bonsai trees.

12

The first postcards were landscapes. Barren deserts spotted with cacti and the occasional buzzard. The same return address spelled out in perfect looping script across the back of each card. Moses Moon had enjoyed watching the postal code burn under the flame of his lighter, back when he and Elvira still lived on Keewatin St., back when they had an address.

"Let's just take the stairs. I got stuck in the elevator once with this dude who wore bunny ears to a party up on the fifth floor. Kept asking me what animal I'd choose if I could be one. When I didn't say anything, he says a ferret. He called me a fucking ferret," Moses said.

Eventually the postcards began to change. Buildings in sepia tones with *Greetings from Arizona* in the corner. Ghost towns and cowboy statues with busted trigger fingers. Lines and lines of houses, a blueprint repeated across the flattened land of suburban Arizona. Moses began to keep the postcards in an envelope, where they remained unread and dormant in his room. He tucked it under his mattress even after they fled the old townhouse, the words remaining benign so long as they were quarantined in that manila envelope. He did not tell his mother.

"You actually live in this place?" Logan said. "No wonder you were never taking us back here. B. Rex always just said to let it go, but I was kind of sketched out. You never actually told us where you lived. This place is like a fucking disease."

Logan was talking again. He'd talked the whole way over here. About the rise of illegal immigration in the city and the broken window theory and the ways you could tell the difference between a Muslim and Hindu Paki if you looked close enough. A lot of his theories had to do with pork consumption and going through their trash. Moses had jammed Texaco's purple hat over Logan's head to cover up the bleeding swastika before they left the butcher shop. Purple didn't show the blood or the hate—just absorbed it. Swallowed it whole. They didn't talk about Mr. Chatterton folded up in the bone can. They didn't talk about Logan's mother, either.

"Well, what did you expect?" Moses said.

"I don't know. Maybe your mom was a spic or something? Fucking revelations happening all over the place today," Logan said. "I guess none of this shit should surprise me. Did you hear they're making another *Terminator*?"

Da Nasty on a Saturday was loud, so loud you felt it down in your gut, in the tiny hairs on your forearms. There were no vacancies. The hallway was littered with bottle caps and White Snake lyrics belted at the top of smokers' lungs. The air conditioners huffed away at full capacity as the meth heads complained about stuffy eyes and phantom itches behind their ears. Someone blasted a porno at top volume with the door open, a woman loudly critiquing the performances of the men on screen. Too soft, she said. Too soft.

"*Terminator*?"

"Yeah, like Part II," Logan said.

The boys walked past Room 227 and the sound of power tools.

"Arnold can't even speak fucking English."

Moses's room was at the end of the hall. He hoped Elvira would just stay in the bathroom tonight. He could play it off as some junkie hiding out in his room, or an old family friend who just needed a place to stay for a while. No, that was stupid. Fuck it.

Logan could say whatever he wanted tonight. At least Moses had a parent around.

"One of your ultimate heroes, after your whole attempt at getting some retribution last night backfired all over your face at the Triple K, is a fucking immigrant in the real world."

"Yeah, but he's German…" Logan said.

"He's fucking Austrian," Moses said.

"I don't care what country he is from. What you aren't seeing here, Moses, is the fact that the American government is so corrupt now, it can't see what's coming," Logan said. "Look, the American government won't even admit how it's playing into the hands of the blacks and the Jews and the—hey, I bet a fucking black dude created Skynet! Just wait for the fucking new movie. Shit, man, you see what I'm talking about? Fucking Skynet. Apocalyptic, four-horseman shit. And Arnold, he's the fucking white reckoning come to set the record straight."

The Judge was alone on the bed, tucked in under the faded flower-print duvet. A thousand washes couldn't get some of the stains out, only pushed them deeper into the fabric until they became a part of the pattern—irrecoverable evidence of someone else's bad decisions. The door to the bathroom was open. Both taps on the sink ran hot and cold. Steam gathered under the fan. The bathtub was empty. The television was on, but the sound was muted and the whole room was too quiet. Bill Cosby waved at the two boys from behind the screen and smiled. Someone had left the door to the balcony open. Postcards spilled across the floor.

"What's with the bowling ball, dude? You got some fetish you haven't told me about?"

Elvira Moon was gone.

13

Alisha Wugg no longer wore any eye makeup.

"I don't let her watch any TV," she said. "I hope you know that."

She still worked in the payroll office at the liquor warehouse, filing away the addresses of every creep who commented on her ass into a folder entitled "Eventualities Et Al." Eventually one of them would have his foot run over by a thousand-pound fork lift, snapping all the toes off inside his steel-toed boot. Eventually one of them would come in drunk and puke all over the scanners before he was fired, losing his wife, house, and custody of three children in the process. Someday they would all disappear. She would shred their file page by page in the storage room with a smile on her face. All of this was eventual.

"Not even, like, *Sesame Street*?" Jamie said.

"Well, what is a Snuffleupagus anyway?" Alisha said.

"I think it's a mammoth."

Jamie Garrison sat across the table from her, his hands fidgeting in his lap. Kansas sat at the end of the table, dividing her peas into separate nations based on size and relative color. The small dark greens would soon outnumber all others, swelling like a tidal wave on one side of her plate.

"Not like an elephant? Or something?"

Alisha was already clearing the table, her thin hands flaking skin from too many showers and not enough soap. She didn't paint her nails, afraid of the chips and flakes.

"Well, without the tusks," Jamie said.

"So just a hairy elephant, and then they gave it a name. It doesn't really make sense to me."

"It's a kids' show, Alisha."

Kansas nodded and began to eat her peas. She saved the vegetables for last.

"I know it's a kids' show, but if I can't figure out what's going on, then—well, I can barely afford the cable. Not that I'm saying—I have been getting your checks."

The checks had been coming twice a month for the last year or so, ever since the night the television got cracked. She had a new box now, humming and spitting out large angry words about God in the living room. The house could get lonely without the noise. And Kansas only talked on her own schedule.

There were no neighbors out here, just old factories for J.P. Chemical and the Osprey Windshield system, discontinued in 1983 after Ford bought them out and closed the whole operation down. An old iron osprey still dangled from a weathervane on the roof with a salmon clutched in its rusted claws. A few miles down the road, the sprawling Larkhill Institute for Mental Health remained closed. Kids still broke in on summer weekends to drink beer and decipher old symbols carved into the walls with dirty fingernails and sharpened toothbrushes.

"You'll keep getting them," Jamie said. "I know what we agreed on."

"And I'm not complaining. That's why I wanted to have you come over again."

The snow had stopped falling outside. Alisha washed the dishes at the sink. The dishwasher was still flooded, and after the plumber showed her an estimate a month ago, she'd kicked him out and screamed at him from the doorway. Something about cheats and liars and the comeuppance provided in the afterlife for every fraudster in his own boiling pot of regret. Something her mother would have said.

Sometimes Alisha would look in the mirror before the sun was up only to see her mother's face, the long lines drawn around her mouth, like channels focusing the piercing file of her scream, magnifying its judgment until all you heard was someone slamming the door and the fact that it was your fault, it was always your fault, don't you realize you broke me? Broke me like a fucking horse. Like a horse that should be put down. Just like you. A nothing.

Alisha Wugg did not want to grow old.

"I saw that thing on the news too, about the boy in the forest. I'm surprised they'd even air that garbage," Alisha said.

"What, what garbage?" Jamie said. "It's been a long day. Right, kiddo?"

Kansas consumed each pea on its own. She nodded.

"The guy they found in the woods," Alisha said. "Partial remains? Is that the way to say it with Kansas here?"

"Like half there?" Kansas said.

"Yes, dear. Do you want to go upstairs and read for a bit?"

The last of the peas disappeared in one movement and there was a gallop up the stairs.

"She still likes books," Jamie said.

"Which is part of why I don't want TV to take that away from her. She is happy now with just her books," Alisha said. "What's she going to do with—well, for example, that boy? Was it a boy?"

The older you got, the more likely something would go wrong. Alisha knew this. The nun confessed she never even saw her mother walking out of the Hasty Mart that day. It was only her third day with the license and her first day driving the priest's new Crown Vic. The crunch of Mrs. Wugg's hip, she told the first responding officer, she thought it was a snow bank, or a pop bottle. Only the screams and the snap of Mrs. Wugg's ulna alerted her to the problem.

"What boy? You need to turn that shit off."

"The one they found in the woods, they had him on TV tonight. Well not him, his mother actually," Alisha said. "She had photo albums and everything. You should see some of the people who've come out. It's pretty amazing—the response. You'd think the fact he was left in the woods for so long was depressing, but it's pretty incredible they were able to find so many people to come out."

"The one with the dental records?" Jamie said. "That dude?"

"Is that how they did it?" Alisha said. "I don't really know how bad the damage was, but the guy on channel eight was saying something like 'extensive desecration' of the remains. I guess it was the teeth."

"Teeth. Yeah. Everyone has them, 'cept maybe a few pill freaks down at the Greyhound."

"Well, your dad for one, Jamie. I don't think he's ever even gone to see a dentist, much less any kind of doctor. Does he have a doctor?"

"He has, just not...well, shit, I don't even see his ass around anymore."

The nun was eventually given six years' probation and had her driver's license revoked for ten. Crying in the witness seat, she swore she would never drive again; the wheel was beyond the realm of her responsibility. She wished to atone, if only she could atone, but Alisha and her brother did not make their names known to the court. Old Mrs. Wugg remained in critical care for three weeks before emerging from a coma.

Somewhere in that three-week haze, Alisha's mother had restructured her life around moments that did not exist, had never existed. Scenes from films and songs from her childhood. It was true she'd been a beauty queen at seventeen, a mother at twenty, and a divorcee by the age of twenty-three. A divorcee lumped with two children and a mortgage on the north side of town with the good schools and the supermarkets with the extra-wide aisles, and the better dentists. All of this was true. She remembered all of these things.

"You don't even call them? What about Christmas?" Alisha said.

"I guess I was there for Christmas. It's not like we're excommunicated. It's just not like I'm calling him up to say, 'Hey, pops, how's it going? Still whittling bullshit and ignoring Mom? How's that going for you, buddy?'" Jamie said. "I don't think he's even answered the phone in the last five years. He lets Mom do that. No way am I calling him. That just leads nowhere."

In the world before the nun, Mrs. Wugg had divorced Harold Evan Wugg after catching him with a neighbor in the family bathtub, her hands clutching a box of chocolate-covered strawberries she'd bought for their upcoming weekend alone. She had sold the house, told her children she loved them and that nothing was ever going to change that. Their father might have left, might have gone off to run some fleabag motel in some other place, some other city, but she wasn't going anywhere. In the world before the nun, she made sure both her children finished high school with honors and watched her daughter learn to figure skate.

"Maybe you should. Just give it a try."

"Oh, you're one to talk," Jamie said. "Look at you giving out advice. Family advice at that. Holy shit. How's Mom? Huh?"

This was where Alisha usually would begin screaming. Sometimes it was directly in his face. Other times it was from down the hall as she threw her shoes as hard as she could at the closet door, restraining herself from whipping them in his direction. She'd read in the paper once about a man who took a four-inch stiletto through the eye. His wife was later charged.

Alisha Wugg did not scream.

"Look, Jamie, this kid, his mother didn't talk to him. She didn't even see him for six years. Six years. Think about how much changes in six years. She didn't even know he was still living in the same town. They were living in the same city, probably the same area, maybe even the same neighborhood, and it was six years she hadn't seen her son. The look of regret on that woman's face...I bet half the people watching ran to call their mom after seeing that kind of thing. I know they did."

Jamie didn't look at Alisha.

"And I know that might sound stupid to you, but you still have both parents kicking around. And guess what?" Alisha said. "You still live in the same town as them, and what's more, they can still talk to you like normal human beings."

In the world after the nun, it was Harold Evan Wugg, extraordinary inventor of the toaster oven, who had left her for another woman, a younger woman, a woman whose sexual wiles and bountiful body had not been put through the endurance, the pain and the suffering of childbirth. A woman with whom he could commune not only through spirit, but body as well, and wasn't that what a marriage was all about? The spirit, yes, but the body too. That was what Christ had asked them for, to commune as both, and as one, their duality wrapped in a single sheath. She had been forced to give it all up for these children, leave behind all the riches and wonders, all the chocolate shipped in straight from Belgium. In the world after the nun, in a bed at St. Luke's Hospice, Mrs. Wugg knew her life had ended the moment she gave birth to that daughter with the tired eyes and the fat ass, the one she saw every other Thursday at two during visiting hours. Mrs. Wugg made sure to tell the world this was not the life she chose.

"What is the point, then?" Jamie said. "I'm a bad man? Boogie man? No love for the family. Is that what you tell the kid?"

"She's your daughter, not 'the kid,' Jamie."

"Why is she calling me up at three in the morning anyway, waking up Renee and everything? I mean, can you not get her under control? Never mind watching TV, how about you keep her in bed for once?"

"Under control? The girl is five. Five. She is so far ahead in so many things," Alisha said. "You saw her reading when she was three, you were the one who…and now you think there's something wrong with her?"

"I'm just saying that maybe, maybe you should—"

"I should do what? Do everything?" Alisha said. "Oh wait, I already do that. I already do that every fucking day of my fucking life, since fucking who knows how long?"

"Let's build you a shrine, then: Saint Alisha amongst the Masses and the Poor and the Drunk," Jamie said. "How many of them do you bring back here?"

Jamie got up from the table but did not look Alisha in the eye. He left an envelope on the counter and stomped out into the snow. Alisha got up from the table and walked to the window over the sink. Her daughter's busted bicycle stood against the railing, its mangled handlebars flashing in Jamie's lone headlight. The front grille of his car was smashed, the bumper distended. The car pulled away, the muffler hiccupping and popping into the dark of the unlit street.

Alisha Wugg stared at her reflection in the glass of her little kitchen. The window was just as unforgiving as her bathroom mirror in the morning. She didn't look at the lines around her mouth this time, only stared out into the snow. She was supposed to go and see her mother that past Thursday, supposed to try and make amends. Instead, she took Kansas to the library. They took out every single book on pirates in the children's section. Kansas had them set up in her room right now, the pages spread open all over the floor. That morning Kansas had told her mother they used to hang captured pirates in metal cages over the ports of cities, the bodies in these gibbets acting like a warning for the next generation of buccaneers and butchers out there on the high seas. Kansas had memorized the passage.

Alisha Wugg did not go see her mother because she knew what she would find. It would always be there, waiting—next week or next year.

It was too quiet outside. There were no animals. She smiled at the glass and watched the cracks grow around the edges of her lips. Alicia did not want to grow old. She knew they would not stop. These lines would move slowly, like a glacier—deliberate and irreversible. All of this was eventual.

14

B. Rex had a new tattoo emblazoned on his neck. It was dripping.

"You didn't do that one yourself, did you, B?" Moses said.

The car bounced over the potholes on the utility road. The neon lights of the highway strip faded behind them as the Buick nursed its way through the slush. No one came down here.

"Yeah. This morning. Had the money, finally, not like it was a big job, but I've been getting stiffed by the folks lately. Think they're still mad about me trimming the hair."

B. Rex had the worst ingrown hairs of the three, mainly due to his refusal of the disposable razor at Logan's house a few months earlier. He brought his grandfather's straight razor from World War II instead, a family heirloom his grandfather kept in the study with his tax receipts and old *Playboy* magazines. B. Rex cut himself eight times before finally accepting the shaving cream and disposable Bick. He wore a hat for a while afterward until the scabs fell off.

"They still won't let you work, huh?" Moses said.

"Nope. Mom says as soon as I start earning my own money, that's the last they'll see of me, and I mean, they're right," B. Rex said. "Oppressive as shit. I can't even take like a shit without my dad asking about the size and color."

After looking under the beds and the sink, Moses and Logan went from room to room looking for his mother. A few doors had opened to confront a haze of smoke and long hair, the bong glowing like a lantern in the center of the room. Other rooms featured women slapping each other on the television while men cheered and smoked cheap cigars and asked when the fuck the strippers were going to show up. They spotted a few girls from school in the elevator, smoking and tugging each other's skirts. No one made eye contact. The elevator dinged and the girls had gone down another hallway where the lighting was offset and the wallpaper had yet to peel.

The night manager wasn't wearing a nametag, and he was too high to tell them if he'd seen her or not. Who? Who is this you look for? Logan asked politely to use the phone and somehow B. Rex picked up. He did have the old Buick tonight, and he was bored like usual. Chemistry was boring, physics was boring, and no, no, he hadn't learned to blow up anything new or how to make anything new blow up. Give it another week and he'd figure it out.

Moses and Logan scoured the lower floor and walked in on old men locked in deep, passionate kisses with each other. They opened doors to women crying over pictures of their children, or someone else's children, or maybe pictures of themselves from back when they were children. No one had seen a six-foot-tall woman built like an Amazon and wearing a bathrobe tied at the waist.

"How much did they charge you? Was it the same place?" Logan asked.

"The place you got your head done, Loogie, except I didn't let the guy with three fingers do it for me," B. Rex said. "I saw your head after he was done with it."

B. Rex met them in the motel room an hour later. He lay down on the bed beside the glowing Judge and listened to Moses explain the whole story of his mother, the bowling ball, the motel rooms, the postcards scattered around the floor, and the fact that she might not even remember who he was anymore.

"Did it hurt? The thing going into your neck?" Moses asked.

"Any more than Loogie's head? No, it didn't hurt so bad."

Moses went through the previous day and the night before—his mother in the bathtub; the fact he had to wash his hands because he and Garrison, the big dude from the butcher shop, hit a lion and had to drag it over to the side of the road and everything. It was a mess, split open like a melon, intestines everywhere.

"14/88. What the fuck is that supposed to mean anyway?" Moses said.

"Obviously, you have not been reading the literature, Moses. And I do know you can read," B. Rex said. "88. Eighth letter of the alphabet. HH. Heil…you know who. You get it? Fuck, this is probably bullshit anyway—right, Loogie? African lion safari bullshit."

They didn't believe him about the lion. That's why they were here now, nosing through the dark and the slush to find the body. No one had reported it on the news. No one had said anything at school. No one even had a lion around here as far as they knew.

"It was like hitting another car," Moses said. "Where else do you think I got all the bruises? You think I did this to myself?"

Logan wasn't talking as much now, just staring out the window. He still had the purple tuque clamped onto his head, but the blood was beginning to push through the fibers.

"Stop, stop, it was there. You can still see it kinda. In the snow."

The car shuddered to a stop. Moses hopped out and walked out into the fresh snow, leaving behind size-eleven boot prints for B. Rex to follow. They kept the car running. Logan wasn't talking anymore. His theories about Skynet and the coming apocalypse had lost their momentum as the night dragged on into morning.

"Shit, no lion here," B. Rex said. "But damn."

A warm patch of earth stood out on the slushy shoulder. Headlights illuminated the wet patch of blood and feces mixing in the dirt. It hadn't frozen yet.

"You sure it wasn't like a big-ass bear or something?" B. Rex asked.

"With a mane and a tail? Rex, it wasn't a bear."

There was no wind. The two of them stood with clouds of steam hovering around their heads. The smog from the Buick floated up into the sky. B. Rex sniffed.

"I never smelled anything like that."

"Well, that's African shit," Moses said.

"Lion shit," B. Rex said. "Real bloody lion shit. Shit. Shit, man. Shit."

"We hit it right up in the belly. Whole thing just collapsed. Goin' like at least ninety down here, there wasn't a lotta snow, and then just fucking *bam*! I didn't believe it at first. And Garrison…"

"He had you leave it here?" B. Rex said. He stopped and stared down at the cooling mess.

"Call the cops? Yeah, all right."

"I get it, I get it," B. Rex. "Where do you think he went?"

"He?"

"The lion. You said it was too big for you and Garrison to drag off to the shoulder. You even listening?"

"It's dark out here," Moses said. "This look like a winter coat to you?"

They turned back toward the Buick.

"You think it just disappears like that and nobody notices?"

The car doors slammed and B. Rex turned the heater all the way into the red.

"It wasn't in the papers," Moses said.

"You don't read the fucking papers, Moses."

"You do after you run over someone's lion."

B. Rex yawned and wiped a hole in the fog on the windshield. The clock read 4:30 a.m. Moses could feel his toes sticking together in his shoes. He stretched and sighed.

"Loogie, buddy, you ready to go find Moses's crazy mom? I'm going to get in so much shit from the parental unit for this," B. Rex said. "Well, all for a good cause. Haven't pissed them off in a while. Been wearing a scarf at home to hide the new tat, my mom says it looks like I'm finally taking care of myself. And my dad, well I think he's pretty sure I'm a fag by now anyway. Hey, Loogie, wanna be my boy toy?"

Logan was asleep across the backseat. Both hands cupped his wounded head. It sounded like his lungs were drowning, but he was just crying in his sleep.

Back in the yellow motel halls, Moses stood against a dirty window and watched the sun rise over whirring police cars in the parking lot. Two officers argued with a naked man threatening them with a rolled-up newspaper.

Logan and B. Rex were back in his room, tucked under the faded comforter with the Judge between them. B. Rex and Moses had carried Logan into the elevator from the car, avoiding the stairway and the broken glass. No one stopped them as they carried his bleeding body down the hall, even though it was full of loud men in tuxedos with the tags still attached. The boys washed Logan's head in the bathtub and he croaked something about being dirty, impure, a fucking abomination, before the soapy water filled his mouth and he spat it up, cursing his mother.

Moses couldn't sleep. He'd paced the halls and watched the night unfold, the police arriving in disparate waves that washed away one layer of dirt only to reveal another beneath it. He stood over the stairwell and dropped beer bottles from the fifth floor, enjoying the brief second before the glass shattered below him.

Moses loved that second. Moses wished he could live in that second, he wished Elvira could live in that second too. He wanted to watch it expand before him until he could not see the other side, but only the center, before the drop and the crash. He wanted to enjoy the fall without the repercussions.

Elvira was always sane for a second, she was always thoughtful for a second, she was always, always unfailingly beautiful for a second, before she grimaced at his face or the television or the fact that another second was traveling toward her where she would no longer recognize her son or her bowling balls or her own face, or remember she was once married to a man named Ted Moon who told her always and forever, amen, in front of everyone who said they loved her once upon a time. Moses wanted another second before that new one arrived, before everything shattered on the beer-stained floor. The carpet at the Dynasty absorbed everything. It was soaked down to the foundation.

The boys would ride out tomorrow and find Elvira Moon and bring her back to waste away under her son's feeble care. Moses knew that was the best he could provide. A place where she could sleep in the bathtub without any questions being asked. B. Rex had promised they would find her. They had smoked out on the balcony and watched Logan twist and turn on the bed, moaning about his mother and the Sioux and the end of everything. B. Rex had puffed his chest out and blown smoke through his nose before he started coughing.

"We'll fucking find her, man. You know where she'd go, don't you? I'll go, and Loogie too. You helped our asses before, told us what the fuck was up. Stopped letting me get my face stomped every time I went into the hall. Got us on the program, you know?" B. Rex said, shifting his small arms around his chest. The wind spat little bits of snow into their faces. "That's why I got it spelled out on my neck, man. Like you said, we gotta be serious. You gotta rub it in their faces, you gotta imprint it in your blood to show them that you're serious. This is no joke."

"So that explains the ugly-ass tattoo?" Moses said.

B. Rex nodded and hugged himself tighter.

"Yeah. Exactly."

"14/88?" Moses said.

B. Rex rubbed his neck and blew more smoke through his nose. He coughed.

"Fourteen words, buddy. 'We must secure the existence of our people and a future for white children.' It's probably all bullshit, but it pisses them off to no end."

"Them?"

"Everybody. Ha. Ain't that the point of all this?"

15

They really did look like ZZ Top.

"You got any trim for us to use?" one of the bearded men said.

Jamie Garrison was still recovering from the night before. He waited for the camera crew to reveal themselves, for some leggy blonde in Daisy Duke shorts to spring up behind the deli counter with a massive sausage in her hands. Then he noticed the popped blood vessels and the dead eyes, and the fact that only one of them was wearing sunglasses inside. The bearded man spoke again and his voice cracked.

"Buddy, you awake, or you still tipsy? I asked if you got any trim."

After leaving Alisha's the night before, Jamie drove around town swallowing all the orange and black pills the Lorax had given him. He banged on the door to the bingo hall downtown, but it was closed. Someone had had a heart attack during Midnight Madness. Each pill he swallowed was like a seed, planting more illusions in his head, until every branch collided with the next and he had to pull over in the parking lot of the Giant Tiger to calm down. Under its glowing yellow sign, Jamie tried to talk himself into a lucid state where lions weren't lurking behind the shopping cart corral and his daughter's teeth weren't marching through the streets together in pairs, all headed for Noah's Ark and the end of the world. Each curb looked like the perfect place to smash your jaw, and he still had no insurance, no cigarettes either.

Jamie had smoked them all staring at the flashing ambulances outside the bingo hall and the blue hair hurling up her entire life onto the chests of the tired paramedics. His mother wasn't there, but she was never around in those moments. He waited for fires to spring forth from rotting foundations, held his head between his knees to block out flashes of his mother's burns, the ones encircling her neck like dried snakes.

He didn't remember getting home, only remembered walking downstairs to find his brother's wife in his bed, her naked back revealing a school of mermaids trapped in a fisherman's net. They waved at him and blew sad kisses from fleshy lips. Renee no longer slept in Scott's bed. Jamie had walked upstairs to sleep on the couch, past the old stain and the laundry drying on the railing. Renee needed to sleep in her bed. She needed to start wearing more clothes. She needed to be all the things he did not want right now. Eventually Jamie fell asleep to the smell of garbage and his brother's voice singing Meat Loaf in falsetto from the kitchen.

"Trim? Like the fat?" Jamie said.

"Yeah. Need it. Going up to the park today. Big day."

"What you need that shit for?"

There were no other customers in the store. It was only eight. In his dreams on the couch, Jamie had watched Alisha walk his daughter up to the roof of the old Osprey building. The wind spun them up to the roof and the crowds below all looked like Jamie. She told Kansas that she could fly, and then a bicycle burst forth from inside her body, its gears replaced with a set of wings labeled PEGASUS UNLIMITED. The wings were bloody but functional, and the feathers glowed like pearls. A bicycle built for two, and no one else would fit into its silken harnesses. Jamie had woken up angry. Alisha always found the better gifts.

"We just wanted to help you out," the bearded man said. "If you're going to be a bitch about it, we can just go somewhere else."

Don Henley had booked Jamie for the morning shift on a Sunday. The store was cleanest in the morning, before the blood worked its way into the grout between the tiles and the dust from the bone saw filled the air with pink fluff.

"Just a long night," Jamie said. "You want trim from the cans, or what?"

The other beard in the sunglasses nodded.

"I guess I can wrap it up for you, or we can—"

"We brought a bucket, we'll just slop it in there," the first beard said. "We know Don. Knew his brother too. Place looks like it's gone to shit since he died. You guys really need to step your game up a bit. Chad always ran it like a pro. A real pro."

"Got that right," said the other beard.

"You feed this to the dogs?" Jamie asked.

Don had inherited the place from his brother after the older Henley forgot to attach his seatbelt on a rollercoaster in Gurnee, Illinois. Chad Henley had hit the ground at an advanced speed, fast enough to push his organs outside his body.

"A dog gets out of hand if you spoil it like that," the one beard said. "Can't teach it nothing. All it'll do is get gut rot. You ever eat a whole roast and then just sit on your ass all day?"

Henley only hired Jamie after he was fired from the warehouse. After Harry "Colon" Collins caught him with Alisha in the bathroom, their faces pressed together and their voices muffled in each other's mouths. Collins stood in the doorway and watched the bathroom stall shake violently, the sound of their breathing competing with the air conditioner. Hairy Colon. Jamie and Brock wrote it on everything. Some of the stores complained about drawings on their boxes, all of them signed Hairy Colon. Fuzzy asses and stick men bending over in front of one another. Harry found it on permission slips and doctor's notes, and on the underside of his desk when he had to climb under there to grab a pen. Jamie was gone before the stall door opened.

"You should see the dog we got now," the first beard said. "We call him Artax. Size of a horse, big white thing. Turkish or some shit. Got him from a farmer. Got nailed by a car the other day—just totally destroyed its headlight, but he lived. One eye is all black now, but he'll get over it. You never want a dog that is taller than you when it's on its hind legs."

"You guys use the trim yourselves, then?" Jamie said.

"Nah, man. You gotta use it for bears."

"Like…to kill?" Jamie said, drumming his thumbs on the counter to match the throbbing sensation inside his skull.

"Kill or catch. What you do is lay it out there for the bear and then—"

"You put it around your campsite," the second beard interrupted.

"Am I telling the story or are you? And take off the fucking sunglasses. You're inside. You aren't blind," the first bearded man said. "This is why I don't wear sunglasses when I'm with you, because then we look like a couple of—"

"The bears, you were talking about?" Jamie yawned.

"Bears love to eat early. And they'll eat any of this shit. Garbage, especially."

"Just pass me the buckets. I'll go in the back," Jamie said. "You want the beef or the pork or what? I'm sure we got all kinds of shit back there."

"We'll go with the beef," the beards said in unison. An older, sadder, ZZ Top.

"No pork? Got kosher bears now?" Jamie said.

"You talk more than Don does. This is why we miss his fucking brother," the one beard said. "You come in and say I want three shanks, a butt, and a bucket of beef navel, and what does Chad do?

He goes and grabs your shit, piles it all neatly in a box for you, asks for the cash, rings up the register, and watches you walk out the fucking door. He knew how to handle his customers. Customers got the word custom in it you see, so customate—"

The one in the sunglasses yawned out the right word. "Customize."

"Shut the hell up," he said. "But yeah, customize yourself to each customer."

"Does it really matter, though?" Jamie said. "I thought bears would eat garbage."

Jamie was tired. Make these two ZZ Top twins work for their beef trim. He wanted to study them—the scars on their hands and the tattoos riding up under the collars of their jackets. Their jeans had holes in the knees, brown and oily in places. No scent of detergent or deodorant.

"They'll eat your ass and then the garbage you left behind the night before. Garbage and rotten meat, top of the menu for bears, and you got little Johnny Appleseed on the news telling me not to shoot it in the face?" the one said. Jamie couldn't tell them apart anymore. "What happens when his kids are playing in the backyard and that thing just decides it's hungry? If you go out in the woods today…you know that song? There won't be no teddy bears. Just monsters. Furry, fast, tree-climbing buggers who can tear your arm off and eat it right in front of you."

"Just give me a few seconds," Jamie said. "I'll get this set up for you guys, no charge. You're doin' me a favor. Getting rid of my garbage."

Jamie grabbed the two buckets and headed back into the cutting room. Only four of the bone cans were lined up in the corner, their black lids firmly closed. One of them must have been pushed outside into the snow. Maybe to get rid of the smell. The meat would be frozen if the night was cold enough. Jamie couldn't remember if last night had been cold or not, only that there was snow and that he'd run over someone's bicycle, no, someone's lion. One of the two. He'd been running over too many things. He could still feel it in his kneecaps.

He was all out of orange pills.

Jamie went through the cans methodically. Most were filled with stock that had gone bad—guts and entrails and chicken kidneys. The other cans were mainly full of blood and a few bits of yellowed pork. Some of the salted back fat had gone off code too and floated like icebergs around the surface. Jamie popped the receiving door open. A couple crows hopped away from the door as Jamie walked out into the melting snow and opened the bone can.

The face looking back at him was shriveled. It didn't smile or blink and its toenails were far too long—a man should never let his toenails get so long. That was the first thing Jamie thought. The second had something to do with a body in one of his bone cans. Arms and legs and everything. He closed the lid slowly and shooed the crows away. The eyes didn't follow him as he closed it. They were dead. They didn't blink or move or say hello. Neither did the lion's. The man's eyes were hazel, they had gold flecks in them and they were dead, rotting somewhere on a cellular level, decomposing in real time. Maybe they weren't here for trim after all. Maybe a pickup instead, something he never should have gotten into. Something Don forgot to tell him about. Jamie closed the door behind him and went back inside. His hands shook the buckets. The crows hopped back onto the dumpster when the door shut.

"Now a lot of it is just trim from steaks and a few whole eyes we cleaned up the other day. I hope that works for you two," Jamie said. The one in the sunglasses was napping on the floor.

"Took you long enough."

"Only the best for guys who knew the big man," Jamie said.

"Man, if you really knew him, you'd know you're always supposed to call him Chad," the bearded man said. "Guy was a Nazi about that shit."

"You don't need anything else from here, I mean, you aren't picking anything up for anyone?" Jamie asked. A new sweat broke out on his brow. "I can check for you in case."

Jamie knew he should just shut up. The other brother got up from the floor and took his sunglasses off. One of his eyes kept staring at the floor, but the other looked straight at Jamie. It was alive, flicking eyelashes and yellow crust crumbling in the corners—alive and probing.

"We just came in to get our shit. You all right if we come by in a couple days? I assume you won't have as many questions next time."

"I'll probably be more sober," Jamie said. "Tell me if you catch any bears, eh? I hear there's all kinds of shit out there in the woods."

"You wouldn't believe some of the shit we find out there, little buddy. If you go out in the woods today…"

The two bearded men laughed and turned to walk out of the store. One of them held the door for a grandmother carrying two baskets in her hands. Her knuckles were large and red, blisters about to pop and drizzle down her liver-spotted hands. Jamie watched the two men jump into a red pickup in the parking lot. It looked like they were cracking beers behind the wheel.

"I was wondering if you had any of the medium mince in today, dear?"

Jamie looked down at the lady in front of him. Cataracts clouded her eyes, but she seemed to have all her teeth. They weren't too straight and they weren't too white. He had a good eye for dentures now, the clacking noise they made when they were loose. Just like that guy at the hobby shop. Brock's mouth could learn a lot from this lady's. He wanted to ask her who her dentist was but instead he asked her how much she wanted.

By the time she'd left, the red pickup was gone. Jamie sat on the floor behind the counter. There were no other customers. Not much was open on Sunday. All his bones still hurt. And he knew that body was a warning, a sign. It had looked at him just like the lion had.

Behind the butcher shop, Mr. Chatterton's body continued to slowly decompose, the cold air maintaining the tight-lipped frown and wrinkles on his face. In the darkness, those eyes stared at nothing but white pork fat and floating chicken kidneys.

16

Moses threw the first stone.

"Yeah!"

The glass shattered, but no one came running to the window. It was noon and the street was deserted. Cars up on concrete blocks filled gravel driveways.

"You fucking suck," Logan said.

Moses knew they should have knocked. He could have done it. Politely asked if anyone had seen a six-foot tower wearing a teal Japanese bathrobe, one of the cheap ones you find at Kmart.

The neighborhood was not the same, though. Plywood patched over broken windows. Piles of bloody carpeting sat outside Julie Brigham's old house, the white fluff looking stained and sad against the melted snow. She and Moses used to walk to school until the cops came for the dogs.

"How about you give it a fucking go?" B. Rex said.

"Do I look like a pussy?"

Logan whipped his rock at the pavement and ran up to the front door. His steel toes crunched against the flimsy frame, bending the chipped wood. It took three kicks to punch a hole through the door. No cars passed on the street. All the trees were almost bare, the leaves blackened and soaked. Moses and B. Rex stood and watched until Logan's feet finally busted the hinges and the door fell inside. The place still smelled like dog piss and split peas. The lingering taint of pine air fresheners somehow made the smell worse, like some sad attempt to deny the stench inhabiting the drywall and the floorboards. Moses hadn't stepped inside yet, but he could feel it creeping down his throat to where the two-legged dogs and policemen fought each other inside his stomach.

"You guys going to come with me or just stand around with your dicks in your hands?" Logan said. "I don't really care either way."

They searched every room and closet for Elvira Moon. Under the beds and behind garish purple curtains filled with tiny spider eggs. B. Rex pushed his head into the attic but found only a baby raccoon fossilized by time. Its teeth were barely formed. Crumbs gathered in the corners, and the floor was sticky around the fridge. There was a picture of the family on the metal door, the father's hands too tight on his daughters' shoulders, the mother's smile a little too crisp, a little too kind.

"First Da Nasty, now this place. My fucking Christ!" Logan said. "Moses, you ever live in a real house, or just shitholes with addresses?"

Moses was inspecting the old couch, the one the new tenants hadn't thrown out. His yellow fingers traced the cigarette burns on the cushions from the nights he'd fallen asleep with David Suzuki whispering in his ear, whispering about lions who eat their young alive to preserve their status in the pride. No new heirs.

"At least it's not a clown house, eh, Mosey?" B. Rex said. "Loogie, did you check the basement?"

"No, I didn't. Got other things on my mind here. These people have three blenders. Three. Excess and decadence for a shithole like this. The machines will definitely have our asses in a sling when the time comes. Skynet will blend us all into one giant shit smoothie."

"I ain't going down there by myself," B. Rex said. "Mosey, you're coming with me."

No dogs ran up the stairs. The sound of squeaking wheels only echoed in the empty spaces between Moses's thoughts as they made their way into the basement. It was brightly lit and filled with homemade weights—cinderblocks and heavy car parts duct-taped together. Framed photographs lined the walls, the family of four flexing all their muscles in tandem, the two girls in front showing ripples of muscle where budding breasts should have been. Short black hairs were barely concealed by the tanning lotion on their chins. The mother's body was still smooth, the muscles toned and barely rising out from beneath her tiny thong, but the daughters looked like men. Their smiles came from their mother, but the enhanced pectorals and wide, ropey thighs came from the father, his own teeth artificially whitened like a streak of snow across his face, his head shaved and glowing like a bowling ball.

"Fuck, man, first time I ever seen this," Moses said.

"Loogie, come check this out! You'll love it. Right up your alley," B. Rex yelled up the stairs.

They heard his boots stomp across the kitchen floor overhead and trample down the stairs.

"I found a calendar on the fridge. They had all this muscle milk shit in there," Logan said. "Looks like no one is coming back here until Wednesday—oh lord, what is this? You can't do that to a kid, man."

Moses didn't say anything. He began to take the framed photos down from the wall. He didn't want to look at these prematurely aging faces, the wrinkles and stretch marks poking through the spray tan like fissures in the earth. He began to stack them on the floor in piles.

Miami Family Nationals, '86.

Corpus Christi Regionals, '87.

Alberta Premium Body Exhibition, '85.

The outfits changed with every season. Silver stripes on a black background during the summer of '88, maple leaves on white during a fall tour of the southern States in '86. The girls were probably only twelve years old now, their bodies pumped full of who knew what bubbling through their arteries, disseminated into young and impressionable cells. In some of the pictures, Moses saw sickly purple veins snaking under the flesh, waiting to pop up from the skin and linger in varicose lines until their hearts burst at thirty-eight, while off-label hormones choked off their natural development like nooses drawn tight around their throats, disguised as championship medals and garlands of plastic yellow flowers.

"What the hell are you doing, Moses?"

Bill Murray would never have done this to his children.

Moses grabbed one of the long poles used for lifting paint cans and stolen weights. With its sharp pointed end, Moses lashed out at the pictures, smashing the smiles and the faces into smaller pieces, tearing through the photographs and the father who was somehow something far worse than a man who ran away to Arizona. Far worse than a mother who couldn't tuck you in at the age of ten. Or a fake father who only existed on the screen, his voice lingering in your VCR to tell you it was all going to be okay, he had a plan to make everything all right. You might even get to meet John Candy, too, if you played your cards right. Moses stopped at the mother's smile—the complicity not quite full, the smile too kind to be faked. It couldn't be faked. It was real, and sad, and horrible, but by then Loogie was laughing and trashing the photos still clinging to the walls.

"See what I'm talking about?" Logan said. "You were right, B. This is sick, isn't it? This is what happens when you start trying to compete with the apes. You see the Easter outfit? The bunny tails? They've got bottles of shitty whiskey upstairs."

"What about Moses's mom?" B. Rex asked.

"We'll find her. Right, Mosey? She's not here, unless you think she's hiding in the toilet or something. She's a big momma. No offense, Mosey. I know you don't want us calling her a babe, but damn, how'd you keep her hidden from us for so long?"

Moses caught another glimpse of the father's smile. He swung the pole again and glass scattered around them. All three were wearing their steel-toed boots, the ones Moses had made them buy after he found B. Rex with a boot print embedded in his chest on the first day of tenth grade. Moses found the boots at Second Chances, a thrift store covered in dust and dead lice. Logan got his own pair when two girls stole his shoes after gym. He had to walk home in his socks. Like his bedroom, they were bright green and filled with holes.

The boots were an investment for the future, for a friendship built on hates they couldn't name until they decided it was everything they were not; it was everything that bubbled and seethed and glared and laughed and mocked their flickering pride. There was nothing else outside that hate, no border left to cross, just juice monkeys in your mother's old basement, and fathers who mangled your mother's hand, and pine resin lingering in all your senses, a reminder of where it all began to fall apart and the fact that she wasn't here. She was gone.

"Fuck it," Moses said. "Let's just trash this hole."

17

Astor Crane discovered the Brothers Vine when he expanded from plants into pharmaceuticals. More money when the drugs were somewhat legal. Prescriptions and half-shipped shipments landed easily inside their pockets. Al and Tommy had survived the purges that drove out most of the bike gangs. The few rats that had jumped ship were found out in the woods with their knees drilled and their mouths filled with bits of their own hands. It was a signature the brothers developed. They had a route to Quebec that bypassed most of the police checks. All the best stuff came from Quebec.

"You find Destinii or what? You guys even looking at her files? You go by LIMH today? Talk to me, boys. You call me from a payphone, I expect to hear some good things."

Even in their forties, the Brothers Vine were still looking for father figures. Astor Crane was happy to fill the role. He'd found them skulking around the Turret after a wet T-shirt contest, mumbling approval at each girl who walked by them. The edges of their beards were wet with beer and they had peanut shells in their moustaches. Astor got them high in his suite and taught them how to talk to women. Neither Vine had had much luck since they were released on their eighteenth birthdays. Three years in prison had led to a twenty-year drought. Astor taught them not to stare and to ask questions—always ask questions. Make the girls feel like you care about them. It doesn't matter if you do or not, but tell them that you do. Believe that you do—you have to believe it or they won't believe it either.

"You found Falcor. The lion…okay, yeah. Good. That's good. Take him to the guy we talked about, the taxidermy guy. I'll go with you when we do it. How about that?"

Astor Crane told Al it was important just to listen, not to try and fix all of their problems at once. He reminded Tommy that the best way to a stripper's heart was through her nose, not his wallet. With careful coaching and heavy doses of cough syrup in their gin and tonics, Astor Crane showed the Brothers Vine they didn't always have to pay for sex, and from then on he was untouchable.

"I thought I made it pretty simple, Al. I thought I made it clear. Find the girl. Yes, it's her real name. You have her? You want to double check? I believe you if you say it's her. Yeah. I know it sounds stupid. Destinii with two I's at the end. Yeah, I know it's a hassle. Write it down if you have to."

Astor opened up worlds where the Brothers no longer just needed each other; he glossed over the broken bits and presented the two of them as grizzled heroes to the women they met on those long treks into French territory. Only half of the girls spoke English. Astor found this helped his cause. He provided the brothers with the narratives they needed. And the shipments did not stop. Not even when Astor was in the hospital. You could rely on the Brothers Vine to follow your instructions. Sometimes, though, they made a mess—the kind of mess that got plastered all over the six o'clock news.

"And I know they found that Condon kid, so don't even get me started. You fuck up once, shame on you. You fuck up twice, well, I'm still not taking the blame. Grab the fucker who got the lion too, if you can. Squeeze our friend with the mustache. Maybe we'll make me a wig out of his hair, my head is getting cold these days. And Al, no more dropping them off in the woods, all right? Condom stole, but he didn't know where the girl was either. And now we got this bullshit to deal with...yeah, I know, things happen. I know. Things also end. Remember that."

Astor Crane hung up the phone and stared out the window. He watched the buses and garbage trucks trading spots with each other down in the street below. He tried not to gaze at his reflection, his scalp shining bright in the glare. The lion was gone, a pile of bones and shit now. Probably some drunk asshole, hurtling toward nothing. It had been a mistake to keep it up at the old mental hospital, a mistake to give the animal its own wing to roam at night.

Someone could have been eaten in the dark.

Lions were scavengers, though. Astor read that when they had him in the hospital, chopping him up and redressing his wounds, telling him he was almost cured. Just one more surgery. One more time under the knife. Lions would drive hyenas and jackals off their prey. They would spook cheetahs and wild dogs. They would make their presence known. They would take what was theirs by right and by might. They would suffer no fools out on the plains.

Astor at least saw a small piece of himself in the animal. A small, nasty little piece, something caught in the corner of its eye. Back when he and Destinii were still trying to make things work, before she'd shacked up with Condom and fallen down an escalator, she told him he looked like one—a lion—in the morning, his red hair splayed out over the bed. He had tried to roar, but could only laugh. He had tried to be kind.

Destinii would need to remember he was kind if they had found her. If it really was her—years locked up in the mental ward promised him nothing. He was getting old. Pieces of him were already falling off, pieces he found in the shower, in the toilet, in the bed when he woke up alone again with the television on, only the hiss of a dead tape to comfort him.

There would need to be some changes. She would have to learn to live by his rules again, the old rules that kept him safe, that kept money flowing into this city, even as Larkhill barked and gasped for more air, for more people, for something to sustain it. It lived on flesh. She would have to learn to be quieter, kinder, softer. Like him. Like him after they chopped and twisted and yanked his insides around one more time. To make sure everything would work for once.

Astor would ask her about that escalator. Once you start falling, it's difficult to stop. Her face had got caught at the bottom, that's what Condom said. Shredded her cheek on the way down. He would ask her about the baby. He would tell her about the lion, how all good things had to end. He would tell her about new things he wanted, new ways he was going to live. There would need to be a baby.

He would ask her why she fell down that escalator.

Astor Crane sat down on his heart-shaped bed and pressed play on the VCR. He watched a vicious nothing tear across the landscape, swallowing everything in its path. He waited for someone to cry out, but the sound was muted. He waited for the Brothers Vine to call.

He tried not to get sentimental about the lion.

Astor knew he needed something more than a pet. He wanted an heir. Something to replace whatever the doctors were scheduled to remove in the next few weeks.

Something wet and mewling. Something he could call his own.

Astor Crane didn't want to die a scavenger, living off of someone else's sons.

18

Mrs. Singh was alone. Her son now went to a boarding school in Toronto, his letters to her growing shorter and cruder with each passing month. Mainly they asked for money. When she called him in the late afternoon on weekends, she heard laughing and drinking and a boy named Henry offering to introduce all the guys to some real prime gash.

Gash. The way he said it made her spine crumple under her housecoat. It was always her son who hung up first, barely saying goodbye before the click. It was the click that made her wrench her hair and cry and watch *Oprah* with the volume up all the way, waiting for someone like her to appear on the screen, to tell everyone just how horrible that click was.

Her husband still worked long hours in the factory that made child car seats. Some nights when he got up early to deliver newspapers, his second job, Mrs. Singh dreamed of going home and holding her sister's babies. She dreamed her father wasn't drowned in three inches of water by the men he opposed on the zoning commission. She dreamed he was still alive, and he would see her on *Oprah*, and it was on *Oprah* where she could tell the world about that click. Oprah would probably clap and tell her to tell it like it is, tell it like it was, because Oprah knew the truth. She knew what it was to be lost and abandoned by husbands and children and the world at large. Mrs. Singh knew this.

And so every night, before she went to bed beside her husband who snored and never cleaned his beard after eating supper, she would sit in the kitchen and attempt to write Oprah letters. Letters about her son and the click and the smell of another woman on her husband's breath. She couldn't prove it, but maybe Oprah could, and all she was asking for was some guidance. All she was asking for was some help from America's number-one talk show host, who never felt ashamed to cry in front of millions on the television screen.

Mrs. Singh wished she was so brave.

She was writing another letter to Oprah about the hopes she had for her new garden in the summer when she heard shouts and stomping boots from next door. She knew her neighbors, with their bulging golden muscles and breastless daughters, were not home. They had left for Columbus on Thursday. But there were sounds coming from their house, maybe raccoons inside the walls. Another shout rattled her writing hand, and Mrs. Singh pulled on her coat.

She did not bother knocking. There was no door, just shattered splinters in the frame. The floor was covered in bleach, and someone had piled all the bodybuilding costumes in the middle of the living room, dousing them in condiments from the refrigerator. Ketchup and pickle brine filled Mrs. Singh's nose as she avoided the puddles of bleach eating through the stain on the wood floor. Someone had torn down all the fire alarms and lined the batteries up like soldiers on the windowsill. Detergent mottled the purple curtains and mustard spelled out MURDERERS across the buzzing static of the television set.

Mrs. Singh told herself to leave, told herself it was the smart thing to do, the right thing to do. All she needed to do was turn around and step out into the cold air. Instead, her legs began to move towards the stairs and the loud noises coming from above—the noises that had drawn Hitler's moustache on photos of dogs and family members without discrimination.

Mrs. Singh sidled up to a bedroom door and peered inside. Three boys with shaved heads and boots too big for their feet sat on pink twin beds, each sipping from bottles held in bandaged hands. One of them had a patch of gauze affixed to his left temple. The boys swigged from their bottles, but their faces twisted with every sip. They were just boys.

"You shouldn't be here."

The one with the gauze on his head belched and laughed when he saw her.

"What the fuck, is it cleaning day already?"

Another of the boys stood up.

"This bitch. I do remember you. You called them, right?"

"I have already called the police. And I will do it again," Mrs. Singh said. This was the voice she had used on her son when he was little and afraid of the moon.

"Yeah, that's what you do, isn't it? That's what she did last time. You're why we moved."

The boy was in front of her now, his shoulders rising and falling and the smell of alcohol on his breath, the same smell she swore filtered through the phone lines from her own son's distant bedroom. This boy in front of her was just another Henry, another corrupter offering his unsavory wares to her impressionable son. All three of them were Henrys.

"You must leave now. I have already called the police."

It was the boy with the bleeding skull and the veiny hands who punched her nose. She felt the bones collapse inward. The pain blinded her eyes. The boy's fists did not stop. Mrs. Singh tried to defend herself but the blows broke down her arms and she could no longer speak through the loose teeth rolling over her tongue. His hands were hard and bony and she heard them pop and crackle against the soft, wrinkled skin of her face, her chest, her veined thighs.

"Logan! Loogie! Get off!"

On the floor, Mrs. Singh remembered when Oprah had wheeled out her cart of fat for the whole world to see. Oprah dividing herself, breaking her body down into separate selves. Mrs. Singh imagined herself now like that fat, beyond the realms of pain. She watched that old reel of the fabulous man in all his bright clothes, his blazer and his sagging skeleton telling Oprah he would die, he would die, because we all die, and Mrs. Singh had watched that at home and cried for the man who would die. Liberace. That was his name. She cried for him because he wore such beautiful clothes, and because he knew he would die. She saw the knowledge he carried with him that day in her living room, whispering the truth in front of millions.

"Logan, Logan, get off, you stupid...look at her face. Look at her, fucking hell. You gotta finish it now. Jesus, Jesus, Jesus..."

Mrs. Singh was fading. The click on the other end of the line rumbled toward her ruptured eardrum. She watched one boy toss the other aside, looked at his eyes. They were looking right at her but she didn't remember them, she didn't remember his voice or his name and then she saw him raise a heavy boot above her face.

"I'll finish it, all right?"

"What the fuck are you doing, Mosey?"

Mrs. Singh didn't feel the crunch. She didn't know her eye socket was fractured, or feel the bruises blooming like spilled red wine across the inside of her skull. She didn't even remember the name of the boy who had lived next door with all his wild robot dogs.

Mrs. Singh was just a wheelbarrow of fat and she was with Liberace now.

19

Someone was protesting outside the courthouse downtown. A lone man with a megaphone and a pharmacist's coat paced the sidewalk. Jamie Garrison drove past the man and his sign, the broken capitals lettered in red ink. He didn't bother to read it. The man screamed something.

Jamie sped up.

After work, Jamie had found all of his underwear folded into tiny parcels on the frozen lawn. Scott refused to say much, still wearing his garbage-man gear, hauling boxes outside onto the dead grass. Renee watched from the window, holding her pregnant stomach. Scott refused to listen to Jamie's explanations about sleeping on the couch, about turning over a new leaf. He told Jamie all that shit was rotted out now. It was already gone. Some neighbors had walked away with his sweaters and a few VHS tapes.

"No need for you to go back inside."

The bone can was still waiting for Jamie. It was patient. Compared to that slowly molting face, the lion was just a blip. It only lingered along his shins and in the spaces between his vertebrae like isolated sparks. If he stood very still, Jamie could barely feel it.

The Condom kid was still all over the radio, his ragged teenage face plucked from yearbooks in someone's basement, so-called friends and former acquaintances emerging like bed bugs from the woodwork to feed off the excitement. Jamie listened to them sob over a body they all claimed to know, while another marinated behind the store in pig's blood and leftover fat.

The strip mall parking lot was empty. The old pickups had moved on to less conspicuous spots. Jamie walked across the pavement with a limp and banged on the glass door. He should never have swallowed all those pills the night before. He banged on the door again. Renee had slept in his bed again, had been doing that on and off for months when she was sleepwalking. Mornings where he woke up to a school of mermaids beside him. It had been a few months since she had thrown herself down the basement stairs. She had bled all over the steps, but the baby was fine.

"Larry, you home?"

The door opened to a cloud of smoke and the Lorax's pink eyes peered out.

"Oh, it's you again. What do you want? And it's the Lorax. If you read the book, you'll see it's kind of inspirational," he said. "In like a sad, defeated way."

"I need to talk to you a bit."

The Lorax bit his lip and pulled the door wide open. He was only wearing a baseball jersey.

"I still got the entire Pirates' starting lineup, if you're interested. Never even been touched by air, vacuum sealed as soon as they came off the printing press. I also got the Maz himself, limited edition, very fancy shit. You know the Maz? Only guy to ever pull off the walk-off homer to win the Series, and he did it for Pittsburgh. No one gets walk-offs anymore."

"Not here for baseball," Jamie said. "It's like croquet to me: a stick, a ball, and a bunch of idiots chasing each other around the field. Look, my knee is still—"

"It's an acquired taste," the Lorax said. "Baseball is a game of waiting and patience. Requires skills like those of a pitcher, kept away from the drudgery of batting in the civilized world known as the American League."

Jamie was already past the Lorax and inside. Someone had piled all the trash into garbage bags. A few loose Darth Vaders huddled on fragments of glass shelving. The Lorax's bare legs were covered in goose bumps and the air smelled like pigs.

"Not even a hello, then? Or a discussion of America's favorite pasttime?" the Lorax said.

Jamie paced back and forth across the small room. He stuffed his hands inside his pockets. The body was still sitting back there at the shop, waiting for him to look it in the eye again. The beards might be there too, with their scarred hands and the cold bed of their pickup truck. Maybe they would bring a bear to dance around his grave. Maybe they would leave him in his own bone can to stew.

"You already run out? How much did I give you yesterday? You have to pay this time, you realize that?"

The Lorax had his top denture out and was polishing it on his Pittsburgh jersey. He walked behind the counter and pulled out a lumpy plastic bag. He whistled while he worked. Bill Mazeroski's rookie card sat on the table in front of him. The Maz was caught mid swing, his eyes closed against the sun.

"I hit a lion. That's—that's the problem, okay?"

"What? First thing you do is come and tell me this?"

The smell of pigs was everywhere. Jamie's father had smelled the same when his sons were young, like blood and puss and shit. Whenever the brothers took a bath, strange colors would swim up out of the drain to circle them. The Lorax kept shuffling through the bag, looking for the bulky orange pills that made the world fade until your daughter's mouth spit teeth like cracked sunflower seeds and everything was blank and hazy. Jamie picked up the baseball card and began to flick it between his fingers.

"I hit a lion the other day. Just fucking hit it. Bam."

"I knew you had a look on your face like you did something. You were wearing a seatbelt? I always wear my seatbelt. Even if I'm riding a lawnmower," the Lorax said, pulling another orange bottle out of his shopping bag.

"A fucking lion."

"I never ask why," the Lorax said. "You should know that. Ask and you shall receive."

"You a priest now?"

"You really hit a lion? I hear all the bullshit, you know. All kinds of excuses: a bad leg, a skiing accident, a wife who is too afraid of doctors to get pills."

"I hit a lion, Larry."

The Lorax popped his teeth back into his mouth. He cranked his jaw back and forth.

"You know I wasn't born with any teeth?"

"What?" Jamie said.

"Of course, no babies are ever born with teeth. How terrifying would that be for the mother? But no, as I aged, no teeth. Just shiny gums. It embarrassed my parents to no end, I can tell you that. They never wanted me to smile in pictures. Figured I would terrify people. When I was like eight they got me the dentures, but the teeth never grew."

Jamie stopped pacing and stood under the dangling fan.

"I hit a fucking lion out on the utility road—like, killed it. Embedded my tires in its rib cage. Who gives a shit about your teeth?"

The Lorax found the bottle he was looking for. "They kept it out of the papers. Did you know that?"

"Your teeth? You featured in the tabloids or some shit?"

"The lion. And the giraffe…well, they killed that."

"A giraffe?" Jamie said.

The little man sighed to himself. He pulled a bag of mushrooms out of his pocket and stuffed two little pods into his mouth.

"You ever go up past Stilton?" he said. "Where the nuke plant is? Place up there been closed forever. Guy calls it a zoo, but it was never a zoo—more like 'exotic farm' bullshit. He got closed down back in...what was it? Like ten years ago. Old nasty place. A lotta llamas."

"New Kenya?" Jamie said. "Abandoned little hole by the highway?"

"That's the place. Bunch of barbed wire and particleboard."

"I checked the paper," Jamie said. "You hit a lion, you wait for that headline."

"No headline though, right?" the Lorax said. "Guy who closed down the place, forget the name right now—he made a show of getting rid of all the tiger cubs."

The Lorax rubbed the bottle of pills back and forth between his hands. Sweat stains stretched down his armpits and his bare feet clicked their nails on the hard floor.

"Kilkenny was sneaky though—that was his name! He kept some of his beasties in the woods and no one really cared. The government sent a few people out to check on him and he was never allowed to reopen, but no one really looked too close. Like an idiot, he left the sign up."

The New Kenya sign still teetered out over one of the concession roads, but it was at least an hour away from Larkhill. Past the nuke plant and the dead trees and the wetlands they kept trying to save every summer with another bottle drive collection. There were tigers and lions on the billboard, faded stripes and raggedy manes. Empty barbed-wire cages visible from the road, overgrown with weeds and solitary sunflowers poking through like massive dandelions.

"So, the lion..."

"He didn't just up and get rid of everything," the Lorax said. "He kept a few. Called them his friends. You start naming animals, you start forgetting they can rip your face off. Animals are never your friends. Food, water, shelter, warmth—that's all they care about. They'll pretend to like you, but they'll never love you, and they will eat you when you die."

The Lorax rubbed his moustache and pulled the baggie out of his pocket again. He mashed up the little gray pods inside and stuffed the whole bundle into his mouth. His cheeks bulged while the dentures worked his food into a paste. It took him a while to swallow.

"Where did it come from? If you actually do know, then I need to know now."

The Lorax stuck his tongue out and dabbed at it with a stubby finger.

"You don't believe in the music of a conversation, do you, buddy?" he said. "You can't even get my name right, or you won't. Do you think we were just given communication to find food and shelter, like we're apes? Have goal. Resolve goal. Sleep. No. Conversation is about the dips and falls, the crescendo and the pause."

Bill Mazeroski was in Jamie's hand. The winner of eight Golden Gloves, the man who still held the Major League record for double plays made by a second baseman. Not to mention his career field percentage of 0.983. The card was still inside its plastic sleeve. It had never been touched by the toxic air of Larkhill.

"You ain't going to say nothing, Brock? How do you like that? Jamie? I call you whatever I want now, how about that? My name's not Larry. It's the Lorax."

Jamie just wanted to go home and sleep and stop thinking about his daughter and those floating eyes following him everywhere. The pills would help. The lion had to be put to sleep.

"The Maz loses his head if you don't hurry up, Larry," Jamie said. "And I know you want to keep the full set. Collectors value this shit, right? It's all croquet to me."

"Oh come on now! I still have a few pods the beards didn't take last time they came collecting for Crane," the Lorax whined. "You want those?"

Callused fingers poised themselves around the Maz's head.

"The lion, Larry."

"What did Mazeroski ever do to you?" the Lorax said. He spat his dentures out into his hand and slammed them onto the desk amongst the loose prescription bottles that rattled with stolen medication. He didn't scrape off the owners' names. "Fine, so you wanna know about the lion. Fine. Give me the card."

Jamie shook his head. The Lorax sighed.

"There was only a male," the Lorax began. "Out there in the boonies—at least in the summer, you know—you can find little grow ops, little spurts of industry in that wasteland. So I hired Kilkenny on and he had all kinds of shit out there on that farm. Actual shit for 'shroom growing. Lion shit, no tiger shit. But giraffe, he had a giraffe.

"Perfect place out there. Isolated, plentiful unmonitored fertilizers. I heard they monitor fertilizer sales these days. Did you know that? Same reason I don't buy hydroponics, they track that shit like it's buried treasure. Kilkenny was growing me stuff, but he was actually growing it for who I grow it for—you know, chain of command—and he got greedy.

"I think that was an excuse, though. Someone really wanted that lion. A pet lion makes you seem pretty badass when the best some other shithead can do is a Rottweiler. Did you know there are more pet tigers in human homes than exist in the wild?"

"So they stole the lion," Jamie said, flicking the baseball card again.

"Weeks ago. I went up there to check on him. Must have taken his ass somewhere. He was always trying to rip me off, and I'm not really a standalone operation. Everyone's gotta answer to someone.

There was blood everywhere, someone fucked with the body too. Be nice to the card, man, please."

"They killed the giraffe?" Jamie asked. He bent the baseball card between steepled fingers.

"I found it out near the plants. A real live giraffe, but dead. They tore up all his stuff, and then of course came looking for me. And now I'm growing everything with lamps from fucking retirement homes and getting all my stuff from pharmacies. I'm barely clinging on here."

The Lorax pulled out his baggie of mushrooms again, but it was empty.

"So how did it end up jammed into the grille of my car?"

"Well, you try keeping a lion cooped up in an apartment or anywhere else. You think it's just going to stay? It stayed with that ginger Kilkenny because he loved that beast, because he treated it like a person. Like a brother. They slept in the same bed. Ate the same food. True love between man and beast."

"So it just escaped?"

The Lorax struggled to push his teeth back into his mouth. One of the canines was chipped.

"It isn't like they're going to advertize it. They'll find it probably," the Lorax said. "They work like dogs for that motherfucker, but it's a lion. A lion is going to do whatever it wants."

Jamie relaxed his spine. He set the card down on the table.

"All right. You can have it back. I still need a favor."

The Lorax stared at the baseball card. The Maz wasn't smiling. He was grim.

"What?"

"Twenty bucks good for a couple of those orange guys? You got the card back anyway. You good with that? I didn't mean to hurt his feelings."

The Lorax opened the drawer again and pulled the dirty plastic bag out onto the table. He caressed the bottles through the bag, but he didn't read the names on the prescriptions.

"Just keep an eye out when you're driving," the Lorax said. "You say it was a lion, but it could've been like a big dog or something, or a kid. I don't want to go to court. You hit a kid, that's homicide. How about eight for you? You can owe me."

Jamie snatched the pills from the Lorax's greasy hand.

"Everybody owes. I'll pay next time I see you."

20

Three skinheads lurked in the back of Yuri's bowling alley, staring at all the women throwing heavy stones down perfectly straight lines. Their shouts mixed with the clattering pins.

"You knew my mother, right? Hey, you, thunder thighs! You knew her?"

"Who do you think you're talking to, boy?" Big Tina bellowed. "Thunder thighs?"

One of them seemed to be crying, refusing to follow the other two down to the lanes. His little arms could barely wrap around his chest. The one in front carried a teal bowling ball. The word JUDGE scrawled across it in black sharpie. The second boy's skull was bleeding from a half-finished tattoo. The bourbon smell washed over Big Tina as she turned to face the third.

"I said who do you think you're talking to, boy?"

The giant woman towered over a busted disco floor. Her team flexed their ten-pin skills behind her while old men put their cigarettes out on the plastic chairs and told dirty jokes with no punch lines. Their boots looked wet. Their eyes looked wet. A world full of weeping.

"You knew my mom, right? Elvira? Kinda crazy lady. You two used to bowl together."

Big Tina was only one who went and saw Elvira Moon after the accident, the one who helped with the prescriptions after Elvira got arrested for public nudity at Paulie's Pins. Big Tina had been the one who picked her up from the station whenever they found her wandering the streets, asking for her husband Ted, asking for her boy, her little boy. That was a while ago.

"I don't know what you're—hold on. Oh, Moses. I thought they just up and took you away," she said. "Jesus. I thought they took you away. Moses, what happened?"

Big Tina tried not to think about Elvira Moon anymore. It was bad enough when she'd quit the Blooming Broads and started her own team. Tina knew Elvira never really forgave her for that. Elvira never understood the bond Tina had formed with Claudia. It wasn't just love, but something else that made Tina's heart stronger.

"No, no, I didn't get taken away," Moses said. "We just left. Why didn't you ever come to look for her? You helped before. And she was so fucking mad at you, I remember that too."

Big Tina quit the league for a few years after her colon surgery, but the game called her back. The clatter of pins, the comfy plush seats at Paulie's, the feel of a good twelve-pound ball resting in your palm—all of these things meant home to Big Tina. Bowling alleys were where she fled from the world in her high school days and ever since. Her mother couldn't ask about boys there, couldn't berate her for wearing pants to school. Her father couldn't call her "my favorite ox." He said it with love, he said it with a smile at the corners of his lips, but it burned her deeply. He'd branded her.

"Well, where did you go? Where is she at now? I had no idea, Moses."

The clatter of ten pins after a perfect strike could break that image apart. It could drown out her mother and her three sisters. The call for another round of beers and the feel of Claudia's warm back against Big Tina's in the middle of the night made it all seem like someone else's life. Someone who woke up at 2 a.m. and told the mirror she hated herself.

"Of course you didn't. We got used to it, I got used to it," Moses said.

Big Tina stared at the boy in front of her and his lumpy shaven head. Big Tina was still at the bottom of the rotation. Her last roll had sealed the win. Another splash of pins behind her broke up the stare. Big Tina knew it was a five-seven split based on the sound. She stopped visualizing Caracas and the beautiful heat and the snaking traffic of its bumpy freeways. Whenever the game got too close, she would envision Claudia's home and the vacation they took every February to escape the cold that encased Larkhill. She knew once she could taste the humid air that her next roll would be a strike. But Elvira was invading that now, her long legs and perfect posture splayed out in a mess on the polished hardwood lane. She wasn't wearing underwear, and her face looked like a child had drawn it. Big Tina tried to focus on Moses instead and avoid the sputtering ghost of his mother writhing under the lights.

"I couldn't do it, it was just too much, too much of everything. And Elvira, she was only floating along—what happened to you, Moses?"

"It's not your business, all right?" Moses said. "Have you seen her in the bowling alleys at all, or like around your old apartment? I know she used to end up there sometimes; you'd drop her off at our old place. The townhouse. She said you never came in because of a dog allergy. You seen her anywhere?"

The kid was talking too fast, words tumbling out of his mouth and trampling the ones ahead of them. Sure, Big Tina saw Elvira Moon from time to time, but only in the corner of her eye. Only when she was in the grocery store and some lady kept smashing jars of beets on the floor, claiming they had stolen her keys. Big Tina saw Elvira when she drove downtown into Larkhill and had to wait at the stoplights. She saw the long legs of women in high-heeled boots strut past, but their faces were never as pretty as Elvira's. She was just born tall, with strong, powerful knees. A lot of people forgot how important knees were in bowling. Elvira was the woman in the waiting room with her head done up in bandages, the old man Big Tina saw on the bus to work who had leaves in his beard. Elvira lingered by the curbs and wrote messages to herself on the inside of telephone booths in lipstick. Elvira was everywhere that Big Tina refused to look.

"No, I don't. Is she missing? She hasn't called me," Big Tina said. "I don't think she'd even know where I was living these days. Kind of dropped off the map after a while."

"I don't even know if she'd recognize you," Moses said. "She doesn't recognize me half the time. She doesn't fucking recognize anybody. Only TV or photos. Maybe."

"I haven't seen her," Big Tina said. "No, she doesn't come around here. You called hospitals or anything like that? The police?"

"I spent like two hours doing that this morning. We did it again two hours later. Nobody answering on nothing. She ain't around. A six-foot blond woman isn't invisible. You haven't seen her at all though? Nothing? You swear?"

"I haven't seen her in ages. Where are you staying?"

"Outside town, just a little bit. She couldn't really have walked anywhere. Sometimes, she gets her mind back for a bit. She'll say your name, or Dad's or whoever, but she doesn't…she doesn't let me know. You have any idea where she might go?"

"They used to take her in at the hospital," Big Tina said. "Back when you guys had the house still. You never even left a note, Moses. Did you ever think someone would find you?"

"What fucking hospital?" Moses said. "Where?"

"Old one. No more funding. They shut it down years ago. She's really gone?"

"She wasn't in her room, in the place, anywhere. We already checked the old house, streets, all the places she used to go. We found you, so that'll have to do for now."

His voice was getting higher in pitch. Big Tina noticed his torn clothes and dirty jacket. Moses smelled like condiments. She tried to think about Caracas and the first time she'd met Claudia instead of the doctors sedating Elvira in a cramped room at the old hospital by the lake. Elvira kept asking Tina why she left, why she couldn't just let them be friends like always, why did she have to take her trophy away? Big Tina focused on Claudia's hips and the way she held a wine glass. So much of the weight hung on her thin wrist. It helped block out Elvira, who would never hold her or tell her she was all that she needed. Elvira liked Big Tina's firm arms and her wide stance, but only because it made the team stronger. It let them win and win again. Half-price wings for life. She only wanted Big Tina for the parts, not the whole.

Elvira had been shopping for a bowler. Big Tina pretended not to see it that way until Claudia came along. She pretended it would only take time, water turning rock to sand. Time and patience were the tools to use. But Claudia never saw Tina as a list of specifications to be fulfilled. She wasn't looking for optimal ball control or unparalleled dexterity. Claudia saw Big Tina in line at the Foodland buying four whole chickens and a bag of corn. She invited herself over for a barbecue, her accent mangling the word between crooked white teeth. Claudia didn't need Big Tina to bowl every Wednesday. Tina hadn't looked back.

"Your turn to roll, Tina," said one of the girls wearing a purple vest. "You ready?"

"You can just skip me, I'm good, I've already got all your asses in a sling tonight."

It wasn't like the old days, with the tournaments and the competitive leagues. All the trendsetters had moved on to lawn bowling or water polo. Some of the old alleys had closed and reopened as diners or auto shops. Those closed too as the years passed. Now the alleys were full of old men who smoked cigarettes with extra tar and liked to inhale the cleaning spray they used for shoes straight from the can. The orange chairs had lost their luster and the carpets bled beer. Strobe lights and disco floors sputtered on and off, but the lanes still clattered and the world still ignored them. Big Tina liked it that way. No one came looking for her in these places.

"The hospital was probably…she might have gone there," Big Tina said.

The flickering green and orange lights announced Rock'n'Bowl was about to begin. Moses's eyes were fading from Tina's face; he wasn't really listening to her anymore.

The hospital pharmacy had been the place where Big Tina realized Elvira was gone from her, gone from this world. Every single shelf was too white, the lights too bright, every pill made to fix something that was wrong with you. There was no smoke, no clatter. That world was stark and bled around the edges like a nail clipped too close to the quick. Big Tina walked the tiny aisles and felt it throb under her skin. People wanted to look you in the eye and examine you in full—like a beached specimen on a steel table.

Elvira had talked to everyone while Big Tina sat and waited for the prescriptions. She explained that her husband never emerged from his room without first being served breakfast, and since she didn't know how to cook she hadn't seen him for years. You got used to it though, Elvira declared. She told stories about the Jolly Green Giant speaking to her in dreams and her long platonic friendship with Bill Cosby, who sometimes needed a weekend away from his family. They talked so much, you know. Bill could never get a word in with those people.

"Fucking closed-up hospital, that's all you've got?" Moses spat. His skull was shining in the orange light. "You shoulda, you shoulda—fuck it. Useless, you're useless, you know that? She ain't here. The fuckin' loony bin. Fucking bullshit, fat bitch."

People had stared and whispered to one another in line at the hospital pharmacy. They pointed at Big Tina; they looked at her wrinkled eyes and the thick set of ankles she inherited from her father. They whispered about farm animals and cattle runs and hopeless cases. Elvira was invisible, but everyone could see Big Tina. No one apologized for staring. Under the white light, she felt like she'd been put on display, split down the center.

"Moses, I didn't—you just disappeared, you know," Big Tina said.

"Tina, it's your turn," said one of the girls behind her.

Big Tina stopped seeing Elvira after that day at the hospital. She refused to pick up her prescriptions and never went to check in with Dr. Albertson for updates on Elvira's condition. Further mental deterioration—she knew the prognosis would not change. Months passed and Claudia found them a nice apartment overlooking the dead fields north of town, an apartment littered with love letters and bright red plants. Tina lay there at night with Claudia whispering about the future and the world they could build in that two-bedroom apartment. A world unto themselves, with no mention of livestock or grandchildren or illegal mass arrests. Across town, Elvira had dropped pills down the toilet and prayed to Bill Cosby to set her free from the fragile bonds of humanity. The constant flush drowned out her trembling prayers. Moses was in the kitchen heating up soup and talking to a postcard from his father. Big Tina slept through all of this, holding Claudia in her arms.

"I said I'm good, guys. I got your asses beat," Big Tina said.

When she turned her face from the glowing scoreboard, the three boys were gone. She could see their scabbed skulls headed out the door, their ragged jackets puffed out by the wind. Journey blared from the speakers and a flimsy, sputtering Elvira Moon staggered down the lane toward Big Tina, huffing shoe cleaner and wearing Christmas lights like a sweater around her chest.

Big Tina closed her eyes and picked up the ball. The familiar weight soothed her nerves and realigned her thoughts. Elvira didn't flee, though. Lipstick drawn up and down her thighs, her long hair filled with needles and prescription bottles, the ghostly image asked Big Tina what a woman tasted like. She stood on the polished pine floor with her legs spread wide apart and asked Big Tina what it was like to hold Claudia in the cold. Sunlight was everywhere inside Big Tina's head, but it was too bright—it made her veins glow under the skin. Elvira smiled with neon teeth. One of them short circuited as she spoke. She asked Big Tina once again.

"So close, Tina," one of the girls cackled as the ball clattered down the gutter.

21

Thomas and Allan Vine were born ten months apart. Each of them weighed precisely ten pounds and ten ounces when the nurse laid their wet, purple bodies on the scale. Each time the same elderly doctor was shocked by the head full of black hair and the massive dimensions of the skull that emerged from beneath the privacy sheet. Gail Vine held this against her sons for the rest of her short life; she held it in the stretch marks and broken blood vessels that her doctor said would heal but never did. The painful split nerves and jagged tears left behind inside her by those two black-haired boys only began to fade during a quilting session at her sister Lorraine's one December, while she stitched the top left corner of her patented turkey design.

"You've only got so many teeth to pull, boy..."

A small blood clot had spent months swimming through Gail's body. It acquainted itself with her left leg for more than two weeks, forcing her to limp around the house as her two wild five-year-olds ran from the looming threat of another bath. The doctor at the clinic dismissed it as a phantom pain, maybe the result of an earlier injury come back to haunt her overly sensitive nervous system. Shrill babies and a looming red-and-yellow sign that asked Gail if she'd ever been tested for Chlamydia kept her from pressing any further. The doctor's office reminded her too much of a courtroom.

The little solid accumulation made various passes through her heart over the course of those months, growing larger as more lonely cells adhered to its blunt mass. Each pass forced Gail to lie down on the couch while her two sons dismantled the television remote. The clot continued its journey, visiting organs on brief excursions that caused Gail to clutch her kidneys in the shower and poke at what she thought might be her liver as her husband slept beside her in the dark. Austin Vine worked for Osprey back then, affixing tiny threaded screws into the blades of windshield wipers for eight hours a day. He told Gail to go and see the doctor again, but she didn't want to. All that steel was so cold and sterile and the paper sheets made it feel like a butcher shop.

"Al, hand me the pliers again. This fucker won't stop moving. Shut your little hole, okay? We teach lessons in a—what would you call it, practical manner? Hands on."

It took five months for the clot's perennial visits within Gail's brain to finally cause a problem. As Gail's fingers went to form another perfect stitch, the clot abandoned its regular route through the cerebellum and diverted down a rather scenic stretch of her frontal lobe, breezing past language centers and semiotic systems until it collided with the walls of a blood vessel unable to bear the load. As smaller cells struggled to navigate the cramped passage, the chronic pain confined in the busted neural pathways and muscle tissue beneath Gail's taut skin began to blink off and on in shorted circuits. Freed from her chronic burden, Gail began to laugh.

"That's a lot of blood. It looks like a lot, I know, son. But just imagine when you spill a glass of milk. Ever watch how far the puddle spreads? It's like that. You'll survive this one."

Gail laughed at her two boys hiding under the table, eating chunks of sponges they had discovered underneath the sink. She laughed at their giant tufts of hair and their small thumbs and the fact that they never learned to say thank you. She laughed at her parents who moved up to Elliott Lake and didn't talk to anyone under the age of forty. Gail just kept laughing, laughing at her sister whose husband had been caught stealing snowmobiles behind the old marina last summer. He tried to drive them away on the pavement but got nowhere. Gail laughed at her own husband and his fading eyesight, the way he tried to kiss her cheek and collided with her nose.

Gail couldn't feel a thing, and it was wonderful. The clot pushed harder, but it could not fit through the tight passage in her brain. Other cells shoved it forward, pleading to circulate. The heart continued to pump them higher and higher into her brain, but there was no place to go. As more pressure built, her laughter descended again. Each cell like a bubble rushing toward the surface of her glass allowed Gail to forget the dread she had attached to those two little boys. She forgot about the lesions in her bladder and the purple marks lining her hips like bad tattoos. Without the pain, she could forgive them all. It would be so easy, but she didn't have the time.

Eventually the clot in her brain had to travel somewhere. Lorraine would later describe how her sister's eyes fluttered and then how her body tipped over the quilt, spilling cranberry ginger ale across the carpet. Like she'd been shot in the head, but there wasn't any blood. The boys wouldn't let go of her after that. Not even when the cops showed; they had to pry each finger off.

Thomas and Allan Vine grew up clutching what remained of their mother just as tightly. They learned to quilt during a rehabilitation blitz at a juvenile detention facility outside of Milton while serving sentences for aggravated assault and robbery. Tommy was sixteen and Allan was only ten months behind him. They only received two weeks of therapeutic quilt instruction before Thomas stole a batch of needles and both brothers were returned to solitary.

"Tom, I don't need a wider set of pliers. I need like a cloth or something. Astor sends us out here and I'm the one with a dirty shirt. You think he's going to pay for the dry cleaning? You think that fucker will even say thank you?"

After their mother died and Osprey moved out of town, Austin Vine had taught them how to hotwire cars with bits of tin foil and knitting needles. He even supplied them with his toolbox and the old .45 he won after a parking lot fight in Winnipeg. Austin's own prison sentence took him to the Millhaven Correctional Facility for twenty-five years after the bank guard didn't get up fast enough one day to unlock the safe. The manager was also too slow. As was the receptionist who kept looking at him after the third bullet had passed through her chest and into the drywall. Her lips still moved, but it was like a chicken after the hatchet came down—a sad, headless chicken. That's what Austin told himself when her ghost returned to chirp an automated greeting into his ear like a mosquito while he rolled around on the cot in his six-by-nine cell. She wasn't saying anything—it was just muscle memory reciting words without meaning. Austin eventually tried to make friends with the voice, but it couldn't carry a conversation.

Austin still wrote letters to his sons, those sons everyone else thought were twins. He told them not to ask questions. The less they knew, the less they could reveal. Tommy and Al didn't spend their cash. They bought all their cars used and lived in the motels below Larkhill. Heeding the wise chicken scratch of their father, the Brothers Vine never stepped forward to fill the void after each round of arrests cleared up the south end of Larkhill for a few months.

They had survived the biker purge after two decades of involvement in Larkhill and positioned themselves in the marinas and the pawnshops as distributors. Al and Tommy routinely rerouted cargo from the shipping docks into trucks for men who never used the same name twice. They paid for everything in cash and spent their weekends in the woods. They'd grown beards in solidarity with their father and still kept his toolbox in their bedroom. The cordless drills were new editions to his set.

"Hey, buddy. You understand us? Hello? You remember our faces, I hope. You got a nice mouth now. A good reminder next time you decide to pull a hit-and-run. You really think a lion just wanders out into the road? This ain't Narnia. Now for the real part...we still got batteries?"

Gail Vine was a vesper now that they only caught in tiny bursts of light, when their brains were deep within the REM sleep cycle. In this state, her two sons could only remember the way Gail checked her makeup, how she tugged too hard when combing their hair, and the cold pillow she occasionally pressed against their faces when she thought they were asleep.

For Tommy and Al, these were good memories. Much better than the solitary confinement in Milton and the hallucinations they found creeping up through the pipes and out of the toilet bowl. All the children they heard in those sterile halls had thick, wet voices. It was the solitary that had bent them both. They each spent three years flooding their cells and setting fire to shredded sheets with light bulb filaments. Almost the full extent of their juvenile offender sentences were spent alone and together in that isolation. Al and Tommy relied on each other to remember they were real after years of isolation in their own private concrete cells.

"I wanna say this won't hurt, but we've always tried to be honest..."

Everything else drifted on the periphery. Illusions of people moaning in the woods and human apparitions that floated like squiggly lines across the surface of each brother's eyes. You could never look at those lines directly—they always fled to the corners when you paid too much attention. It made it easy to snap a finger off or disembowel another Bandido out of Winnipeg. The dirt washed out of your clothes and no one ever asked about the smell. Eventually it all faded and the only evidence remaining was the cash in your pocket and the figment of some fatty tissue clinging to the dull bit of your drill. And the drill bits were always dull.

"Almost done, you just gotta hold still. Al, you wanna grab his feet for me?"

Sometimes when they tried to sleep, the brothers saw those dead faces pushing through the stuccoed ceiling to stare down at them. Flooded toilets kept flushing in their dreams, but their solitary cells never let them drown in all that waste. Whenever the ceiling spoke, the white masks would tell Al it was not his fault he grew so big inside his mother's belly. Broken lips and distended eye sockets of dead associates told him about his girth and weight after the nurse had plopped him on the scale. Ten pounds and ten ounces. Just like his brother. It wasn't their fault, the ceiling said. Genetics.

"You wanna wash up here or wait until we get back to the motel?"

The body on the basement floor jerked and spasmed. Red bubbles rose and fell from the leaking hole inside its face. Teeth lay around it in a small circle like thrown stones from an ancient, complex ritual. This was a message they were told to send, spelled out in jagged holes and dripping pus. The lion was still dead. No one could bring it back. Astor still would not forgive them fully. The washer and dryer were spattered with blood; there were no words inside its patterns. The Brothers Vine slammed their toolkit shut and looked at one another. They had left this one alive, according to Astor's instructions. They checked to see if it could breathe, small lungs heaving beside the empty lint trap. Tom kicked the body.

"Two down in one night," Al said. "Let's go check on the bear before the sun hits."

The body tried to speak, a single tongue probing for some teeth. It wanted to ask why.

22

They didn't always scream at each other.

"Holly Condon has recently come forward with her own campaign for an inquest into her nephew's death, calling for increased pressure to be placed on local investigators. Mrs. Condon has asked the media to refrain from rampant speculation about her alleged history of substance abuse..."

Most of it happened quietly. A few socks bundled up in the corners. Laundry left unfolded. A broken dish swept under the fridge. Small signs of neglect that neither of them acknowledged. They lingered in the corners like ammunition. Kansas sat through it all, her eyes a constant witness to the petty negligence shoved under the couch beside her Dr. Seuss and Berenstain Bears. At four years old, she did not speak, but her small ears noticed the television volume was a little too loud when Mom was trying to sleep. Her fingers found hairs stuck to the soap in the bathroom after Dad's shower. Kansas would stare at the tomato sauce left to dry on the stovetop till it was hard and black. Her lips remained closed. The house filled with future fuel for the coming confrontation, but Kansas didn't say a thing.

"Despite last year's corruption charges within the Larkhill Police Department, Sergeant Harold Klemp has vowed to follow up on new developments concerning the Condon incident. Local residents complain their safety is still at risk..."

Blood clung to Jamie after work, and Alisha's hands were covered in tiny paper cuts. Her skin seethed each time she ran water in the sink. Each small incision hid from her eyes, but the nerves felt everything. Jamie brought a smell into the house she couldn't wash out of the sheets, and her skin chapped with the detergent.

Jamie knew Alisha would run the dryer late into the night while he tried to sleep, reading her horoscope from outdated magazines in the basement. Alisha was a Gemini, so she practiced another face in the warm laundry room. The yellowed pages always told her something was split inside her, cracked like a bad mirror. It wasn't her fault, though; it was the stars and the moon, foreign planets that whirled on some axis she could not control. The schism sliced through her neural matter was not a choice; it was a fate handed down to her by something cosmic, unknowable. The new face was for her mother. It was flat and did not show any pain. The eyes looked past the hospital bed and the lips shunted any ill will back down into her stomach.

Alisha Wugg didn't really believe in twelve human variations cast down from the heavens. She didn't avoid Scorpios at work. Astrology wasn't real, but it made things easier.

"Even with the recent discovery of two more bodies in the south end, Larkhill police refuse to speculate about connections with the Athabasca remains, while acknowledging the growing anxiety displayed by residents at rallies in Foxe Park this weekend…"

Jamie wouldn't even drive her to the hospital. He sat at home and waited. She wasn't a human, she wasn't her mother; she was a person who sought to dismantle Alisha every time she walked through the door. Every motion was open to critique, Kansas just another target she tracked with deadly accuracy.

The child was a mistake, a mute that would only haunt them until they died, according to Alisha's mother. Her mother's teeth were rotting because she refused to brush—who would look at her anyway; her hair was still long, but growing white in the dark; blind in her hatred like a fish that only knows the salty depths of its own cave, she snapped at anything that moved. Her teeth were well worn with age, but sharpened by the fresh offering her daughter made every Thursday, baring her heart for another bite that would refuse to heal.

"Now we'll move to the phones to find out what you have to say. The number to dial is 1-800-KRS-CALL. Again, that number…"

Jamie never said this aloud; he said it with wet laundry piled on the floor. He said it with an empty tank of gas in her Corolla and rings of water on the coffee table. Little neglected pieces grew into a barrier neither of them could breach, accumulated spite packed densely beneath their feet. The carpet wore down under the weight until floorboards poked out. Small incisions invisible to the naked eye spread from Alisha's hands across both their backs; they chaffed and burned under the bed sheets every time someone moved in their sleep.

Alisha said her mother was a Gemini too—two-faced, shattered, corrupted deep down into her brain stem. It was easier to believe in floating planets spinning fates instead of what the doctors said. The nun's tires had unleashed this second half Alisha faced in the damp visitors' room. She brought her daughter sometimes to try and break through to that other face her mother refused to show, the one that had raised her and sewn together all those awful ice-skating outfits.

Kansas became a shield to deflect some of the blows, soundless and unmoving. She was four. Half of the old lady's words could barely penetrate her mind. Alisha's mother ranted about children who sucked sustenance from their mothers. She was a sacrifice, a fresher piece of meat to toss into the flame. Kansas bore it all until the orderlies arrived and wheeled Mrs. Wugg away, her lips still funneling hate down the hallway. She could hear it in the parking lot and on the long drive home, bouncing over the airwaves and polluting every song.

When Kansas finally spoke, it was at the dinner table. Her food was organized by color in a half rainbow across her plate. Methodically, her head counted each piece in silence.

"Bitch."

When a child speaks its first word, the parents are supposed to celebrate.

"Did she just…"

Kansas whispered to her food, "Sloppy, rutting bitch…"

All the barriers collapsed in a sad pile of wet thermal underwear and ceramic teacups. Jamie's voice rose and cracked against the ceiling fan. A horrible, vicious thing. A fucking monster that needed to stay locked in its cage. That's what she was, that woman. She was all bile and it burned Alisha, it left her ragged and weeping in the bathroom at 5 a.m., you think he couldn't hear it through the door? He could hear everything; it was like an animal in a pit whimpering to be put out of its misery. Did she want to feel this way? Did she get off on it? And then to bring your own daughter, to expose her to such a poisonous, vicious thing. What did she think she was doing? Did she want Kansas to grow up like that? To have it injected into her? No one deserved that shit. No one should be born into it.

Kansas sat in the kitchen, her mouth closed once again. The fight swirled through the living room and toward the massive television that kept Alisha Wugg awake at night with dreams of soap operas where the comas ended and the dead came back from the Amazon with treasures in hand. In that world, the world she watched some mornings when the rain was too heavy outside and her head felt like it would explode, she knew it would all pass. The plot must go on, new hopes built from mysterious cures and identical twins. And here was Jamie, and he was smashing each of those hopes on the floor, crunching the pieces under heavy black boots that woke her up in the middle of the night. The plot was snapped. It was all in shambles. He wasn't listening. She tried to warn the girl about what she could become. A fist shot out in her direction. It cracked the television and spluttered. The splintered screen watched them but didn't say a thing.

Another fist—through a painting this time.

Another fist, but it was hers. It whacked against the top of the television and Alisha's screaming realigned itself. Her screaming found a single focus and bore down. Out. Get out. Take your fucking mouth out of this house. I will not let you talk about her, I won't let you say it. Just get out. Out. Out. Kansas ate her food in the kitchen while they screamed back and forth.

Jamie packed his clothes and Alisha kept saying *Out, out, out* like it was a spell, like he could be cast away because he had said so many fucking things. Out, out, out. He'd said things she didn't want to see, he'd pulled up rocks and dug into the dirt beneath and pulled out all these squirming poisonous things and then shoved them right under her nose, and he didn't care. He laughed. He'd do it again. He would do it until she stopped going back to the poisoned well and drinking in all her mother's rotten words about ruptured varicose veins and the inevitability of divorce and the spectre of failure looming over us all. She was a failure. No one was going to refute that. All the rocks were flipped and Jamie refused to put them back.

"Now, I know we have already covered this, but I'd like to bring the discussion back to animal control. I mean, do we actually know this was done by humans?"

Jamie turned off the radio. He was parked outside Brock's house and its bright teal garage doors. Somewhere to stay. The street was filled with cars. Frost gathered on the windshields. Jamie swallowed another orange pill and pulled himself out onto the front lawn. Garbage lined the curb up and down the street. Rot crystallized in the air.

The door to the basement was open. Wet sounds blurted from the laundry room below. Jamie made his way down the steps. Underneath the hum of the washing machine, he could hear moaning and another voice mumbling something. It sounded like a lullaby. Farther away, the roar of Maiden's "Number of the Beast" beat against Brock's door. The record was too fast. The settings were wrong. There was detergent all over the stairs.

"Brock? Jack-O, buddy, you all right?" Jamie said.

There was an indent in the dryer the size of a man's skull. Brock lay on the floor, his knees leaking puss and blood and some other fluid Jamie couldn't recognize. His mouth was open and Karina was on her knees, clutching him to her chest. Teeth were lined up on the floor like small soldiers, their dark roots filled with brown blood.

Karina was still dressed for work.

"Brock! What the fuck, buddy?"

Brock tried to sit up on the floor. A perfect hole was punched through each of his kneecaps. The smell of detergent barely covered the copper scent. Fluid seeped from the holes. Karina kept talking, her voice breathing in low whispers. Her hair smelled like formaldehyde.

"I came down to do the laundry. My parents, they come back tomorrow," Karina said. "And then I saw his face, oh my god. He keeps talking about giants."

Brock spat blood out onto the floor. His gums were ragged and split, a new Halloween mask permanently affixed to his face. The teeth on the floor looked too big for his mouth. Fluid pooled in deep holes toward the back of his gums. Jamie spotted a tongue pushing through the bloody mess like a blind fish.

"Karina," Jamie said. "You gotta go."

"No, I need to stay. You see his face? He can't stay like that."

"You need to go and you need to call the police and then you can come back. All right? Call the cops. Do it. You need to tell them someone has broken into your house, you need to tell them they have badly beaten your friend. Tell them we need an ambulance."

Karina nodded. Her awkward office shoes clunked up into the clean air above. Jamie turned back to the remains of Brock's face.

"Buddy, buddy, man. It'll be all right. You just gotta focus on something else."

"Fucking beards, man," Brock dribbled. "Thought I ran over their pet."

Jamie's hands almost pulled away from Brock's head, but he resisted the urge. The tongue popped up again from the mess and tried to speak.

"Huge motherfuckers. I mean, they were just be-beasts. They came right, riii—right in and just, ba-baaam. I didn't even—couldn't see 'em."

More blood welled up and ran in thin lines down Brock's chin. His T-shirt was soaked.

"They had this fucking drill…"

The words were drowning on their way out of Brock's mouth.

"Just spit the blood out, Brock. Just spit it."

"Fucking hu-hu-hurts, man," Brock drooled. "The fucking knees, man…."

Brock had done his share of stupid things. He liked to race the trains at night. He told Jamie they reminded him of owls when they hooted at him in the dark. He and Jamie had grown up near the train tracks that ran through town. The same tracks claimed one kid every year until the city council topped the safety fences with barbed wire. Brock told Jamie he could hear everything they had to say, but it was always written in a rust—sounds of livestock and stock-car parts and a million sheep transported to the slaughter. It traveled through the rails. Chlorine gas and computer monitors. The tired wheels didn't click or clack into Brock's ear at night. They bleated.

"Said I killed. I know I didn't..."

"And they...how big were they? You gotta talk to me until someone gets here."

Brock spat. "Said I ran over Falcor, their pet, man. What the fuck is Falcor?"

Jamie lowered Brock back to the floor. He reached into the dryer and pulled out a pile of sweaters that still smelled like booze. The stink never left you—it just retreated deeper into the fibers. The booze ran deep; it inhabited your pores. Jamie knew if they cut him open half his organs were going to be pickled and full of brine.

"What are you doing, J?"

"I'm trying to soak up some of the stuff."

Karina was there beside him, pushing pillows under Brock's head. Jamie swept up the teeth and set them on the dryer. He could trace Brock's nose and eye sockets in the dent. He imagined ZZ Top smashing Brock's face into the dryer again and again while a crowd cheered and waved homemade signs from the general admission seats. They came here for the lion. Jamie sat down on his haunches and watched Karina clear the red from Brock's face. It welled up again when he tried to speak and she hushed him. Scattered pages from her love letters were lying on the floor with handwriting like rivets on the page.

"You called the cops, right?"

"Yes, I called the police," Karina said. "I called and called, and they put me on hold, and then finally someone answered."

"You called what? The station?"

"I had to find it in the phone book, and then I had to go through a directory once I got through on the line, and then—"

"You didn't just fucking call 911?"

"You told me to call the police."

The room tasted like the bone cans. Jamie rinsed them out every couple weeks, the blood rising in founts under the spray of the hose, the lemon suds barely concealing the rot. The runoff ran down into the sewer grates, trickling its way through the alley. In the summertime, you could watch the bugs follow it, the gnats and mosquitoes hovering above the mess in confusion.

The ants never hesitated.

The long wail of the ambulance siren trickled down the stairs. Brock's tongue pushed up again from the mess and tried to speak. Jamie hushed him. Karina kept humming. She soaked the blood with each sweater and then neatly stacked them beside her.

"Hey buddy, buddy, you need to just breathe, all right? No, no, through your nose, okay? Let's keep it clear, let's keep it clear. You just gotta nod when I say things, all right? Just nod, that's it."

Jamie looked down at Brock's face—what was left.

"Brock, look at me. Look at me, okay? I said look at me, Brock, for fuck's sake, okay?"

Larkhill had done this to him. Same thing it did to everyone else. No teeth and busted kneecaps—an accelerated decline.

"You shouldn't be yelling at him," Karina said.

"I'm going to fucking say whatever, Karina. Okay? Brock, I'm going to go, but don't freak out, all right? I'm not actually leaving. You just gotta stay here."

"Guuh—no!"

"No, no, I am not leaving you," Jamie said. "Just—just close your eyes. You'll be fine…I will figure this out, all right?"

Jamie left Karina holding Brock on the floor. Outside, the air was still cold and filled with garbage. The siren grew louder. Jamie began to drive away from the house, headed toward the Village Plaza with only one headlight burning in the dark. The radio was off and the trains were hooting at him from somewhere out there in the cold. Jamie knew Brock could hear the wheels in his fingertips, even if the doctors could never sew his busted ear back on correctly. It was a vibration, not a sound. A transmission delivered along molecules of marrow up into your bones from the root source of the rails. You could feel it rattle in your skull. Brock said it looked yellow when he closed his eyes. It looked like anywhere but here.

There was an abandoned ambulance in the parking lot. SATIN RULES!! was sprayed across the back doors, the words colliding with LARKHILL MUNICIPALITY typed out in faded red stencil. Someone had removed the front seat and set it up on the roof like a recliner. Jamie Garrison smelled smoke as his legs carried him across the parking lot and past the frozen condoms scattered on the broken asphalt. Brock swirled around his head, mixed up with images of lions hunting children. The parking lot had no working streetlights. Smoke threaded through the night sky, but there weren't any stars. Only the moon forced its way through the clouds and made everything blue and cold. Jamie's hands kept clenching involuntarily.

"You can't even keep a fucking fact straight, can you? Fucking junkie motherfucker…"

Jamie slammed the door open. A chair stood in the middle of the room. A broken pair of dentures lay on the floor. The bottom palate was split in two. Broken orange prescription bottles and sandwich bags littered the ground. Scattered dustings of crushed medication sprouted from the tiles. Trails of smoke pushed their way into the room through the hole the Lorax had carved into the wall. Jamie recognized the smell. The Lorax's fungi were burning with his lamps.

"Mmmmmm! Mmmmmmuuuu!"

The Lorax was naked. His arms and legs were duct-taped to the chair. His eyes stared at the ceiling as Jamie tried to pull the gray tape off his mouth. The tape pulled off skin and hair with it, leaving tiny beads of blood behind. The Lorax coughed up a mess of half-eaten mushrooms and broken yellow pills straight down his chest. Jamie noticed all the baggies were empty, the prescriptions too. The Lorax coughed again and more gray mushrooms fell into his lap.

"Oh, Larry, you dumb motherfucker...what did you do?"

All the baseball cards were torn up into little pieces. Jamie climbed the counter and looked for a pair of scissors, a knife, even a broken piece of glass sharp enough to cut through the thick gray tape. More of it was wrapped around the Lorax's torso too, pulled taut against his sagging belly. The exposed skin was red and blistered. The Lorax stretched his mouth out.

"You ever—ugh, blah—you ever watch the Pirates this summer?"

"You know who did this shit?" Jamie said. "You fucking told them, didn't you? And you can't even get that shit right! Where are your goddamn scissors?"

"There was this game this summer. I mean, what a game," the Lorax said. "I don't know if I can stay a true fan after watching it. There are no scissors. You know that, Jamie. They aren't stupid. No knives either. Nothing sharp. You shoulda seen this game though, buddy."

"A knife? You got nothing here?"

The Lorax kept talking.

"You don't watch baseball, do you? Back in June, and my Pirates, I don't even know why I like the Pirates, do you? It's kind of like cheering for a corporation if you think about it too hard, so of course I don't. I'm just surprised you're here. I thought you'd be gone before me, Brock or Jamie or whatever."

Jamie kept digging through the drawers. The smell of burning fungi wafted through from the old dentist's office. A picture of two wolves began to melt in the waiting room. They watched Jamie through the hole in the wall, trapped behind their glass frame.

"Not even, like, an X-Acto? A razor?"

"Earned ten runs in the first inning, first inning. Insane," the Lorax said. "Just insane. What a game it coulda been, right? Ten runs.

Game is over. But no, they just had to fuck it up. And that's what happens. You try to get ahead, but it's over. You're never golden, you slip up. Like the whole giraffe thing."

"Larry, I want to fucking untie you before the whole place goes up, if only to kick the shit out of you, but you aren't helping."

"So why isn't your face fucked up?" the Lorax asked. "I never did lose my teeth. What did I tell you? Oh, I've got a lot of stories. Like the one where I crashed my bike into the green box on my street, or when I bit down on a roll of change. Truth is they plucked them like fucking raspberries back when Crane was bein' all crazy. Pop. Just 'cause I did a little biz here and there on the side. Only a little though. Like raspberries, man. The teeth. You ever pick raspberries?"

The Lorax's voice was still calm and level. Jamie slammed another drawer.

"Larry, I need you to shut up and think."

"They made me eat it all, you know—all of it. I had to eat it all, Brock…Jay…what do you even know? Even the insulin pills. You sell those to the kids who don't know what they're getting."

Another drawer. More shredded baseball cards.

"Who did I tell what?" the Lorax asked. "The guy with the lion. Kilkenny on the farm. They killed him dead. But the Pirates in this game, I tell you, man, it just goes to show you can't bet on a guaranteed thing."

Jamie gave up on the drawers. The smoke gathered around the ceiling of the room. Pig shit and dying mushrooms. He staggered away from the back wall and began to pry at the tape while more mangled mushrooms and pill capsules fell out of the Lorax's mouth and onto the dirty floor. The Lorax didn't seem to notice the chunks dripping from his toothless face.

"It was June eighth. I remember 'cause it was my birthday, and they took me out to get wasted, both of them. I had this kid working for me, Condon—Astor's old bitch boy—but couldn't get him to come out. Just stayed cooped up in his place and never comes out. So just me and those bearded fucks. And we got ten runs in the first inning. Barry Bonds whacking home runs and killing it out there. And it's against Philly, fucking Phillies. All their fans are assholes. Ten runs. I'm not even from Pittsburgh. Never even been there, but I'm watching this game 'cause it's my birthday. And they popped my teeth like raspberries. Pop. Just like that."

More smoke filled the room. Jamie tried jamming his keys into the tape, but they wouldn't cut through the thick fibers. On his knees, he began to saw back and forth against between the Lorax's wrists. It was quiet outside the sound of crackling drywall.

"Shut the fuck up, Larry. Shut the fuck up for like five seconds," Jamie said.

"I had to tell them, you know, had to—it wasn't like a choice, you know. It took a lot to steal that beast. You wouldn't believe how much Kilkenny cried before we finished him off, guy was all water. Musta pissed himself. But that game Rooker, the guy calling that ballgame. That was his name. He was calling it in Philly."

"Larry, you gotta help me with this shit. Try to lean back or something."

"They made me eat it all," the Lorax said. "Even the little weird hormone shit they give the guys who wanna sprout tits. But not Jim Rooker. He was calling the game. He said he'd fucking walk home from Philly if the Pirates lost. Counting your chickens before they die, right? Or eggs? 'Cause that's what they did, they died right there in front of everybody. Embarrassing.

"It was like watching an execution in slow motion, but baseball is always in slow motion. It was my birthday, and they'd just got the lion too. The team blew the lead, ten runs. Do you remember? They were supposed to get you too. They didn't even warn me, didn't even bring the drill. Never used tape before. That was new, that was very new…"

The Lorax droned on at a steady volume as the room got smaller and smaller.

"Larry! I'm trying to—"

"You. They were supposed to get you first and then they got me, because Crane knows. I'm like a free agent. I play out the contract and the contract ends. They really, really made me eat it all, man—"

"That wasn't even.... You can't keep one thing straight, can you? You even recognize my face? That wasn't even my fucking address on the prescription..."

The Lorax was not listening to Jamie. He wasn't even listening to himself.

"That game. Don't matter how far you're ahead. Don't matter. It isn't over till the fucking ninth inning. Yeah, they found me. And I always wanted to be a big deal, you know? This operation here, this was just a beginning. This wasn't an end. I wanted to be like a Mazeroski, the Maz. I wanted that big walk-off. I could hold it on my own out here. I still hung out with them after that too, even after they took my teeth. They tore up my Maz, too. Eight-time Gold Glove winner!"

Smoke was everywhere. Jamie backed up from the body in the chair. The voice kept pushing at him through the smoke. The same droning voice that told those two all about the lion and the address. It was the wrong address, and now Brock had no teeth at all. A busted fucking jack-o'-lantern, the kind you find shattered on the street after Halloween, and the voice kept speaking inside that cloud of smoke laced with pig feces and burning fungus. The ceiling tiles rippled and began to fall. Jamie dodged the smoking panels and crawled toward the door. Sweat smeared the smoke onto his forehead.

"They coulda left me anywhere," the Lorax said. "That's what they do—like a warning. You don't need to sign it because you know who it's for and what it means and they shoulda gone to you first, not me. But they knew, they always know. You can't blow a lead like that. No one gets the walk-offs. No walk-offs for anybody, just more of the same. I can't—you still there?"

The body back at the butcher shop was probably frozen. The bone can wasn't supposed to be outside. The voice kept coughing and Jamie pushed his way through the door. The thick fumes made his eyes water and he hacked on the pavement outside. His spit was black and chunky. The Lorax kept talking, his voice finally rising as the flames began to nip at his bare, pimpled skin. His voice spat the words into the haze while Jamie watched the whole plaza smouldering.

"It was my birthday, and they took me out to the bar, and there was a ten-run lead in the first. You can't stay fucking ahead, though. Never. Final was fifteen to eleven and the announcer said he was gonna walk home all the way from Philly back to Pittsburgh. All the way. They didn't even take me to the woods and let me crawl, you know that? Just left me here."

Jamie stumbled back toward his car. He didn't hear any sirens, just the voice of the Lorax tunneling into his brain. He could hear his lungs crackling from the heat, the smoke choking each individual cell until they collapsed on top of one another.

"The announcer walked home and they wouldn't even let me crawl out of my own."

Jamie climbed into the car and turned up the radio. His knees popped with the static. He couldn't find a station. A lone flame swayed from the roof of Harry's Holistic Hobbies like a sputtering signal flare. Jamie closed his eyes and tried to start the engine. The cold air clutched it tight and the motor sputtered in convulsions. He needed to return the message.

"It doesn't matter how far you get ahead, Brock. Brock, yeah? Doesn't matter, not until the ump says you're done. You can't end it till then—and it's always too late."

Jamie let static fill his ears instead. The body was still waiting for him. A letter they didn't bother signing. He was the one who ran over the lion. It was addressed to him. Jamie wiped his hands across his lap. Each finger left behind a sticky red mess.

"It was my birthday, and they took me out for a drink..."

Jamie drove out of the parking lot. He didn't bother to signal when he turned onto the street.

Police would later assume it was insurance fraud tied to the estate case. The bed sheet curtains across the street remained closed as the Lorax burbled and melted in the burning dark.

23

The bullet ricocheted four times before embedding itself in the skull of Francis Paul Garrison. It first bounced off the temple of the cow on the killing floor of the Tillson Abattoir and then ricocheted into the rafters. It then struck a two-inch-wide steel beam that fired the slug back down at sixty miles an hour, where it eventually collided with the concrete floor and sprang back up toward Francis's face. As he tried to protect himself, the lead passed directly through his left palm before burrowing deep into the bone between his temple and right ear. Medical staff on site agreed it was too dangerous to remove the slug, and Francis Paul Garrison quit two months later without any explanation. No cows rejoiced. There was always someone else to pick up the gun.

"Dad, you need to open the door and let me in," Jamie said. "It'll honestly take five minutes. Just open the door. I will leave you be, all right? Open the door."

"It's almost two in the morning."

"I can tell time, Dad."

"Your mother's asleep," Francis said. "She can't be disturbed. You can't just come whenever you feel like it and disturb the schedule we have here."

Jamie's father was never the same after that bullet passed through his hand. In the first few months afterward, Francis sat in the living room with his cigarettes and let the smoke eat a hole through the ceiling. He no longer cared to watch his embattled Leafs lose season after season, and he stopped trimming his hair. The only reason he cut his nails was the annoying click they made against the television remote. He left the clippings in his lap.

The hole in Francis's hand never fully healed. You could poke your pinkie finger through it when he was asleep, but he didn't close his eyes very often. Francis Garrison did not believe he deserved to participate in the world after that incident with the cow. He had interfered enough, caused enough sorrow, eaten from the wrong tree in the wrong garden during his time on this earth. The problem was knowledge, he decided. Knowledge of that gun and everything else—the machines of man had betrayed him. Francis sat in that chair while the Cold War crept past and watched men try to destroy each other with all their hard-earned knowledge packed into warheads and submarines. He still ate meat, but he never asked about its origins. He had uncluttered his mind of all the useless facts his cells had collected over the years. Each synapse was issued an expiry date.

"I'm already halfway in the door anyway," Jamie said. "I promise I won't waste any of your precious fucking meditation time or whatever. Go sit by the TV and I'll find it myself. I just need the gun. The old one, all right? Just for a few days. You going to let me in or what?"

Jamie had watched his father recede for years, the old man's inaction burning pancakes and abandoning laundry until ants began to treat it like a home. Mrs. Garrison did her best to stay out of the house, spending shifts at the bingo halls downtown, where the glass was covered in greasy facial imprints from the homeless. Two of these illuminated fishbowls sat on King Street, their clouded interiors beckoning with heaters and a two-dollar minimum to sit down at the tables. Jamie's mother's hands were covered in green dabber ink like liver spots, and the second-hand smoke made her smell like the bathroom stalls at work—musty and overgrown with mildew. It was better than home, though, and the lump in the corner who refused to turn the television from anything but the news. Francis Garrison watched it on mute.

"You want what?" he said. "You can't have the gun. It don't even work the way it did..."

Jamie pushed past his father into the living room.

Francis never got rid of the gun that propelled that fateful hunk of lead into his skull. He kept it as a reminder of his hubris. That's what he told his sons before he stashed it in their house on Olive St. A reminder of his pride and all the fallout that was to come. Never interfere. You must let nature take its course—it will decide your fate. This is what he told his sons while their house burned down. They had found him standing on the front lawn smoking and watching it burn in the dark. The rifle was in his hand.

Don't interfere. This is what he told them in the hotel room downtown while their mother was treated for third-degree burns; the chain she wore had melted the skin around her neck, a cross branded between her breasts. Jamie remembered emerging from the smoke and that figure on the curb with an ember in his hand. Francis hadn't bothered to wake them up.

It was in that downtown hotel room with the Magic Finger beds that Francis explained why he couldn't interfere. He'd done it once before, and look what had happened. A line of white through his black hair traced the bullet's path, the skin beneath a meaty pink that pulsed like a vein. He pointed to his skull and sat on the hotel balcony, watching toads drown in the hotel pool as the chlorine overwhelmed their systems and burned their porous skin.

"Don't give me that old spiel about it bein' broken. You had it out at Christmas," Jamie said. "Mom had to tell you to put it away. Do you remember Christmas? Fucking had the TV on the whole time. It'll just be for tonight. And Mom isn't even here, is she?"

"She is. They had a heart attack at the hall. I keep tellin' her she's going to have one if she keeps breathing in that smoke every night. Soot in her lungs like I tell her. She wants to kill herself all slow like that, she's welcome to it."

The clutch of silence and muted news on the television had seeped into every little room in that row house. It was Janet Garrison who went out and worked, worked until she finally got her pension and could flee as well. The post office set her free after forty years with a fractured disc and collapsed arches in both her feet. Francis Garrison ate whatever she left in the fridge and slept in the living room. He did his own laundry while she was out of the house but washed it in the kitchen sink. Janet did not believe in divorce. It was easier to pretend he was a ghost than file the papers and drag what was left of her husband into a brightly lit courtroom. Everything would be on the record after that. Anyone could access the stenographer's account of their dysfunction.

"Well, I won't bother her. Jesus Christ. Where did you put it now? Is it in the kitchen again? You should just give it up. Throw it away if you don't want me asking for it. I got nowhere to be. I can look for it all night," Jamie said. "You hear anything from Scott at all?"

Francis Garrison retreated to his chair in the corner.

"So you're going to shut down again?" Jamie asked. "Like a robot. All right, fine."

Jamie could still see Brock's mouth split open with that little tongue pushing through the fluid like a worm. He could still see the lion mashed under the grille of his car, its vacant eyes. Jamie didn't know what the Lorax had told those two men from the butcher shop. Who else could they be? The Lorax could have said anything with all those mushrooms jammed into his cheeks. Jamie slammed another cupboard and kept looking. He smelled like smoke.

Francis didn't move. On the television screen, a woman bellowed from a pulpit made out of scrap plywood. Homemade signs fluttered behind her in the breeze. The close angle of the camera made her look massive; you could see small black hairs raised along her upper lip. Her teeth gnashed and she paused for effect. The crowd was smaller than it looked, pumped up with occasional banners and one guy in a motorized wheelchair driving around in circles. He looked more lost than angry.

"Leave it alone, Jamie. You can't just take whatever you want," Francis croaked. "It ain't yours to take. It's like anything else. Like a microwave or a satellite dish. I keep my eye on it."

"Just tell me where you stashed the gun, and I'll leave you alone to whatever you're doin'. You can do whatever you want with that TV. Mom doesn't use it anyway."

Jamie found the rifle underneath the sink, held against the wall by pipes and a stack of iron wool. His father crept up behind him in the cramped kitchen, waving his hand at Jamie like it was a talisman. The light passed right through the hole in his palm, a reminder of cows split down the middle and pigs boiled to clear the bristles off their snouts before their throats were cut.

"Just relax, Dad. You need to take a seat before you hurt yourself."

Jamie had seen this hand routine before, and he still had Brock's broken jack-o'-lantern face floating behind his eyes. He tried to push past his father with the butt of the gun—a Remington Fieldmaster, .22LR caliber. It had belonged to his grandfather first. Francis Garrison held fast against his son, trapping him in the doorway. He hadn't brushed his teeth.

"You're going to make a mess with that thing. Like everything else you do," Francis said. "I'll throw it out like you want. Just give me it. I'll be the one to throw it out. Things come back at you if you ain't careful."

Jamie knew his father always kept one in the chamber—just in case he got tired of waiting for the end. He saw it when his father cleaned the gun. Sometimes the eventual dissolution of this world was not eventual enough.

"So it came back and bit you in the ass—so what?" Jamie said. "So does everything else. No one is trying to take your TV or your microwave or whatever else you think we want. Not taking anything but this, I swear. Mom needs to put a leash on you. Jesus…"

"You don't know what you're doing with that," Francis said.

Jamie shoved past his father and found his mother standing in the hallway. She was dressed in the green pantsuit she wore to the bingo halls. Her eyes were hidden behind a pair of sunglasses, the ones she wore after a good long cry in the bathroom with the tub running. The stoop of her back was reinforced from years of lifting packages onto conveyor belts and sorting through Christmas letters to Santa Claus.

"Mom, can I use the phone?" Jamie said. "I just gotta make a call and the old man ain't helping. Don't worry, it's not long-distance—let go—and it won't take too long."

Janet Garrison brushed past her husband. Her eyes didn't even flicker over his hairy face or the rifle clutched in her son's hands. That gun was always bouncing around the house. She had slept with it beneath her bed for the last week before Francis moved it again. Sometimes she wished it would fire once of its own volition.

"Sure. As long as it's not long-distance, you can call whoever," she said. "You still staying with Scott?"

Janet began to put on her shoes in the kitchen, the large orthopedic ones the doctor advised would reduce the strain on her lower back. Unlike most of her friends, Janet had yet to crumble entirely. She attributed it to a lack of cigarettes and a healthy dose of All-Bran each morning. It was only her feet that looked truly old—like dead roots.

"Scott's gotta sort some shit out with that wife of his, so I'm letting them kinda air everything out," Jamie said to his mother. "Phone is still in the back bedroom, right?"

"Where do you think you're going, Jan? It's two in the morning!" Francis said.

"They've moved the games to the high school," Janet said. "I can't sleep after watching Audrey keel over like that, and I'm not staying here to watch the two of you go at it again. I've already seen that before. Many times.

"Its fine, Jamie. You do whatever you need to do, just make sure your father eats something, and for God's sake don't bother returning that thing," Janet continued, ignoring her husband. "Shoulda been taken out of this house a long time ago. Take the TV too, if you want, but he probably won't go for that. You tell your brother I said hello, okay? We never see enough of him around here, but I understand why. Oh, don't tell him that, though. Just say hi."

Janet stood up and began stomping out the aches in her feet on the kitchen floor. She pulled her coat on and slammed the door behind her. The wind battered it around the jamb.

"Jamie, you gotta listen to me. You can take the TV, how about that?"

The hallway was short and crowded with black-and-white photos of the dead. Jamie opened the door to his mother's bedroom and sat down on the bed. The walls were crooked, the corners mismatched. Jamie could hear his father grumbling, but he knew the man's muscles had wasted away. Francis couldn't even hold the gun straight anymore. Jamie dialed Don Henley's number.

"Y'allo? Jesus, two in the morning, I coulda been sleeping. Y'allo?"

Don Henley didn't sleep. He napped.

"Donnie, it's Jamie."

"Oh, man, you gonna bullshit me about shifts again?" Don said. "I told you, I can't get any of the other guys to work. Sunday mornings. There's like no customers anyway."

"It's not about that, it's—there's too much to explain. Never mind. All right. Listen to me," Jamie said. "You know two guys, big fuckers with beards. Sometimes they come in the store, I guess? Sound familiar?"

"Look like ZZ Top? Those guys? Should have guitars on them, right?"

"Yeah, exactly," Jamie said. "They come around a lot or what?"

"They give you trouble? My brother knew them better than me. They been 'round forever, back when we still had bikers in town," Don said. "They aren't even twins. Irish twins, same year but different birthdays. I think. Their momma musta pumped 'em out real quick, I can tell you that much, and—oh, for fuck's sake Gloria, no I don't need another ice cream sandwich. Just let me talk to J here and then we can get back to—"

"I don't need their whole life story," Jamie said. "I think I mighta pissed them off a bit today, and then all this weird shit…well, I just wanted an expert opinion."

The line went quiet for a little and Jamie noticed the gun in his lap. He moved it onto the bed, but didn't like how it looked sitting between the pillows.

"What did you do? They used to do a lot of the booking for the ring, you know, in the backyard, and they do a lot of—well, they got hands in all kinds of things," Donnie explained. "The Brothers Vine is what my brother liked to call them. They got hands in everything. Brothers Vine. Used to come by for trim."

"They came by this morning, and I gave them some for hunting bears."

"Sounds about right. What exactly did you do?" Donnie asked.

Jamie put the gun on the floor and remembered what he said to the Lorax.

"Spit it out, buddy. I got fucking *Rocky II* in the VCR here and it isn't as shit as I thought it'd be," Don said. "I might even finish watching it tonight. What did you do?"

"I think I, um, ran over their dog. Big-ass dog. In my car last night."

"You did what?" Donnie asked.

"Dog. Ran it over. Told some guy about it, and then Brock, he ended up like..."

There was a low whistle down the line and some whispering. Don spoke into the phone again. His voice was quieter now. Jamie kicked the gun under the bed. He didn't want to see it.

"You know when I worked back at the warehouse? And when I was running the weekly Toss-Up Throwdowns in the backyard? They had a finger in that, and they needed to or I woulda been done faster than a goose in a trailer park. Blam," Don said. "Where do you think all the stolen booze from the warehouse went? You think I didn't forget to check off certain containers? Never the number-one brands, of course. Where do you think that would go? Brothers Vine.

"They don't even care about the money. They don't even work for themselves. Used to be hooked up with this real mild, skinny dude. He lived in one of those big apartment buildings off Olive, the ones they wanna condemn now since they're only twenty years old and already falling apart. What I'm saying is, they got fingers in lots of pies and they are dirty fingers—so you don't wanna just say sorry, you know?"

"So what do I do?" Jamie asked. "I can't exactly track them down."

In his mother's mirror, Jamie saw the body in the bone can, ice crystallizing over the nostrils. It smiled and bobbed in the meaty slush.

"I don't really know. These are major fuckers. Been around forever, they're like a cleaning crew—just dealing with everyone else's mess," Donnie said. "They don't cause too much of a ruckus—in and out. I had them do security once when we had the ring set up, like a few summers ago, but it was worse than Altamont. They do not fuck around.

"I say lay low, take some time off work, you can borrow a bit of cash off me, but don't tell anyone where you're going. Just be safe. It's just a dog, so they probably won't kill you, but I mean the last kind of—Gloria, I can hear you standing at the door."

"What if I wanted to apologize? I don't want to have to worry about this chasing me for the rest of my life. How do I do that?"

"Shit, they been living at Da Nasty for like ten years now. Room—uh, shit, hold on a second, I had it from the last time I had to call them. You know they might kick your ass, right? They ain't Santa Claus."

"I know, I know. You think I'm happy about this?" Jamie said.

"It's Room 227. I think. They been there for years, like I said. Not likely to change."

"So what should I do? Beg? Bring a new dog?"

"You should really—oh, that is not fair, Gloria, I get one nosebleed and you bring it up fucking now? That was like a year ago. I told you, the dry air and my nose," Donnie said. "We just need to get a dehumidifier and I am still talking to Jamie, so can you give me—"

Jamie hung up the phone and picked the gun up off the floor. Somewhere one of the next-door neighbors kicked over a kitchen chair and someone in another unit was running up and down the stairs. Jamie didn't like the green wallpaper his mother kept on these walls. It didn't hide the water stains. It didn't hide anything. He strode down the hall, switching the rifle from hand to hand. He'd never really fired it before. He wasn't exactly sure where to buy rounds at two in the morning, either. And there was still that body waiting for him, and it was a sign after all. A calling card. He'd been right. The Lorax was right, everyone was right. Jamie wanted to be wrong for once and have that be the right answer.

"You shouldn't take that."

Francis Garrison sat alone in his chair, but the television was still playing. He raised his hand at Jamie, but there was not enough light to pass through the hole. Jamie shook his head and pushed his way out the door. His father yelled his name, but Jamie did not turn around.

Outside in the cold, Jamie Garrison kicked at the tires of his Cutlass and ran a hand over the busted grille, searching for a piece of mane. The stars were out and the hood of the car was covered in frost. The body in the bone can waited for him in the dark, waited for whoever opened its heavy lid. He waited for his father to stagger outside, to the light the house on fire once again. No one emerged.

"I am never driving that fucking skinhead home again."

Jamie tossed the gun into the trunk. He was going to need a tarp.

24

Moses never told his friends that true skinheads didn't shave their heads. Sure, their hair was short, but real skinheads were never truly bald. They got a one or a two buzz from their mother's electric razor in a small apartment on a council estate where they lived with senile grandmothers and their father's ashes on the mantel. They rolled their pants up over their boots and had tiny crosses tattooed on their foreheads. Some of them, at least—Moses knew that much. They loved Sham 69 and the smell of tobacco and they flipped you off with two fingers, not one.

He'd found pictures in the library after a few months hanging around in the Triple K parking lot. The library was a way station filled with busted spines and strange stains underneath the microfiche readers where the old men lingered. The teeth were what surprised him. All the photos were black-and-white pictures from soccer games and riots. The teeth looked so white. Some of them were even straight. The English were supposed to have the worst teeth. Moses had spent his nights naked in the motel bathroom prying his jaw open and examining his mouth.

He knew his teeth weren't white enough and his hair was too short.

"You never said it was abandoned," Logan said.

"I didn't say anything," Moses said. "It was four fucking years ago."

The moon led the way. Moses walked through the grounds of the old hospital with his friends trailing behind him. They didn't have a flashlight. Most of the windows were broken. Moses chucked a rock at a remaining pane. He didn't get a chance to see his face in its reflection. A few scattered tags marked the territory of teenagers who'd made the pilgrimage before them. The Larkhill Institute for Mental Health had only been shut down for four years, but it could have been decades. A lack of funding and a receding population in the city had sent hospital finances spiraling down until basic maintenance became a problem. It was at this point the provincial government stepped in to transition many of the faltering patients into new facilities. Many were reassessed and allowed to return to their homes and families. Elvira Moon had only been at LIMH for a few weeks before she was released and welcomed back to work. Two weeks later she quit taking her medication, and after a month she was quietly released from the company. That was when she started buying up all the busted dogs.

"You really think she would come back? We could barely even find it," Logan said. "Place is like the end of the Earth. Is she a homing pigeon? Caw!"

The boys had parked the car on the road out front before hopping over the chain-link fence. Six buildings leaned out over the grounds. I LOVE YOU TERESA was spray-painted in purple across the front door of the administrative offices. Someone had tagged FAGGOT underneath it in neon green. The letters looped over one another. Moses felt bad for Teresa, but he kept walking. Maybe the rain would wash it away. It was too cold to stop.

"Let's just hold up, all right. Ruining my jacket on all the fuckin' branches," B. Rex said.

"Don't be a little Jew, B. Rex," Logan laughed. "You got the cash to buy a new one."

Logan was the one who clung to it the hardest. Not just the haircut, but all of it—all the speeches and the heritage movements. That was the sneaky way to say it, according to B. Rex. A heritage movement—the phrase was a dog whistle. Only those attuned to its frequency would pick up the necessary meaning.

Moses provided the rhetoric for the boys, words he found in pamphlets and Ayn Rand newsletters left on the bedside tables of slumbering women in the Dynasty. He found missives from the businessmen who never tipped and brought plastic sheet covers for the motel beds. Moses gathered inspiration as he and his mother fled the ghosts of group homes and observation wards, stumbling from one motel to the next. Even at school, Moses found the words he needed scrawled into the cafeteria tables, sprayed inside bathroom stalls and dangling unsaid from the upturned corners of his teachers' mouths. Moses didn't need all those words, but he held onto them like used-up batteries. Drained of their power, but still filled with the necessary acid. He spat them out in large gobs.

"Fuck you, Logan," B. Rex said. "Can't even see out here. And I don't like leavin' the car out by the road like that. It's like a big sign for the cops. Like, hey, look, somebody's home!"

"I'm not the one who stomped the old lady's face," Logan said. "You know that, right? You remember that, Moses?"

They weren't going to be like the KKK. It wasn't about blacks or Catholics or fags. That was too easy. Back at the motel, Moses had stayed up late and listened to old men talk about weekly lynchings in the Southern states. He saw the photos of children posing beside the bodies of flayed black men. The kids' grins revealed gap-toothed smiles. It made him sick, but he kept watching on the blurry satellite channels the motel got for free. He watched until he didn't feel sick anymore, and then he watched it again.

"She was asking for it. She…she…"

"You fucking killed her, Moses," Logan said. "Now we ain't going to say anything…but like, you can't say it didn't happen. You took the bitch out. It was cold, man."

"I didn't do it like that," Moses said. "I wasn't the one who started whaling on her. She was an old lady, she didn't even—she shouldn't have been there."

"Well, I just threw a few punches," Logan said. "B. Rex can back me up; I just threw some punches, that's all. I didn't kill nobody."

Moses wanted action. B. Rex lent them old books by angry white men from the States and neo-Nazi pamphlets his dad had hidden in the garage. They laughed at the overblown fears and words like sand-nigger and camel jockey. Moses knew this wasn't what he wanted, but it was a place to start. It was filled with all the fear they had; it spoke to those little angry bits they hadn't organized into thoughts yet. Madison Grant, David Lane, and Frazier Glenn Miller Jr. made them laugh, but Moses could repeat some of their speeches word for word.

"You threw more than fucking punches," Moses said. "She was on the goddamn floor!"

B. Rex didn't say anything. He kept poking at the holes in his jacket.

"I didn't finish it though. I didn't go crazy just 'cause some old lady came into my house," Logan said. "It wasn't even your house anymore. You don't live there now, Moses, you know?"

"Then just go home. Go home, Logan. Oh wait, you fucking can't, can you? No one is fucking coming home. Get that through your fucking head. You got something better to do tonight, go ahead, but you'll be walking. And it's a long fucking walk."

"So what, I'm supposed to live in a motel with you and your crazy-ass mother?"

It wasn't Elvira's fault either. She might have prayed to Bill Cosby and loved her bowling balls like children, but she never hurt him. She didn't call him stupid or mock his high voice, or ask when his balls were going to drop. She still knew who he was sometimes. Elvira wasn't the reason for any of this, and neither was Ted Moon. He was just an envelope full of weird promises and lipstick kisses on napkins and postcards. He was just dust and fucking hawks circling the city and waiting for Moses to die. Ted Moon could do whatever he liked. Moses didn't write him back, and he wasn't dying any time soon.

"She's fine, she's not even…she's not that crazy. You haven't even seen her yet."

"Then why are we running all the fuck over town?" Logan asked.

"It's fine with you to run into bowling alleys and smack people around, but all of a sudden it gets dark and you're afraid? Is that it?" Moses taunted. "She's going to be here. This is where her doc was…"

"Is that what the giant dyke said?"

Moses Moon knew it wasn't about skin or accents or the way someone walked. That wasn't the reason why they were here with their scabby skulls and in-grown hairs. It was to build something of their own. Something new. They needed to make it new, and the only way you did that was harvesting the past. Pulling up all the broken things your parents had buried and killed and making them your center. Turn trash into your cosmos—either worship it or burn the fucker down. Moses wanted to pull everyone down to that level, and it was easiest when you were already on the edge of the radar. It was easy when you sucked cock or spoke Cantonese or cut hair for the two hundred black men in town. It was easy to slip off the map and end up in the small little place, crowded with everyone else's misery and bleeding from open pores you couldn't close. That was why they bought the big heavy boots and ran razors over their heads and stabbed pens into their tiny bird chests. Start at the bottom of the level, start in your own tenements and tattoo MADE IN LARKHILL on the line above your skull. Let the ink settle and blur till you can barely read the letters. It was best to start at the bottom, and Larkhill was dead weight.

"You can suck my cock," Moses said.

They would tear it down, and then it would be new.

"Like you even—"

Moses tackled Logan, and then they were rolling around in the dead leaves and melted snow. He pinned the smaller boy underneath him and raised his fists. One, two, three, and there was blood pouring from Logan's nose. Logan coughed and tried to choke Moses but then B. Rex was tearing them off each other, using his short arms to hold them apart and laughing.

"You know how stupid this is, Loogie? I am going to get my ass kicked tomorrow by the old man. The cops are already probably at my house. Now I have to babysit you two? No, not going to play it this way. You two can throw your little pity party some other time. It's fucking cold. You get that?"

The two boys flopped down on the grass. Logan wiped the blood from his face while Moses massaged his throat. From one of the brick buildings, they heard something bang against a wall. It groaned in the darkness.

"Where you going, B. Rex?" Moses asked.

"To find your fucking mom. You coming or not?"

The double doors were painted industrial green. B. Rex yanked one door open and pushed his way inside. Moses and Logan followed him down the hallway, stepping around small holes in the floor and pink tufts of insulation. There was a painful light coming from down the hall. A small sign on the wall read WARD 3-W. They passed a nurse's station covered in old schedules and crowned with a busted clock. It was always 7 a.m. in WARD 3-W.

There was another thud from farther down the hallway, toward the light. B. Rex kept striding forward. Moses wanted to sit down. He could feel his stomach turning. Elvira had tried to run away many times before, but Moses always caught her waiting for the elevator. Elvira pretended she knew where she was going, but she was never wearing any underwear. Sometimes she said it was a job interview at Scotiabank. Other days she had a hair appointment. The nightgowns she liked to wear didn't cover much; Moses found it hard to find extra larges at the second-hand stores. It seemed like only small people handed down their clothes. People got fatter with age. The ones who got thinner were usually sick, their bodies retreating away from poisoned bones or squeezing the last bit of energy out of each fat deposit until there was nothing left.

Elvira had refused to wear underwear. She would flush it down the toilet or chuck it out the window. Sometimes she used it like Kleenex and left it bunched up in the garbage. On those mornings when he caught her in the lobby, Moses knew everyone was watching her as she paced back and forth across the threadbare lobby rugs. They were leering from the collapsed La-Z-Boys and couches scattered around the Dynasty's busted lobby. Moses didn't know what his friends would find in WARD 3-W, but he wanted to stop walking. He wanted a homemade quilt to wrap Elvira up in before he turned the corner and found B. Rex and Logan staring at her half-naked or worse. Moses lingered behind his friends as they neared the light. There were strange stains on the floor and deep gouges in the pale green linoleum.

"You gotta see this, Mosey," B. Rex said.

It used to be a cafeteria. Long, chipped tables were pushed into the corners and orange chairs were stacked up to the ceiling. The majority of the floor was covered in a thick mulch that smelled like manure. Tall stalks of green filled the room, urged higher by the powerful lights above them. Racks of hydroponic equipment were drilled into the ceiling. The air was moist and stuck to their skin. Large wet stains sprouted from the walls and long tubes of aluminum ductwork crisscrossed the floor. Mold grew on every surface in a sickly half-rainbow of greens and browns. Moses allowed his spine to relax slightly. His mother wasn't here. She didn't like plants; she had told Moses she didn't trust them. Plants could stop providing us with oxygen at any time if they decided they'd had enough.

"You ever seen anything like this?" Logan said. "It's like the fucking Emerald City. I'm just waiting for some flying monkeys or some shit. Breathe it in, buddy. This is going to be good. How much do you think we can take before they notice?"

They were lucky it was wearing a chain.

"Probably five plants each or some—"

The bear burst out of the tall plants, its patchy fur revealing stringy muscles underneath. Teeth snapped in front of B. Rex's nose and then all three were running toward the door. The bear bellowed and crashed after them through the stinking plants. Logan lost a boot in the thick manure but kept on going. The bear rose up on its hind legs and bellowed again, revealing a scarred chest covered in seeping gashes and cigarette burns. A few butts remained embedded in its chest like dead tapeworms. One eye couldn't focus—it stood still in the middle of that roaring face.

The boys didn't remain to observe this new specimen. None of them had ever been this close to a bear. Only B. Rex had ever been to the zoo. They scrambled away into the darkness as the animal continued to bellow and roll its thick neck against the reinforced chain tethering it to the wall. Someone had welded it in place.

The boys stumbled down the hallway, crashing into fallen ceiling tiles and office chairs. Logan's bare foot hit the cold linoleum with a splat as his breathing filled Moses's ears. The bear roared again. It was all fur and teeth and seeping wounds. Some of the cigarette butts looked fresh—they were filled with day-old puss.

The heavy green doors lay ahead. B. Rex led the way, his stubby legs pulling him closer to the cold air outside. As he yanked the steel door open, a large hand grabbed him by the neck and threw him onto the frosted grass. Moses and Logan emerged behind him and were lifted off their feet by two sets of heavily tattooed hands.

"Whoops," a voice laughed. "Where you runnin' to?"

Moses couldn't breathe. The hands were locked around his neck. He knew the police didn't tattoo their hands. They didn't have bushy beards or snakes encircling their thumbs. B. Rex tried to stand up, but a size-twelve work boot pushed him back down onto the wet grass. A red pickup was parked beside the crippled building. It had mud splashed up to the windows. Logan let out a wheeze as he struggled with his own headlock. The moon outlined their bodies.

"If you go out into the woods today, you better not go alone!"

The man was singing into Moses's face. The other one laughed. He recognized the man from the ice machine. The man dragging the garbage bags and power tools down the dirty hall.

"It's too bad she didn't get one of you. She's been hungry."

The other man laughed again.

"We saw your car out by the road. A Buick, right? The bowling ball yours too?"

The Judge was in the truck bed. Moses tried to speak, but he couldn't get the words out. The man tossed him onto the ground and pulled out a roll of duct tape. He bound Moses's hands and ran a piece of tape over his mouth. It stuck to his teeth when he tried to speak. The man tore another length of tape off the roll and kicked Moses in the testicles. He blacked out and smoke filled his eyes.

In the haze, Moses watched himself roll around in the grass and his mother kissing men he didn't know with stomachs shaped like bowling balls. He didn't see their faces. The lion from the side of the road warned him it was all going to happen again. Another repetition. Moses tried to drag the lion out of the way, but he could see the headlights coming. The lion spoke, but Moses couldn't hear it over the sound of the horn. His face hit the back of the truck as the three boys were tossed into the pickup.

"Usually we'd just leave you out here, but can't be doin' that no more," one of them said. "So you're going to have to come along for now till we figure it out. Patience, little bears. Ha."

The two beards stepped away from the truck bed and slammed the cab doors. Lying on his back, Moses Moon stared up at the sky. A lion in the stars stared back at him—just the pain roiling across his eyes. B. Rex moaned from behind his own duct tape mask. Despite the burning sensation in his wrists and the rash he could feel forming around his lips, Moses tried to breathe through his nose. In and out. He hadn't been eaten by a one-eyed bear. He hadn't been killed by two giants or chopped into pieces. Not yet. In and out. The truck hit a ditch as it drove away from the scattered hospital buildings and slammed Moses's head against the floor.

He had wanted to start at the bottom.

The back of the truck was filled with old screws and small stones that dug into their skin. The Judge stared at Moses with its three tired eyes. The ball didn't blink. Real skinheads didn't shave their heads bald. Moses would tell Logan and B. Rex the truth if this all ended up just being a dream. Real skinheads didn't live in Canada. They didn't even wear steel-toed boots anymore.

The two giants were still singing in the cab up front, one of the windows open. The beard in the passenger seat pounded the roof with a fat hand and belted out the lyrics. Moses prayed to Bill Murray for deliverance. He prayed to his favorite Bill Murray, the one from *Stripes*. Maybe this was just a rerun. "We are the wretched refuse," Bill Murray had said. "We are mutants. Something's very, very wrong with us." Moses Moon closed his eyes and listened to Bill's voice as the truck hit a patch of gravel. *Something's very, very wrong with us.*

"If you go out in the woods today, prepare for a big surprise!"

At least no one had seen Elvira Moon without her underwear.

25

They named her Kansas because it didn't remind them of anything.

"It's just a blank. I mean, have you ever been there?"

Outside the emergency exit of the Dynasty, Jamie unloaded a body wrapped in blue tarp from his trunk. He dragged it to the bent door and tried not to breathe in the smell. The parking lot was quiet. Sunday night was never too wild at Da Nasty. All the emergency exits were busted after years of raids. Teens taped over the deadbolt slots to sneak in after dark.

Jamie yanked the body inside. Donnie had said 227. He pulled the tarp up the first few stairs. One of the feet kept popping out. Its long toenails rasped against the floor. Jamie tried to shove the foot back inside the bundle. They used the tarp in the summer to keep raccoons out of the dumpsters at the butcher shop.

It had taken Jamie a while to get the body out of the bone can. The top layer was like frozen slush. Thick chunks slopped over his chest as he'd pulled the corpse free from the ice. Jamie drove the car with all the windows open and tried not to look at the man's face. Despite the cold, it had begun to collapse in places. The lion had been so much easier.

They named her Kansas because it was a flat place. A quiet place nobody ever decided to visit. Even before the nun ran her over, Alisha's mother said it sounded too sparse, too barren. Why not something pretty? Jamie had met enough girls with names like Lily, Lotus, and Rose. Outside the petals, he knew there was nothing pretty under there. He knew those names and the way they clattered down the stairs after too many drinks, the way they shrieked for cabs and tucked Dilaudid into their bras when the cops raided the bar.

Kansas. Nothing grew there but grain. If you asked someone to draw Kansas, they might just draw a straight line across the page. Or a tornado.

The rifle was wrapped up in the tarp with the body. Jamie didn't know where else to put it. The stairs were filled with broken bottles. He tried to avoid the bigger chunks of glass as he dragged the body up onto the first landing. Jamie nudged the door open on the second floor. The hallway was empty, but voices shook a few of the doors. A woman at high volume discussed the benefits of a low-protein diet as Jamie pulled the tarp behind him. It slid much easier across the orange shag. He could barely see the wet brown trail the body left behind. The carpet absorbed it all.

Jamie saw the door at the end of the hall. He wasn't sure what he meant to do with the body. He was just returning the message.

Jamie knocked on the door. A dead giraffe. They'd killed a giraffe, according to the Lorax. Her name was Kira, and Jamie wasn't sure what sound she made when she died. He didn't know what a giraffe sounded like. Jamie pulled the rifle out of the tarp and waited. There was only one bullet. He couldn't do anything about that. Maybe some bond would trigger a collapse if he shot the first one he saw. He'd heard of these things happening to twins. Brothers separated at birth whose wives looked the same and shared names—men with dogs and children almost identical in their looks and personalities. Maybe the nervous systems were interconnected. There could be a bond in the chemical structure of their brains. They weren't twins, though; they just looked like it. Irish twins with busy parents.

Kansas was the right name for a daughter who didn't speak until she was four. She absorbed everything she read, but she rarely spoke unless it was on the phone in the middle of the night. In the dark, no one could see the teeth shuffled together along the bottom of her jaw. She collected tracings from her library books, pirate faces and the outlines of anteaters. The anteater was her favorite animal. Kansas told Jamie it was because the name explained exactly what it did. Why couldn't all animals be like that? What did a zebra mean?

Kansas was a blank slate for anyone to draw upon, except it wasn't drawing. They were etching things into her every day. Burning little marks she wasn't even going to notice until it was too late. Her grandmother had already started the process—tiny little slits in the surface that would remain benign for years before the chipped portions started to show.

With his rifle aimed at the door and a body soaked in pig guts behind him, Jamie Garrison understood tonight might mark his daughter far worse than any grandmother had.

There was no answer. The televised voices continued their diatribes in the hallway. Jamie knocked again and tried the doorknob. Locked. The doors in Da Nasty were thin. It was too expensive to replace them every weekend. Jamie raised a foot and kicked at the knob. A jolt of pain traveled up his leg, the lion returning to wrack his spine. He fell backward onto the cold, hard corpse behind him. The stiff body didn't complain. The door had moved slightly. Jamie wound his foot up again and felt the particleboard give a little more. The tiny bones inside his foot rearranged themselves around the knob. Jamie bit his tongue against the pain and tasted blood. He had no more of the Lorax's pills. With a third kick, the door snapped open and he dragged the body in behind him with one hand.

The television was filled with static. Two queen beds stood beside each other against the far wall. Each one was neatly made and covered in a homemade quilt. Bright reds and greens made it look like Christmas. The furnishings didn't belong to the motel. Matching green lamps and bright white dressers sat in front of the locked balcony doors. A workbench and two toolboxes leaned against the television stand. There were no family pictures.

It was too clean. Jamie had expected cigarette burns and pools of Jack with dead houseflies on the floor. He wanted to find them passed out drunk in front of pay-per-view with their hands in each other's pants. He wanted to press the gun into the fat rolls on the backs of their necks and wake them up slowly from a naked slumber with their guts hanging over the side of the bed. There weren't any stains on the ceiling, no condom wrappers on the floor. Jamie tossed the gun onto a bed to thumb through a stack of medical files on the bedside table. Women's faces gazed back at him from hospital gowns and leather restraints. Prescriptions, toxicology reports, and therapists' notes were mixed into a pile on one of the beds. None of the pictures were labeled.

Jamie dragged the body over to the far bed and unwrapped the tarp. The face looked up at him from sagging sockets. Bits of pig fat clung to its lips. Jamie held his breath as he scooped the body up and laid it on the bed. The skinny legs were rigid and bent at odd angles. He had to press on them with all his weight to crack the knees into place. On the right leg, he heard the knee pop and a gout of purple fluid hit the ceiling fan, sputtering around the room. Jamie didn't pause. The arms were easier to adjust. He got the body into a sitting position and piled up knitted pillows to support the slippery back. He spent another five minutes trying to turn the head toward the door, pretending it wasn't a person. It was too purple and mottled to be a person. Jamie yanked at his dead model's neck to face the entrance, but it wouldn't budge. He wanted the brothers to look their prize in what was left of its eyes when they came home with drills in hand.

Jamie's reflection in the screen was covered in wet splotches and his arms looked black in the static. He tried the bathroom door, but it was locked too. Jamie sighed and tried a fist against the wood. It did not move. He used the same foot as before and felt the bones give again. This wasn't a regular Dynasty door. The lock was heavier and the wood was too solid. The pain forced him to curl up on the floor for a few minutes, breathing through his nose till the urge to puke passed. He could smell the purple stains on the wall creeping toward him. It was just like cleaning out the bone cans in the summer. That was what he told himself as he wound up again. Just cleaning out another bone can. There was always more waste to come. The door gave away and so did Jamie's ankle.

The woman in the bathtub wasn't wearing much. Her long legs stretched over the edge of the tub, covered in blue and yellow bruises. Her lipstick was messy and stretched up to her nose. She pulled her teal housecoat tight across her chest. Long blond hair filled the tub around her. The water was running and she kept one hand under the warm flow. For a few seconds, Jamie thought she was a man. Then he noticed the long, tapered fingers and the swell of her hips crammed into the back of the bath. Her legs were shaved and she had a ring on her left hand. The diamond was missing. Jamie didn't move from the doorway.

Elvira Moon waved hello and climbed out of the tub.

The woman from the tub walked up to Jamie and reached out to touch his face. Her back was wet from the bath and she had fine wrinkles stretching out from the corners of her eyes. Her large hand wrapped around his cheek. The light made her skin look yellow.

"Who—did they bring you here?" Jamie said.

"I don't know you," she said. "You weren't supposed to come in here."

The tall woman sat down on the toilet with her knees pressed together. She began to hum a prayer to herself. When she got to the end of a verse, she began again. Jamie couldn't make out the words. He tried to get her to speak again.

"Are you…can you at least give me a name?" he asked. "I need to know what they did. Was it the brothers? Those guys? They did it to you?"

Jamie grabbed a quilt from the other room. When he returned, she was washing the lipstick off of her face. She pretended not to see him in the mirror. The woman didn't belong in this place. The lock on the bathroom door was too stiff. Someone had spent money on the new door. Her underwear was gone.

"Do you know where they are? Do you know if—are you going to talk to me?"

She ignored him and continued to wash her face.

"Elvira."

"What?"

"I'm Elvira. You wanted my name, you got it, okay?" the woman said. "You don't need to ask so much. So many questions, and if you are looking for him—I know I was looking for him until I fell in here. I know where he goes when he doesn't want to see me anymore. I know where he goes. He goes away, but not as far as he thinks. Downtown is not so far away."

There were two of them, but they looked so alike with their beards. She was just confused, Jamie knew that. She could have thought she was seeing double in that state, whatever state she was in. Especially if they had their sunglasses on the whole time, but he didn't want to think about the whole time. He didn't want to think about any of it. Jamie thrust the quilt in her direction. The woman ignored him and splashed more water on her face. Jamie pushed the quilt at her again. It was covered in turkeys and pumpkins, but the pumpkins were green and the turkeys looked skinned. Christmas colors for the wrong holiday.

"Just put this on," he said. "Where did they find you? How did they find you?"

She couldn't see the body on the bed from inside the bathroom. Jamie knew the twins could return at any time. He opened the door a crack and looked down the hallway. It was still empty, but there were newspapers sitting in front of the doors. Photos from the rally in the park took up the front page. Jamie could not stay here any longer.

"I know he can't hide. He left and he tried to hide. And hide me too."

Elvira wrapped herself up in the quilt and pulled it over her head like a hood. Her bare feet were almost bigger than Jamie's. She turned off the taps and closed the bathroom door.

"You know where they are?" Jamie asked.

Elvira nodded from inside her new wrap and scratched her leg with one long foot. Jamie grabbed the rifle off the bed. Elvira didn't notice or didn't care.

"Can you—um, can you show me? I need to find them. Him. Can you do that?"

"I can show anyone, but no one will let me. I know the place. You want me to go with you?" Elvira asked. "I don't want to stay."

"I'm your friend, okay? I am. I am. You just need to…you need to come with me."

They stepped out into the hallway. There was nothing Jamie could do about the busted doorknob. They would know someone was here either way. He had traded in his corpse for a six-foot woman without any underwear who couldn't look him in the eye. As they made their way down the stairs, Elvira kept talking and smiling. The words bounced off the walls. Jamie knew she wasn't talking to him; she wasn't talking to anyone but herself. It was the same thing Alisha's mom did during visiting hours at the hospice.

"It's the tall place downtown with all the bad chandeliers, but you have to take me with you. You don't get to leave me here," Elvira explained. "They don't even let dogs in there. They think they're so fancy, but even fancy people got dogs. I don't want to be left places, okay?"

"The tall place? Pillaros?" Jamie said.

"No dogs allowed," Elvira said. "That place. That is where he goes. Dusty, nasty place, but it's where he likes to go. They have the big elevator in the back to get up to his room."

"Where they go? Is that where they go?"

"Where he goes," Elvira said. "It's where he goes."

"You gotta be more quiet," Jamie whispered. "Can you do that for five minutes?"

Elvira was already ahead of him on the stairs, her feet skipping around the broken glass. Jamie followed her slowly, taking the steps one at a time on his fractured foot. He held the rifle against his chest and tried to keep a grip on the railing. There were only twenty steps to go.

Alone in his old living room, Jamie had courted name after name in the dark with rum burning the corners of his mouth. Each name had tasted wrong on his tongue. The name Elvira had only come up once during the whole process. Alisha had banned all those old names immediately. Carmella. Mabel. Margaret. She didn't want her daughter prematurely aging while all her classmates remained Jennys and Susies, fresh-faced and pink-cheeked until eternity or high school, whichever came first. Jamie pushed for those older names the next morning; they were free from his unpleasant midnight associations. Free to do whatever they wanted on their own time. Those names were protected from the hopeless fates he saw swooping down to pluck Melissas and Donnas off their pink tricycles in broad daylight, to plunk them down with busted teeth and three children twenty years later in a subsidized apartment with electric heating and a clogged bathroom sink.

"You're so slow, we'll never find him if you take the stairs like that."

Elvira wasn't safe, though. There were already stories written there.

"Just wait, Elvira. Can you do that?"

Jamie began to take the stairs two at a time. Kansas was a blank space, but it didn't mean she was safe. She was grain and flat sunsets and a line across the horizon, but there were still basements in Dodge City. Wichita had closets no one wanted to open. There were hidden things he'd never seen and bodies in the rivers, cold cases forgotten in Topeka.

It was the fifteenth step that he misjudged. The broken foot collided with a brown bottle neck that snapped under his weight. Tumbling down the stairs, Jamie felt his right foot crack against the railing. Elvira started laughing and clapped her hands. Jamie clutched the rifle close to his body as his spine rippled down the concrete steps.

Kansas was a blank space for anyone to fill in for themselves. She was already boxed in by the margins they'd drawn around her in that tiny house out on Baseline Road.

Jamie hit the bottom of the stairs in a pile of bloody clothes and prematurely aging bones. He closed his eyes against the pain and tried to stand up against the drywall. His right foot did not agree with this decision.

"Are you going to get up?" Elvira said. "We need to go. He won't be there for long."

There was another option. Kansas could fill that space in for herself.

Jamie braced himself against the wall. It was a fall; just another fall. Jamie grabbed Elvira's hand and tried breathing in and out his nose while he attempted to stand. Elvira pushed the busted emergency door open. The world was covered with blurred lights that refused to focus. Jamie limped after the woman in the quilt, following her into the dark. He used the rifle as a makeshift cane. Pigeons sat on his car. They fluttered back up into the shit-stained balconies as the slouching figures approached the car in the motel's single shaft of light.

26

This was far worse than a missing lion. "Just stay quiet for now, or we'll really have a problem," Al said.

Neither brother could avoid the figure glaring at them from across the room. The three smaller boys cowered between them in the doorway. Each one had his hands tied together and a piece of tape over his mouth. They shuffled from foot to foot.

There was a body in Al's bed. It was almost looking at them, but the eyes were dried out and one was oozing down a purple cheek. The walls were splattered purple too and the bathroom door was busted. Tommy's quilt was missing.

"Al, you gotta check this out," Tommy said.

The exposed sheets looked too white for the room.

"Who the—fuck, the bathroom! Crane is gonna fuckin' flip!"

Logan Chatterton recognized the body. Ducking under arms tattooed with obese reapers and small Guatemalan children wearing skulls for masks, he dove across the motel room floor. The two bearded brothers could only stare as he jumped up onto the bed and tried to speak through his gag. Logan's bald head nodded back and forth with the words he couldn't push past the tape. He ran his stubbled skull against the dripping face and guttural noises worked their way out of his chest. The swastika on his head was leaking again.

"Get the other two into the bathroom," Al said. "Used to be so much easier when we got to make the decision. I said get them in there, Tom.

"Get offa there! Another freak. Last thing we fuckin' need."

Al tore the tape off Logan's mouth and threw him to the floor. Logan scrambled away across the carpet on his knees, his chin covered in rug burn. The beard followed him and dragged him back against the wall. Logan kicked his feet against the hard shins behind him. His one bare foot connected with the bone. Logan's voice kept bleating at the body on the bed.

"I didn't mean it! I didn't mean it!"

"I said shut up!"

"I didn't mean it!" Logan said. "She didn't even want to look at me! I don't want to be like them. I don't want to have part of them in me, like Frankenstein. Did you want me to be like Frankenstein? Like pieces of everyone else? 'Cause that's what she told me! Part of whatever fucking tribe! I was already a freak enough, and now I've got their blood in me too?"

"Shut the fuck up!" Al said.

Al threw him down onto the floor again and Logan tried to crawl away under the bed. He kicked at the large hands trying to yank him out and kept yelling at the purple body.

"And then she just walked away, but you didn't even say anything, 'cause you knew! I didn't cut her open. I just smashed the mirror, but then she got cut, and she looked at me like…fuck!"

The bearded man was too strong.

"She looked at me like when she looked at you when you went outside! And I saw the fucking blood in her, just scum fucking water, fuck! Let go! Let go! Let me fucking go!"

One spring sliced through Logan's index finger as the giant man yanked him out from underneath the bed.

"You got it in me now, too!" Logan said. "Fuckin' scum water!"

One of Logan's flailing feet connected with something soft. He heard Al groan from behind him and climbed back onto the bed.

The quilt was ruined. Logan's arms were still tied behind his back. He leaned his face against what remained of his father's left ear.

"I didn't mean any of it. But she left and then you came home, and you meant it all!" he spat. "And she knew that it was not going to stop. Nothing perfected, everything half-finished, even me, like—like a fucking frog!"

Al Vine wrapped his hand around the boy's spluttering mouth and dragged him off the bed. The kid had to go. Al just wanted some silence. Ten years ago, the Cardinal Inn had evicted them when some kid from Trois Pistoles tried to pull the same kind of freaky shit.

"Shut the fuck up, you—don't bite me!"

"Just toss him, Al! She's gone anyway. We gotta bring all this to Crane to fucking clear it," Tommy said. "One kid in the woods and now, fuck, he wants to rubber-stamp all our shit."

"Enough. Kid, you need to shut up now!"

As Al released him into the air, Logan Chatterton was still sorting out the look in his mother's face after he had broken the bathroom mirror.

"Oh fuck, are you kidding me, Al?" Tommy said. "The fucking TV?"

The buzzing and hissing died slowly. The kid's body was limp and his neck bled over the fake oak varnish. Al kicked at the short, skinny legs but didn't pull him out of the massive television. The static was gone. Tom Vine dragged the other two boys out of the yellow bathroom, shoving them onto the floor. The carpet caressed their knees as they stared at what was left of Logan—smouldering and six inches deep inside a television set.

"Well, what do we do now?" Tommy said. "Crane said no one, not without an order or a decision. Oh, fuck, he is going to be pissed. First the girl, and then this?"

"He didn't even know about the kid," Al said. "We don't gotta say anything."

"No, but he'll find out," Tommy said. "And we can't do three at once."

"We bring them with us. They can fucking tell him the story, all right?" Al said. "We gotta pack them back up and take them, but whatever. Beats having to explain ourselves. We found them with the bear, we come back, we find the door's busted, Crane's lady is gone."

"Was it his lady? Files are a mess."

"I know what he wants, but he can't always get it. We couldn't get him the tiger, right?" Al said. "And he just had to deal with that. She might not be the right one."

"It's the right one, man," Tommy said.

Al Vine grabbed the chins of the two boys on the floor.

"You're going to tell him exactly what happened. You don't even need to lie. You just tell him how your friend went crazy," he said. "Tell 'em how we came back here and all that shit was busted up. The bathroom door off the hinges, and your friend, he was just—well, he was crazy. He'll listen to you guys, it'll sound better."

Logan hadn't moved since they were dragged out of the bathroom. Small sparks still crackled from inside the box. The floor was wet under the boys. B. Rex had pissed himself.

"We're going back outside," Al continued. "And it's almost morning, so keep it quiet. We'll take the tape off your mouths in case someone sees, but not a word."

Tommy Vine grabbed the drills and tested the batteries. They were running low again.

"None of this shit holds a fucking charge. You got a receipt?"

"No, we didn't keep it," Al said.

"Fuck. They won't take it back, then. No returns without a receipt."

Al slammed the door. The Brothers Vine were going to have to change motels. Even with a DO NOT DISTURB sign dangling from the broken knob, you could smell the bodies from the hallway. The staff at the Dynasty was familiar with these smells. They would call the cops when the shift changed over in two hours. There were no real names on the registry.

"Should I grab the quilt?" Al asked.

"It's got that dude's ass all over it," Tommy said. "I don't think that's gonna wash out. And the fucking dry cleaner at Helena's is still giving us funny looks after we had to drag that kid down to the woods. He just ain't saying nothing yet."

They would need a new dry cleaner, too. One of the boys in front stumbled and face-planted into the orange carpet. Al booted him in the tailbone.

"Get up, get up," Al said. "I'm gonna go grab the toolbox."

Al turned and headed back to the room. When they had killed the giraffe, he remembered Kilkenny crying in the woods. The smell was similar then too, the animal shit hanging like a cloud that stuck to everything and followed them back here. Astor had told them it was part of the job. Al didn't bother looking at the purple body on the bed or the boy in the television screen. He had seen all of this before. Tom had seen it too, creeping around the edges of his vision when he shut his eyes at night.

The television still popped and crackled. Al grabbed the toolbox from the corner. He reached out a hand for the quilt, but the slumped body made his tattooed fingers retreat. Al didn't want to believe in ghosts—he had enough voices in his skull. The body lay with its arms spread wide open as if to embrace him. Al backed away from the bed and closed the door. Astor would want answers for this shit. He would want to institute some corrective measures. To make a point. They would need the other boys to prove this was all just one big misunderstanding. This was just another roadblock. The door slammed shut, leaving the two bodies in darkness.

Inside the television, Logan Chatterton's eyes were closed. He wasn't staring at anything.

27

The clerk didn't even look up when they stepped inside.

"He only stayed on the top floor, and he didn't even stay," Elvira said. "He just comes and goes like he wants, never stays, never even writes to me. Because that's Ted. That's him."

The Pillaros wasn't the tallest building downtown, but it was one of the oldest. Its windows were rarely washed, and its all-day breakfast was frequented by the early birds from the methadone clinic who liked to catch a meal at 3 a.m. Elvira Moon did not raise a single eyebrow amongst the staff when she barreled through the front doors with Jamie Garrison limping in pursuit. The rifle was shoved down his right pant leg; a temporary solution to his busted foot and the pain recoiling up his femur with each step. No one gave him a second glance.

"Don't take the elevator, he tries to get out that way every time," Elvira said.

"I can't take the goddamn stairs! Get back here!" Jamie said. "My foot, we gotta go up the elevator! I said get back, Jesus Christ, like a child. Where did they find you?"

In the car Elvira had told Jamie all about Ted, about the pills she had started flushing down the toilet, about Ted's favourite foods, about the flavour of cake batter compared to actual cake. She could not stay on any topic for long. The pills had turned the water purple in the toilet. Someone had stolen her bowling ball. She needed it back. Elvira tried to show Jamie the crack Ted left inside her, but all Jamie saw was a frayed bathrobe and the fear inside her eyes, flickering on and off.

"I told you, he'll see us on the elevator," Elvira said. "He's waiting. Can't go up that way."

The Pillaros' halls only looked cleaner than the Dynasty's because of the lighting. Small chandeliers dangled every few feet from the low ceilings. The incandescent bulbs could not illuminate all the stains and broken doorknobs like the Dynasty's fluorescent glare did. Everything blurred in a haze around the edges as Jamie Garrison dragged his broken foot after Elvira Moon. She was still wearing the quilt like a parka. They were on the third floor with seventeen more to go. He could barely keep up.

"Now, I don't remember what room exactly, but there is only one room on the top floor, I think, because that's where we were. And there was a waterbed. Did you ever have a waterbed?"

They were on the fourth floor now, Elvira plowing ahead with the red and green quilt wrapped around her shoulders. Jamie had begun to count the spots that appeared before his eyes whenever he leaned too heavily on his right foot. After the third staircase, he counted twenty-seven big blotches and three smaller ones that disappeared before he knew if they were real.

"Elvira, we are taking the goddamn elevator now," Jamie said. "I know, I know that he won't know we are coming. Right? Right? No, wait for me! You can't keep going!"

"But he'll just leave! We have to surprise him," Elvira said. "He has a whole speech ready, and he'll tell me he didn't mean any of it, but that it had to be done, and then, and then…"

"Did you call him before we decided to come here? No," Jamie said. "Let's just get up there. I will do the talking. I will sort this out. You just stand and—well, do something."

"I do lots of things. I sew. I cook. I even do my own taxes. Deductible for children, deductible for friends, deductible for charitable donations...do you like dogs? You can't get a deductible on them, but if you run it through an organization they will let it go."

The Pillar was quiet. Jamie pushed the elevator button while Elvira explained dog discipline and the best way to shave their bellies if they got infected with worms from eating their own shit or some other dog's shit. Ted never called her after he went to Arizona. This was where they had their honeymoon, she said. This was where love was supposed to live. The wallpaper was dark brown and small photographs of farms hung on the walls—all the old properties that the town had built over. The barns were gray and bent under the wind. Jamie pressed the button again with his thumb.

"He knows the elevators, he'll take the bigger one, and then he's gone," Elvira said. "Ted knows the elevators."

Jamie yanked Elvira into the tiny elevator before it struggled up the guts of the Pillar. Small feet scurried around the outside of the tube. Jamie hit another button. They were headed to the twentieth floor and the penthouse suite. He flexed his good leg and tried to stand on his toes. The right foot dangled limply above the floor. Jamie pulled the rifle out of his pant leg and let his hands get used to the weight. Elvira had stopped talking once they stepped into the elevator. Jamie tried not to think about the size of the Vines' hands. He hadn't even recognized the body the two bearded men had left behind in his bone can.

The elevator doors opened on the twentieth floor. The walls were a much darker shade of mauve. There was one door at the end of a very short hallway. All the light fixtures were made of fake pewter and stuck out from the walls at odd angles. The ice machine's hum cut through the artificial silence.

A skinny man in a robe waved at Elvira as she and Jamie stepped out of the elevator. Long, winding scars traveled up from his belly button and into webs across his chest. The man's skull looked shaved down to the skin. He grinned at them with a full mouth of discolored teeth and shook his ice bucket in the couple's direction. The elevator doors closed behind them with a ping. Elvira pulled the spoiled quilt up over her head and stuck her gaze to the floor.

"This isn't Ted. Look at the hair."

"I wasn't—ahem—really expecting anybody," the man said. "I think you might have the wrong floor. This is the honeymoon suite, the penthouse. You must have the wrong floor."

Astor Crane gazed down the rifle barrel now tucked under his pale chin.

"But I suppose I could ask you all in for a drink. Would that help?"

The lone strand of hair on his head was red and stringy.

28

Elvira Moon ran down the hall into the honeymoon suite. The hotel staff still sometimes called it a penthouse despite the heart-shaped bed. This was where Ted Moon once walked away from her. Jamie could only watch her run. His leg was still screaming every time he moved.

"You gotta relax, buddy."

Astor Crane laid a hand on the rifle barrel bobbing in front of his face.

"You seem a little too high-strung. How about—now, just swing that away from me. Just like that. There we go."

"She said—fuck. She said they'd be here," Jamie said. "Elvira! Hey, get back here!"

"Who would be here? No one on this floor 'cept me," Crane said. "Hasn't been anyone else up here for months, really. I've got the place as long as I want. She probably isn't going to come out of there if you yell at her, you know."

Jamie swung the rifle barrel down at the floor. He could barely hold it straight.

"You have no fucking idea the night I've fucking had," he said. "Just back off, all right."

"Well, after you graciously jammed that gun up in my face, how can I refuse?" Crane said. "Manners. You ever notice no one has them anymore?"

"Oh fuck off. It was a mistake, all right?"

The almost bald man turned to walk down the hall.

"Wait up!"

Jamie limped after him. The rifle returned to its original role as a cane.

"What happened to your leg?"

"I said I had a night," Jamie said. "I just need her to help me find them. That's the whole problem—she can't tell one apart from the other."

"You look a bit shaky," Crane said. "You wanna sit down for a second?"

Elvira Moon lay naked on the heart bed.

"You gotta—what did you do with the quilt?" Jamie said. "She doesn't even realize she's got everything hanging out there, you know? I shoulda just waited there for them."

Astor Crane carried his bowl of ice over to the bar. He plopped three cubes into three heart-shaped glasses and pulled out a bottle of Canadian Club. The suite's floor was littered with VCR cases and small ashtrays overflowing with bottle caps and cigarette butts. Prescription bottles were lined up neatly on a windowsill with a schedule taped to the glass above them. On the massive television screen in front of the bed, *The Wizard of Oz* played on mute.

"You bust in on me and start waving shit like that around, there is bound to be a misunderstanding," Astor explained. "So I think before you run off with the princess and the pea here, you need to at least introduce yourself. Let's try this out, like human beings enjoying the early hours of a Sunday morning. Or is it Monday? Must be Monday now."

Jamie set the rifle down on a pink loveseat.

"All right, but I can't really stay."

Astor offered Jamie a drink. He took the strange glass but didn't sip from it.

"No, let's start brand new. My name is Astor. I live here. And you are my guest. So is your friend. Now, what did you say your name was?"

"Jamie. Does that work?"

"Jamie, yes, that works. You can take a sip of that, you know."

Jamie wanted to spit it out, but swallowed instead. "Look, we can just get our shit and get out of your hair and then…"

"Very funny…"

"What?" Jamie asked.

Astor pointed to his fuzzy scalp.

"Come on, man," Jamie said. "You know I didn't mean that."

"Nobody ever does. Can you let me know when it's five thirty? I need to take another round of meds. Disgusting stuff, really. Horse pills."

Jamie sat down on the loveseat and placed the rifle on the floor. He took a bigger sip and tried to avoid looking at Elvira. "Look, uh Astor, we aren't looking for you. Or anybody really. I'm looking for twins. Well, not real twins, like pseudo twins," Jamie explained. "And I found you instead. And Elvira, well, she had it in her mind that they would be here."

Astor remained standing. He gazed at the television while Jamie spoke. Dorothy skipped through red flowers with her three friends. The lion was a little out of step with the other two.

"Twins? You don't look like you're in any condition to be chasing some twins around. Look at your foot," Astor said. "And you haven't shaved either, I can see that. You really think two girls are going to go for that…and the gun?"

Jamie swallowed his drink and crunched an ice cube in his mouth. "Not girls, they're old guys. Like forty-something. And they were supposed to be at the fucking Dynasty, but they weren't, and then I found her there, and she was out of her gourd."

Elvira stood and began remaking the bed. Her long hands smoothed the sheets and tucked them under the upper ridges of the heart-shaped bed. Astor ignored her.

"My buddy says they call themselves the Brothers Vine or some stupid shit like that. Sounds like wrestling names to me. They could be wrestlers actually, I guess. Tatted up like crazy, too, but they don't ride bikes. Any of this ringin' bells?"

Astor leaned back on the bar. His skin looked transparent in the blue flicker of the television. The scars up and down his chest could have been rotten veins floating to the surface, like bodies in the water. Jamie sucked on another ice cube.

"Oh, I know they don't ride bikes," Astor said. "Brothers Vine. Tommy and Al. What did you do, exactly, to piss 'em off, eh?"

"So everyone seems to know these assholes but me?"

"They can be pricks, I'll admit that. But they get things done."

Elvira was finished with the bed. She leaned against one of the windows and looked outside. The sun was starting to emerge on the horizon. Little figures limped from corner to corner on the roads below. Elvira left the window and headed toward the bathroom. No one stopped her. On TV, Dorothy had fallen asleep within sight of the Emerald City, her red shoes matching her lips as she drifted off into another dream within a dream.

"Get shit done?" Jamie said. "It's overkill if anything."

"You ever watch a lot of these kids' movies? I mean, like really watch 'em. They let me have a VCR in the hospital for a few months. Calmed me down at first, until I started paying attention."

Astor turned his gaze away from the television screen.

"I know you looked at the scars. Don't worry, it's not like I fell into a meat grinder or nothing. This is just what happens with the cancer. Sometimes they gotta go inside and pull some pieces outta ya. I watched these movies after they cut me open. I watched them over and over. It helped with the chemo, too. All the stories work out in the end, but they don't actually when you think about it. Even in Oz, those farmhands are looking in the window all creepy and leering. You know? If you were there, and you were there, and you were there, then who the fuck was the Lollipop Guild the whole damn time? The internal logistics alone can mangle your mind."

"Cancer?" Jamie said. "Really did a number on you." He eyed the rifle on the floor, but didn't move from his position in the loveseat.

"Adrenal cancer, to be specific," Astor said. "Adrenaline, right? The stuff that gets your heart pumping. Fight or flight, right? Actually something in your brain, I think—the fight-or-flight part. But the adrenaline contributes, and mine was all over the place. Adrenal glands going crazy. Up and down, side to side, fluctuating like a motherfucker. I was smashing coffee cups when there was too much milk. And your adrenal glands, they are inside you, inside the trunk, you know, like a tree. I had these tumors—"

"Like on the glands?" Jamie asked.

"Exactly. Benign. What a fucking word. I must have had them for years.

"Some of the other guys were jealous I had the VCR in there, but I had to watch them all leave while I stayed and they cut more and more out of me, because the hormone levels weren't balancing out. The tumors were telling my body, go, go, go! Firing on all the wrong cylinders. They'd gone malignant on me. Each time they cut me open, I'd wonder what was going to be left over after. Wouldn't you?"

"Yeah, I guess it wouldn't exactly be pleasant," Jamie said.

"They still got me popping pills and going in for radiation. I swear my balls are going to fall off if they keep this shit up. All virility shot to hell. Now that's a good word. Virile."

"You got it," Jamie said. "Like I said, when you're right, you're right."

Astor swallowed, then poured another glass. The lines on his chest swayed in the blue glow.

"Well, I did wonder what would be left, what would be left of Astor Crane once the knife went inside, and what would come out?" Astor said. "You see that scar traveling around my belly button? They called that a 'necessary' procedure. The kids' movies, they were supposed to be an escape. You can escape in a movie, right?"

"You wanna see something get blown up," Jamie said. "Or something funny like Belushi." Jamie was fumbling for words. He was out of ice cubes to distract his mouth.

"I watched *The Wizard of Oz* over and over," Astor said. "I watched *Robin Hood*, I watched *The Land Before Time*, I watched the fucking *NeverEnding Story*, which was just false advertising, you know? Ugh, how many times the nurses made that fucking joke. I started picking up on some weird shit in those movies. The radiation has got me puking out my eyes."

Astor gestured with his glass. Droplets splashed onto the screen. Elvira dropped something in the bathroom and slammed another cupboard shut. Astor ignored the noise, but Jamie shook himself and tried to stand.

"Maybe I should go check on her. Don't want her to mess up your pills."

"None of its mine—it's the hotel's stuff. Got my meds by the window, so who gives a shit?" Astor said. "What a piece of work she is though, eh?"

"This shit just landed in my lap. I didn't even see any of it coming. Let me grab her."

Astor Crane placed an idle hand over the Tin Man's face. He was wearing heart-shaped slippers on his feet. His heels hung out the back of each fluffy organ.

"That is how it works. Just like the cancer," he said. "Out of nowhere. Just like you stepping out of an elevator and swinging a gun in my face. Nobody is supposed to be ready for it. You don't wake up in the morning and decide to pump adrenaline into your bloodstream for five hours straight. You don't just decide that today is the day you'll get run over by a truck. The truck is there and your eyes lock on the headlights like a deer…and then you go down. Or a raccoon. Or a house cat. Doesn't matter. Splat. You don't see it. You weren't meant to, either. Just another dead dog on the road."

"Or a fucking lion," Jamie laughed. "You never know."

Astor Crane grinned and massaged the thick scar tissue scaling his stomach. Flying monkeys tore apart the scarecrow on the screen. Straw and bits of felt fluttered in the air as the scarecrow shrieked without making a noise. With one heart-shaped slipper, Astor slammed his foot down onto Jamie's right ankle.

"That happens too, doesn't it, Jamie?"

Jamie shrieked—a sound he hadn't heard before—and scrabbled at the floor for his rifle. Astor kicked the gun away with another heart-shaped foot. Tears filled Jamie's eyes. He saw four blurred versions of Astor Crane toss the gun from one hand to the other and check its sight.

"My fucking foot—"

Astor Crane leaned in toward Jamie. His eyebrows were barely visible in the gloom. Little red hairs poked through transparent skin. The veins underneath were blue and his eyes were wet and pink. All the blood vessels were broken. Something yellow was dripping from the corners.

"I don't know how you stumbled in, but that's okay," Astor said. "You can just walk out on that leg now. It'll hurt, but you can do it. Grab your friend, too. I'm sure the cops will love to see you two walking down the street. That was the second break, wasn't it?"

"I fuckin' told you we could just leave," Jamie said. "Oh Jesus, it's snapped."

"They'll put a pin in it. Slap you back together. Good as new, like Robocop," Astor said. "Who doesn't want to be Robocop?"

Jamie tried to take a swing at Astor, but the smaller man danced away. He ran a hand over his chest scars and walked to the window. The line of prescription bottles had times drawn on their caps. Five thirty was dumped down his throat and then he began to talk again.

"Leave a man in a bed for that long and see what happens. The docs gave me a list, but how do you expect a man to keep track of that? And yes, you do have to listen to this. It's just a fucking foot," he said. "You'd think I castrated you."

"You fuck," Jamie said. "I'm going to barf on all your shit."

"I did that too. All over the place. And I was spewin' words all over the place too. Lions, and tigers, and bears, oh my! Delirious as shit and just singing along to keep myself from getting sick. Singing along to all that shit. Lions and tigers and bears, oh my!

"And of course those dipshits take it literally. Wonder twins, wonder twins both of them. They only survive because they're too stupid to take any initiative beyond stealing a lion. And then the beast gets run over, of all things. Steal the lion, give it a name, and watch it get railroaded by some drunk in the middle of the night. Or you, I guess. Were you drunk? We're gonna get the head stuffed now because you kind of have to at this point. All this bullshit because of me fucking singing while high on whatever they had me on. It wasn't like I made a special request."

Jamie coughed and tried not to think about the swelling in his boot. Astor kept bouncing the rifle up and down on the bar. His hands didn't look out of place on the barrel. "You're gonna get it stuffed," Jamie said. "Why? Jesus, I can't even feel my toes."

"Because you bond with an animal. Even if you didn't want it and you think it's a stupid idea and it smells like shit, you bond with it because it eats from your hand," Astor said. "They had a bear, too. We didn't name it though. She was too dumb.

"All because of a stupid codeine high with me babbling about the fucking *Wizard of Oz* in the recovery ward, I get two pets like it's a present. I never asked for a fucking lion."

Jamie groaned and tried to massage his busted ankle.

"Gotta get him stuffed because some people don't know how to drive," Astor said. "A dead lion. Kept them just outside the city, too, where we grow the plants. And of course, the Lorax was trying to ruin all that shit. We had the hydro set up perfect. We tapped right into the main line and bypassed the meter. But the Lorax is always trying to run something on the side, never ever a team player. I didn't really care as much as before though. Wild, you know? I wouldn't have just broken your foot back in the day.

"But I come out of the hospital and it's gone. The wildness. They took it. They took something. Something that I needed, and they left all these lines on me. You see? Look at them."

Astor pulled back his robe and pointed at the thick, rigid tissue burrowed into his flesh.

"I want you to look at them. Women want to touch them, but they don't really want to know. They want to imagine what it was like, but not ask me. It was like swimming underwater while they played music. They play music while they cut you open, did you know that, Jamie? A scalpel is like another instrument for them. Only in the right hands does it ever play true. Nobody wants to say they got fucked up by a violin. I don't, at least. Not by a symphony."

There was pink light streaming in through the thin curtains. It clashed with the blue of the television and made Astor look purple as he paced back and forth in front of Jamie. On the screen, Dorothy was yelling at the man behind the curtain, and he was bellowing into a machine that echoed through the Emerald City. Jamie's ankle had puffed out of his sock.

"I'm slower now. I'm kinda glad I don't have a kid because like, how the fuck am I supposed to be surprised anymore? There is just nothing there, nothing. I can't even blink."

There were three hard knocks on the door. Elvira stopped making noises inside the bathroom. She stepped out into the suite and pulled on the ruined quilt. She ignored Jamie and Astor. Her long blond hair was swept across her face. Astor readjusted the rifle in his hairless hands. Three hard knocks again.

"You guys going to come in or stand out there?" Astor yelled. "Come in! COME IN! Are you hungry, Jamie? I'm always fucking hungry, but I can't keep anything down. COME IN!"

There was spittle on Astor's chin. It was pink and thick.

29

Two skinny boys with bruised skulls and razor-burned scalps fell into the honeymoon suite. Duct tape bound their thin wrists together behind their backs. Jamie recognized Moses's head, the lumpy plateaus that rose from the boy's forehead to the crown. He didn't say anything though, and Moses kept his eyes on the plush red carpet. Astor still twirled the gun from his skinny wrist and watched everyone in the blue glow. The other boy's pants were wet. He moaned. Behind these two sad bundles, the Brothers Vine entered the room with a bowling ball and a power drill.

"That's the one, man. How the fuck did you get here?"

Elvira stared at them from the bathroom door. She didn't recognize the bearded men pointing at her, the ones who'd grabbed her under Astor's deluded demand.

"That's the one, guys?" Astor said. "You think that's the one?"

Astor was pointing the gun at the two brothers now. Al spoke up.

"Like you said. We went and dug up all that shit. All the paperwork. Found the pictures, too. She was the best one. Hard to match up the photos and shit, but that's the one. We woulda brought her sooner, but you were in the hospital. Can't bring a lady like that to hospital. They'd just lock her up all over again."

Astor Crane sighed. He ignored the two sad piles on the floor. The twins were always bringing their experiments home. He had insisted they weren't supposed to kill anyone anymore after the kid in the forest. Not like it helped too much. The boys on the floor looked close enough to dead and smelled like piss.

"So this is supposed to be Destinii?" Astor said. "And what did she say her name was? Did you even bother trying to ask her?"

"She said Elvira, but I bet that's what she tells half the cops who pick her up," Al said. "Most do the same if they don't want a record. We checked the files, too. It's her."

"Did you even look at her face?" Astor said. "When I described her, did she sound like she was six foot and blond with shoulders like something out of a fucking comic book?"

Jamie tried to stand up and Astor tapped his forehead with the rifle barrel. He slid back down into the loveseat. The two boys in the corner were shivering. Astor hadn't raised his voice. The room was quiet. It was too cold for any birds to begin chirping at the sun outside.

"We went through all the stupid file cabinets and that's what we found," Al said. "And we found these kids too, and they were fucking everything up."

"I asked you if you thought that was her," Astor said. His teeth clicked together.

"It's fucking her, all right. It's Destinii," Al said. "It's the goddamn girl, all right? We found her. So give it up."

This time the bullet didn't ricochet. Jamie felt the air blast into his left eardrum as the slug burst from his father's Remington and into the center of Al Vine's face.

The back of Al's head burst outward due to the incoming force of the lead and the imbalance of pressure within his forty-five-year-old skull. As it bored through bone, blood, and the soft tissues of his brain, Al Vine lost consciousness and the ability to feel that little cylinder of metal ripping open his skull, splattering his fine motor skills and spatial sense across his brother's face.

Jamie wasn't sure who started screaming first, but even with his eyes closed, he knew Astor Crane was the only one in the room smiling. Elvira's screams were the loudest until she slammed the bathroom door behind her. There was a thud as the bowling ball hit the floor and Tommy grabbed his brother. He kept tugging on Al's beard.

"It's not her. You got that, Tommy?" Astor said. He kept his voice level. "Not her. That's the wrong one, like usual. What do we do? Any ideas, Tommy? Any ideas, anyone?"

Tommy Vine could easily have plucked each limb off of Astor like chicken wings. He could have licked the bones and asked for seconds without even straining his gut. He didn't, though. Tommy lay in the corner with his brother and kept slapping the corpse's head. Al Vine did not respond. An artery between the two had been snipped, something no one else could see.

"I ask for one thing to get done and they can't do it right," Astor said. "You can't trust the paperwork. Hospitals screw up all the time. Wrong photo with the wrong patient.

"I gave them a description. Short, dark hair. Lots of scars up and down her arms, and one fucking missing cheek. See her sometimes downtown, but she doesn't recognize me. And they bring me some woman from the jungle who isn't wearing any panties."

Tommy Vine moaned by the door and began to bash his head against the wall.

"What is he doing?" Jamie said.

"Relax, Jamie. Just be glad you didn't spend three years sitting alone with your brain in a hole. They say it hurts the smart ones worse, so maybe you woulda had nothing to worry about in solitary. Lose all ability to connect with that outside world. Only thing keeping each of them alive was the other."

"Aren't you going to stop him from doing that?" Jamie asked.

"One down, the other follows. Dominoes. They used to tap messages at each other through the walls. Apparently they had a very intricate language all their own."

Tommy wound up his head and smashed it into the wallpaper. He left a bright rose behind on the wall before he wound up again and reapplied the pattern. Astor strutted over and poked at Tommy with his gun. The big bearded man was focused on the wall, didn't acknowledge the barrel probing his ribs.

"And you're just going to…"

"Oh, come on, no one heard it," Astor said. "Even if they did, who's going to say anything? I could rent out this whole place for the next year or so if I really wanted. But that would draw too much attention. Somebody dropped a case of beers, that's what I'll tell them. No one else is even on this floor. It's the fucking honeymoon suite."

Moses and B. Rex lay very still on the carpet. They were covered in specks of Al Vine.

"Remember when you were a kid?"

The rifle was poking at Jamie's crotch now, sorting through the wet patch Jamie had created when the gun went off. Someone handed the scarecrow a brain in the blue glow of the screen.

"Everyone was a kid once. No one comes out of the womb smoking and cursing their mother. So you were a kid once. We all were, even that blubbering asshole over there."

Jamie stared at Astor Crane's heart-shaped slippers and tried to think of Kansas.

"I remember hearing some other kid crying. The kind of stuff that makes you want to look away or pretend it's not happening," Astor said. "The horrible deep-rooted kind of shit you see at really bad funerals for babies. Never go to those, by the way.

"So I'm maybe nine and I'm listening to this crying. And it fucking hurts me to hear that crying. It drives something inside me like a splinter right under the tip of a nail. And I can't fish it out, stomp it out, chop it off. It's inside me and it burns and I can't do anything about it. What am I supposed to do? It makes you feel helpless. You are nothing in that moment. You are the speck in a world that fucking hurts. You are that speck, you understand?

"And I'm listening to this fucking kid wail his lungs out and I'm imagining what that feels like and I know that if I could take that pain away from him, I would. I would take it, and I would put it inside me, I would swallow it fucking whole and let him walk away from the whole thing unscathed. Un-fucking-touched. And now I don't have that feeling anymore. You know that movie, the one I told you about? *NeverEnding Story*?"

"I don't think I've seen it." Jamie coughed. "I don't really watch a lot of kids' movies. Astor, you don't need to—you could just let me and Elvira and whoever else leave."

"No, you see the movie is kind of fucked for a kids' movie. I mean, most kids' movies are, when you get down to it, but in this one, the villain is just the Nothing. Nothing. Non-being. And so I was lying there watching this mystical shit, and I was thinking that's where that feeling went. The Nothing has swallowed it all, but you can build it again, the fucking princess in the movie says. And I'm lying there with holes in my gut and too much opiate in my brain, and I want to burst, and I know where that feeling went. And I know I gotta remake it. Remake it like the stupid kid did in the movie.

"I was going to have a kid once, but I didn't want one. Who wants a fucking kid? But maybe with a kid that is how it works, that is how you take that pain and swallow it and make it fucking new, because in fact you are so much bigger and so much stronger and you know what the world has in fucking store, and it's nothing good. So, I don't have that kid, but I could. And I got those idiots to go out looking for the mom-to-be.

"Her name was Destinii. Who the fuck names their kid that?" Astor said. "It wasn't like she picked it. Her parents named her sisters Johanna and Rachel. I guess they got bored, that musta been the thing. Years ago we fucked, and boom. Pregnant. Scary shit. You know anything about that, Jamie? Get a girl pregnant? Fuckin' end-of-the-world shit."

"No…well, there was a scare one time," Jamie said. "But no, I don't really have any kids."

"I did not want the baby. She fucked this Condom kid I had working for me, nothing major. I don't even know if he could get it up, dumb as fuckin' bricks, but loyal. And so I start saying, hey, maybe it's his kid, maybe you should be with him.

"We get them a place, we get everything nice and cozy, but she doesn't want to be with him. She wants me, and guess what? Next thing I know she's bouncing down an escalator and loses half her face. They take her off to the asylum, and then boom, no more baby. And no more nothing. And I wasn't happy like I thought I would be. You understand this?"

Tommy Vine whacked his head against the wall again. He was babbling nonsense words in the same rhythm as Astor. No number of words could cover up the mound of Al Vine in the corner. His blood had begun to dry on the wall in brown patches.

"They caught Condon, the stupid kid, but they can't even get it together to find out where Destinii went. They can't be bothered to do anything right.

"The thing about a gun, Jamie, is that it's so messy. Efficient, but when you factor in clean-up costs, time, and resource management, you come out on the loser's end of the bargain," Astor Crane explained. "Now the pseudo twins, they had to go. Like the Lorax—you ever meet him? I think we still have all his teeth somewhere in a jar. Sometimes you have to make cuts."

Everything was bathed in pink. Dorothy was clicking her heels, but Jamie wasn't going anywhere. His ankle still bleated pain up into his brain and he could almost see the shards of bone stippling the skin from the inside. The barrel of the rifle was directly between his eyes.

"Now this might wake a few people up. If you'd met me in the hospital, you coulda helped me find her instead," Astor Crane said. "Wouldn't it be grand to have that hypothetical kid? With a girl named Destinii, too. I got a deep want inside me. That ain't ever going away.

"That want will eat you alive."

Elvira didn't want to stay in this bathroom anymore. She pulled herself up off the heart-shaped toilet and laid a hand on the knob. She could hear a voice out there; it wouldn't stop talking. The Judge was lying on the floor outside. She was never going to get that perfect game. She would be left wondering why forever as she lay on other men's rounded stomachs, but they would never be like Ted's. They would be so cold and hairy and rumble in the night.

So she picked up the teal bowling ball. There was that man there in their suite, it was their suite and it used to have a waterbed and Ted Moon was supposed to leave messages underneath the mattress. *Come and find me. I am ready*, but of course he wasn't ready, never would be. There were no postcards from Ted. And the man out there wouldn't stop talking. He thought he could just talk and talk and talk, but Elvira had some things to say too.

Yes, she did. Something about family, and a son he had left behind and a life he could have had. And Ted Moon didn't care, this man didn't care, he kept talking, and he was wearing stupid slippers, Ted was always wearing stupid slippers too, she had just never noticed that before.

There was a teal bowling ball in her hand and Elvira remembered how to roll like she had in the big leagues. The ball flew out of Elvira's hand and nothing stood in its way. There was no alley, just pure air.

All twelve pounds caught Astor Crane in the left temple and his skinny body tumbled down into the plush red carpet. His finger pulled at the trigger, a muscle reflex pulsing from a confused and damaged brain trying to evaluate a situation far out of its control. Astor's lips tried to sputter something about flying luck dragons, and then they stopped altogether. There was no bullet in the rifle. Only one was ever in the chamber, and it was the same bullet now embedded in the drywall where Al Vine's head had been.

Jamie tried to spring up from the loveseat, but his foot caused him to crash down onto the floor beside Astor. The skinny body convulsed a little, but there was no movement in its blue eyes. A torn bit of scalp revealed the damage to his head. The teal bowling ball rolled away into the corner, its three eyes refusing to gaze back.

"Moses, that's you, right?" Jamie said. "Moses?"

"Yeah, it's—ugh—me. Is he out?" Moses asked. "Is he down?"

The two boys were still lying by the door. Tommy Vine didn't move. His lips were stuck open and he didn't blink when the television flickered. Occasionally, he tugged at his brother's beard and moaned, but the sound got trapped halfway up his throat. It was more like a gurgle—a clogged drain trying to swallow.

"He's down, he's down," Jamie said. "There won't be any more of him, all right? He's out."

"Like knocked out?"

"Like fucking dead, Moses," Jamie said. "Can you move at all?"

"We can kind of roll around, but they taped the hands pretty good," Moses said from the floor. "B. has been trying to break it out, but he's kinda given up. They thrashed us pretty good on the ride up in the service elevator."

Jamie crawled across the carpet and grabbed a piece of glass from one of the broken bottles near the bar. Moving on all fours, he dragged his right foot behind him. The pain was pointed and insistent, but it was tiny. It was something he could swallow by himself. Jamie didn't need the Lorax to help him now. The glass in his hand was sharp. As he neared the boys by the door, Jamie got a look at the hallway. The elevator doors remained shut. Jamie began to saw at the tape binding the two boys. He was careful to avoid slicing through their pale wrists.

"Where did you find her?" Moses asked. "We were looking everywhere…"

He looked at Jamie while he shook out the static blood in his arms.

"What do you mean, where did I find her?" Jamie asked. "You mean Elvira? She was hidin' in the bathroom where the big hairy dudes were living. Too much to explain. You know her?"

"Yeah I know her," Moses said. "I recognize her, um, from the motel."

Elvira did not check on the body splayed out on the floor; she knew it wasn't Ted. Ted didn't have a collapsed left temple and didn't leak all over the nice red carpet. Everything else was blurry. While Moses shook out the needles in his fingers, Elvira started with what she knew best to reorient herself. The big toe always came first. This was a fact she could trust no matter where she was. This little piggy went to market.

Astor Crane watched her from the floor but did not see a thing.

"She live there or something? They had her locked up in the bathroom, and the first thing she does when we get here is run right into the bathroom," Jamie said. "Look, I don't wanna hustle anybody out of here, but I can't crawl out by myself exactly, you know?"

Jamie was working on B. Rex now. The smaller boy wasn't talking. He smelled like ammonia and the tattoo on his neck looked infected. The small numbers bled around the edges.

"You just—you wanna go?" Moses asked.

"Yes, and fucking now," Jamie said. "Someone is gonna come up here eventually. Maybe to flip the sheets or something, and I don't want to be seen with two dead men and a third—is he dead? Has he even moved? Hello? Buddy! Fucker! Beardo! Hello!"

"He's been like that since the other guy got his face blasted," Moses said.

"Well, good, the things they did to my friends," Jamie said. "They deserved this shit. All right, now shake it out. Shake it out hard. Your wrists look like they're purple."

"They are purple," B. Rex mumbled.

"Well, rub them or something. Don't just stare at them."

Jamie Garrison pulled himself up on the back of the loveseat. His right foot flopped back and forth when he kicked out his leg. He had seen worse in the warehouse. He'd tell the doctor Brock had backed over his foot with a truck. Crushed all the little bones and snapped the ankle. They would put him back together. Rebuild him. Astor had that right at least.

"Look, I can kind of hop," Jamie said. "Moses, you grab one side of me. And little dude, you wanna grab Elvira from the bed there? And don't touch the body. Just leave him. He isn't going anywhere now."

B. Rex nodded, but Moses grabbed him. B. Rex didn't meet his eyes.

"Just go with Jamie. Take the elevator and go. Don't say anything, just go, and then don't say anything to anyone," Moses said. "You weren't with us at all. Not me and Logan. You got the car stalled or something stupid. You can drive him home or to his car, right, J?"

"You going to meet us down there or what?" Jamie said.

Moses watched his mother move from one foot to the next, pointing with her finger.

"You're just going to slow us down anyway, Jamie," Moses said. "Look at your foot. So you go first, and I'll stay here with her until I can figure out how to get her to move."

"Just grab her and then we can go," Jamie said.

"You wanna try moving her by yourself? With your foot, J?"

Jamie pulled out the keys and dropped them into B. Rex's hand.

"Moses, we can get her to come," Jamie said. "I don't want you staying here and then doing whatever. Don't take it out on that bearded guy, if that's what you're thinking. You don't need that on your back any more than you need these other two fuckers."

"Just go, J," Moses said.

Elvira lay back on the bed and began to roll around in the satin sheets. Jamie thrust out an arm and B. Rex ducked under it. He could barely carry Jamie's weight. Moses watched them shuffle down the hall toward the elevator doors. Every other step, B. Rex had to reach out and grab the wall.

The elevator opened. Both figures stumbled inside. Moses closed the door to the honeymoon suite.

30

Moses Moon didn't touch his mother. He sat in the purple loveseat and poked at Astor Crane's body with the rifle. The television was still muted. Everyone on that screen was probably dead by now. They all fit in with the rest of the suite. Even the chandelier was made of tiny fake crystal hearts that lit up and spun around above the bed. Moses traced the trail of fluid leaking from Astor's brain with the end of the barrel. It worked its way around the ashtray islands overflowing on the floor. The carpet absorbed it all.

Elvira had wrapped herself up in the red sheets on the bed and was snoring. Her large chest rose and fell in time with the noise. Moses hoped she didn't dream of anything—he didn't know what they had done to her. Elvira Moon would eventually forget these men, like everything else before them. Everything except Ted Moon and Arizona.

The honeymoon suite was windowless on three sides. The Venetian blinds were tilted to let in the light. The city stretched out beneath each window in long gray lines like an old strip mine filled with rainwater. Little figures blundered into each other down below and asked for change. Twenty floors up, not much sound made it through the thick double-paned glass. There were no balconies at the Pillaros Hotel, no pigeons to wake you up when the sun rose and you realized you were alone again. It must have been the pigeons at the Dynasty that drove them to it. The soft cooing reminding you the rest of the world had somewhere else to be, but you were there alone for twenty dollars a night with five television stations and a watercolor print of Irish setters staring at you from the wall. There was no continental breakfast, and the free soap made your scalp itch. The Dynasty had locked all the balcony doors, but people still got through. The windows in this hotel did not open wide enough for anyone to jump.

Moses was tired of rented rooms. He didn't want to deal with headboards rattling against the thin, non-insulated walls. He ran his hand over the medication lined up under a window. Astor Crane's handwriting sketched out a schedule on a piece of the Pillar's breakfast menu. According to his drug regimen, he would only sleep in two-hour sessions. There were five different pills to take in a constant rotation. A note reminding him to see Dr. Kostich for another round of radiation therapy was taped up on the glass. Moses tapped it with the rifle and then tossed the gun behind the bar. It crashed into some heart-shaped glasses and a few bottles tipped and spilled onto the floor. The carpet swallowed that too.

Moses planted his head against the glass window. He liked the cold. It made it easier to think. Mrs. Singh hadn't looked right at him when he stepped on her face. Her eyes were closed. Moses knew he hadn't stepped, he had stomped, but still, her eyes were closed. There were pieces of him, tiny skin cells left behind all over that house. There were footprints affixed to Mrs. Singh's face. Everyone had seen them at Yuri's bowling alley—watched Logan shout at Big Tina and B. Rex cry over what was left of Mrs. Singh. B. Rex was gone, but he couldn't wipe the numbers off his neck. There was so much pus around the edges. Moses had seen it dripping down his friend's neck. A scarf wouldn't be able to hide the smell if those numbers got infected. They were going to slowly eat his flesh the longer B. Rex hid them from his father.

Al and Tommy Vine were still piled in the corner by the wall. Tommy was breathing, but he hadn't moved since Astor crumpled to the floor. The bearded man had grown tired of whacking his head against the wall. His sunglasses were broken and drool slipped out the corner of his mouth. Bits of his brother still stuck to his face and poked out of his beard.

The Judge wouldn't look at anyone. The ball sat in the corner and stared at the wall. Moses Moon picked up the piece of glass Jamie had found on the floor. He ran it over his palm but didn't press down against the soft white skin. There were still purple bruises on his wrists. Elvira groaned in her sleep, and Moses sat down on the bed beside her. He ran a hand through her tangled blond hair and tried to undo a knot above her left ear.

The world outside looked wet. Stuttering lines of cherry light covered each body on the floor like spoiled film. Dorothy was awake now, and she remembered everyone who was in her dream. You were there, and so were you. Moses rolled the jagged glass up and down his palm. Bill Murray wasn't saving anyone. He was standing on the sidelines. He was cracking jokes and smirking for the cameras while Logan shuddered inside a television. "We are the wretched refuse," Bill Murray had said. He was lying—every time he spoke, it was someone else's words.

Moses wanted to see Logan again, but all he could find were Logan's fists and bleeding nose staring up from the ground. All he could find was Mr. Chatterton in that bone can, gasping for some air. His face was purple and Logan was trying to tell him he was sorry. He was so sorry. Everything was wet. Everything slipped through his hands. There was nothing to hold onto.

In the afterbirth of morning, Moses sat on the hotel bed and stroked his mother's hair. He tossed the jagged bit of glass onto the plush carpet. Dorothy was talking on the screen. Moses listened to the faint noises echoing up from the streets below. He could hear sirens in the distance and someone was yelling hurry up, the bus would be here any minute, any minute now. A car failed to start and a dump truck was reversing down the alley next to the hotel. Moses focused on the yawning whine of the sirens. He stood up against the window and pressed his ear against the cold, pink glass. Elvira yawned and stretched out her arms to hug the air. She clutched what she could grab and pulled it tight against her chest. Moses Moon listened to the wailing. The moisture gathered on the glass and then began to fade. He agreed with that voice yelling in the street.

Any minute now.

Larkhill, Ontario
1990

31

Half the kids on the frozen playground had bright yellow grocery bags tucked into their boots. Jamie Garrison sat on a bench and tried to ignore the ice melting beneath him. A breeze kept snatching bits of his newspaper and tossing them into the brittle branches above him. He had to use two hands to hold down a single page. Kansas was somewhere in the mess of kids trying to climb up the slide instead of traveling down it. She was wearing an orange snowsuit and a blue scarf around her face. By Jamie's estimate, she had fallen down the slide five or six times.

There was no snow falling, but it covered the ground in one large pockmarked sheet, disguising the dead leaves and pop bottles until April arrived and the sewer flooded with the runoff like last year. Scott's basement would probably flood once the snow melted, but Jamie had his own place now. He was nestled on the seventh floor in the Gillman Arms with an inclusive lease. Jamie liked to run the shower even when he wasn't home sometimes, but there was mold growing in between the tiles on his bathroom floor.

Moses Moon was still on the front page every day. The high school photo they used didn't show the shaven head or the purple wrists Jamie remembered from the honeymoon suite. Moses Moon was smiling in this picture, his lips stretched too far. He was even wearing a shirt with a collar. The buttons were mismatched and one side hung lower than the other. The sun watched over the kids with Jamie and began to melt some of the ice on the higher branches. Droplets split phrases like aggravated assault and first-degree manslaughter into inky blots that ran down the page and darkened Jamie's fingertips. Kansas fell down the slide again.

The cops had come by a number of times since they found Moses on the top floor of the Pillaros Hotel with two and a half dead bodies in the room. The half is what bothered the prosecution. Tommy Vine couldn't talk; he only dribbled and wrote the name Al over and over on napkins. His diet consisted mainly of pureed foods and well-mashed potatoes administered every six hours in the extended care ward at St. Joe's. One of the prosecutors described him as a "husk" to the jury and prodded Tommy with a finger to prove his point. Objections were overruled. Without the beard, Tommy Vine looked like any another fat old frog with drooping lips. Most of his tattoos were hidden under the wrinkled brown suit two nurses forced him into after they changed his bedpan and wiped him down.

When investigators found Jamie elbow deep in pork picnic shoulders at Henley Meats, the questions weren't about his car outside the Pillaros on the night in question. Neither of the men asked about the Lorax burning alive with duct tape encircling his gut or how Jamie's father's rifle ended up behind a honeymoon suite bar. Francis Paul Garrison had never registered the gun.

The detectives were interested in the character of Moses Moon—his work habits, personal hygiene, his sociability. Had he seemed evasive or suspicious in the days preceding the night in question? Was Jamie Garrison aware of any accomplices or acquaintances that may have frequented the workplace? What was his home life like? Were there any early signs he might have been capable of these attacks?

In the first weeks after his arrest, Moses had been accused of a variety of crimes. Everything from stolen hubcaps to forced abortions were tossed in his general direction, but few of the allegations stuck. One of the most damning pieces of evidence came from a size-eleven boot print lifted from a fifty-year-old woman's face. This was Exhibit A in what prosecutors called a drug-fueled killing spree that stretched across Larkhill over one devastating weekend in December 1989. The manager at Yuri's Bowling Emporium was able to identify what remained of Logan Chatterton, who was found with his father in the Dynasty Hotel. The elder Chatterton had been reported missing by his dentist when he did not appear for a follow-up appointment to replace a faulty crown. Moses Moon was suspected in both cases, but there was not enough evidence to pursue either investigation to the trial stage. They remained open homicides.

Jamie answered no to every question. He was in fact very unaware of Moses Moon as a fellow employee, and even more so outside the workplace. The boy had seemed quiet and well-mannered while on the job. His attitudes toward minority groups and alleged racial intolerance were rarely if ever observed while he was employed at Henley Meats.

Jamie did not mention B. Rex, the piss-soaked boy he had driven across town after they left the hotel. The kid had cried the entire time, tried to explain something about an old lady. When they found his car, the driver-side window was smashed and the seats were soaked with melted snow. The kid had honked when he drove away, and Jamie knew that boy could not have clamped a foot down on anybody's throat. When the officers asked again about accomplices, Jamie just shook his head.

Teachers talked about a Brett, um, a Brett something, one detective said. The connection, we understand, is tenuous at best after speaking to the boy's parents. It seems they spent a few days together after school, but we don't have any real evidence against him at this point.

Jamie couldn't remember anyone named Brett. He watched the investigators from the window of the butcher shop when they left, waiting for one to write down his license plate or check his tire treads. Neither of them stopped to take a look and so he went back to separating the picnic shoulders. Texaco Joe was on vacation. He told everyone he wanted to see Houston for himself. Don still had Jamie working Sunday mornings and never spoke about that 2 a.m. conversation in the dark. He was watching *Rocky II* that night. That was all he could remember.

Another page fluttered away from Jamie into the branches overhead. Kansas teetered halfway up the slide. Alisha gave him weekends now. She was working at the arena teaching skating to the five-and-under set, dealing with diva mothers and anxious fathers worried about sons who couldn't skate after five minutes outside the womb.

Kansas slipped and tumbled down the slide again. Jamie watched her rattle off of two other kids before she hit the bottom in a pile. He waited. His daughter shook her head and began to climb again. She could do this for hours on end if he let her.

One of the photos in the paper showed Elvira Moon before her bowling ball accident. She stood before a banner at Paulie's Pins with three other women. Her hair was curled and she clutched a bowling ball below her breasts. The winners of the fifth annual Woman's League Half-Price Wings Tournament were all smiling, but Elvira was the only one looking into the camera. Her teeth looked much whiter in grayscale. Jamie had trouble recognizing the face without the blue and yellow bruises or the roving eyes that had rarely made contact with his face. Although the ongoing trial made allusions to her involvement, an early plea deal with her own public defense team severed any ties between her case and any new developments surrounding her teenage son.

A bunch of small, bundled children were gathering near the swing sets. Kansas gave up on the slide, and Jamie watched her orange snowsuit plod toward the circle. Alisha was dating someone from her building named Carl now, and Brock liked to call him Hot Carl when Jamie wasn't around. Brock had dentures these days and enjoyed scaring children with them at the grocery store or standing in line at the movies. He had refused to cooperate with police, but now went to the dentist once a month for follow-up examinations. Karina's parents had let him move upstairs, but the two could not share a bed. Her parents would be able to smell the formaldehyde clinging to his skin whenever they touched. Jamie only lent out his apartment once before realizing it was impossible to get that smell out of the sheets. Brock took to renting out motel rooms down by the highway for special occasions.

Alisha didn't talk about Hot Carl much when she dropped off Kansas on Friday nights. Neither of them talked about her mother, or Jamie's parents, or the night Renee fell down the stairs for the third time while Scott was out at work. It was art projects and Triceratops and the best way to introduce Kansas to the wonderful world of the Hardy Boys. She had already finished most of the Nancy Drew at the library, but wasn't ready for Judy Blume yet.

Kansas spent every Saturday with her dad, but his apartment was small and it always smelled like leftovers. Grandma had taken her to the bingo hall once to change up the scenery, but Alisha could smell the smoke in her daughter's hair for three days afterward. Green dabber ink didn't come out of Kansas's skin very quickly either, and so that was the end of bingo night.

It was Saturday, and the sun dangled above the park. Jamie kept his orange girl in sight while he read about Moses's refusal to take the stand and a lack of fingerprints on the trigger of the gun. Astor Crane was a footnote near the bottom of the page, his name referenced in regards to three disappearances and one kidnapping charge involving baseball bats and a toolbox. No family had stepped forward in his case.

Photographs of Moses Moon's tattoos appeared in the nation's tabloids, blurry and subtitled for the farsighted. Apparitions of the White Eagle Army manifested in Halifax and Nelson, according to various letters to the editor. Most were the ghosts of mohawked kids and angry neighbors spraying GOOK onto corner stores.

Jamie tried to hold the paper still, but the wind snatched it from his hands. He watched the pages flutter away into the branches, joining plastic bags and lost birthday balloons. Half buried at the base of a strangled maple, a sign for Connor Condon leaked purple ink into the wet snow. The words were faded and hand-drawn; they barely fit across the cardboard placard.

It had been months since the discovery of the body, but there were no leads to follow. Connor's mother still wandered the halls of the courthouse, but she had run out of things to say. Usually she just lay her temple against a fake marble pillar before guards asked her to leave.

Petitions wilted on the walls of churches and community centers. The names that remained on those petitions were never called upon to testify in the park again. The weather had grown too cold, the wind too strong. Only the lost man in his motorized wheelchair returned with a sign. He was picketing the lack of ramps in local libraries and his own petition had swelled to five thousand signatures since the first protest back in December. Jamie had signed it the week before while Kansas chucked snowballs at chickadees. Each little ball fell apart in the air before it hit the ground. The birds didn't notice.

A red coat fluttered up from the middle of the circle. Jamie abandoned Moses on the bench and walked across the frozen gravel. His right ankle clicked with each step. Three pins and a number of surgical staples still held the foot together. The nurse in the emergency room hadn't questioned Jamie when he blamed it on a tractor. Out in the snow, the children were quiet and no one was laughing. Jamie could see a boy attempting to take off his jacket, stumbling around in a tiny circle. He had the heavy coat halfway over his head but couldn't get it around the tip of his chin. Kansas joined the circle, watching the boy try to remove his coat.

Jamie Garrison glanced back toward his bench and the fluttering pages condemning Moses Moon to twenty-five to life without parole. He was being tried as an adult for three murders, one of which was considered a premeditated act for which he exhibited no palpable remorse. The prosecution remained firm in these assertions after the verdict was read aloud to cheers and the sobbing of Mrs. Singh's son in the front row of the balcony.

It had been three months and there was still no mention of a lion. No reports of a taxidermied head discarded on the streets or found in someone's garbage can. Jamie waited for a jogger to spot the bloated cat's body floating in the lake beneath the ice. He checked each page every morning for a glimpse of the beast, but he found only Moses—Moses Moon smiling from a high school photograph. Another gust of wind blew through the park and tossed all the pages into the air.

With his back to the children, Jamie stumbled after his fleeing newspaper. The boy continued to fight with his jacket. He was running out of breath. It was hot inside that coat.

The neon snowsuit circle stood around and watched him struggle.

Acknowledgments

Thanks to Miriam Toews for all her guidance while I bashed my way through the first draft and somewhere into the second.

Thanks to Jeff Parker for the constant support and for reading the early draft while riding the subway in Russia. I plan on rewatching *Splice* soon.

Thanks to Rosemary Sullivan for her support and guidance at the University of Toronto.

Thanks to my editor Guy Intoci for the edits and advice through the whole process of turning this into a book. Thanks to everyone at Dzanc, including Steve, Dan, Michelle, and Meaghan. You made it easier to be a Canadian in America.

Thanks to Chris Bucci for embracing ZZ Top when many others declined and for continuing to support my work.

Thanks to early readers and advisers like George Pakozdi, Brendan Bowles, Jennifer Birse, Karen Principato, Daniel Mittag, and James Rathbone. Thanks to all my friends who have supported my work along the way, from workshops to readings and finally to these pages. Thanks to Victoria Hetherington for all the support during the editing process and Naben Ruthnum for the day-to-day advice.

Major thanks to all my family, especially my parents Ed and Shelley, for their unending support and encouragement. A lot of this started with the Hardy Boys.

I also want to thank the Oshawa Public Libraries, specifically the Legends and McLaughlin branches, where the majority of this novel was researched and written. Thank you for keeping your bathrooms clean and your water fountains running.